RUSTY NAIL

ALSO BY J.A. KONRATH

Bloody Mary

Whiskey Sour

A Jacqueline "Jack" Daniels Thriller

RUSTY NAIL

J.A. KONRATH

HYPERION New York

Library of Congress Control Number: 2006925772

ISBN 1-4013-0088-X

Hyperion books are available for special promotions and premiums. For
details contact Michael Rentas, Assistant Director, Inventory Operations,
Hyperion, 77 West 66th Street, 12th floor, New York, New York 10023, or
call 212-456-0133.

FIRST EDITION

10 9 8 7 6 5 4 3 2 1

This book is for Mike Konrath, one of the coolest guys on the planet. I love you like a brother.

RUSTY NAIL

1 oz. Scotch
1 oz. Drambuie

Pour ingredients over ice in an
old-fashioned glass.

Stir.

RUSTY NAIL

Indiana 1976

T HE SOUND BEGINS. Again.

Alex, eyes clenched shut, pillow pressed to face, can't escape the repetitive *slap-slap-slap;* it penetrates the thin apartment walls and saturates the cotton batting.

The wailing starts, the cry of a sick dog, increasing as the slaps come louder and faster.

Father will call soon.

Alex rolls out of bed and tiptoes through the door, every painful squeak of the floorboards hitting like a blow. Slowly, so very slowly, Alex creeps down the hall.

Beyond Father's room is the back door. If Alex can make it outside, there's a chance. Perhaps spending the night in the barn, or at a friend's house to escape the . . .

"ALEX!"

Alex jumps at the sound, Father's voice drilling in and pinning feet to floor.

"Alex, get in here!"

No choice now. Run, and Father will hear and get angry. Alex doesn't want to be the recipient of God's penance.

The child heads back to Father's room.

As always, the sight is ghastly. Father is kneeling on the floor, clad in dirty jeans and bare from the waist up. His back is glistening with sweat and something else; streaks of blood leaking from angry red welts.

"I'm a sinner, Alex. A terrible sinner."

Alex stares at Father's hand, sees he's using the scourge—a multi-tailed whip with tiny metal barbs on the ends. That one isn't so bad. Father has implements that are worse. The one Alex fears the most is the old brush handle, the bristles replaced with thin nails, rusty from years of use.

"Take the whip, Alex. Show me God's wrath."

Alex hesitates.

"Now!" Father's eyes burn, promising the threat of Redemption.

The eight-year-old holds out a hand and takes the scourge.

"You are the instrument of God's vengeance, my child. Give me His penance." Father's voice trembles, cracks. "Punish me for my terrible sins."

Alex swings the whip.

Again.

And again.

And again.

Father's keening grows in volume, and Alex beats him faster and harder, wanting to get it over with, wanting it to end.

Finally, Father cries out for mercy, and then he pulls Alex next to him, both on their knees, and they both pray and pray and pray to the Lord for forgiveness and salvation and deliverance from evil.

Father's sobbing eventually softens, then stops.

"Ointment."

Alex fetches the salve and rubs it into Father's wounds, coaxing whimpers.

"Reject sin, Alex. Reject Satan's ways. Don't end up like me."

"I won't."

"Promise me."

"I promise."

"Good. Now get the hell out of my room. I don't want to see your ugly face for the rest of the night."

Alex runs outside, hands pink with blood, brain awash with terrible feelings of guilt . . . and disgust . . .

. . . and something else.

The night is hot, the sticky summer air smelling like garbage, the field behind their house dark and quiet. The tears erupt, and Alex wails, head in hands.

A cat, a stray tabby that hangs around the farm, bumps Alex's leg and purrs. Alex holds the cat close, wiping tears onto its fur.

Next to the barn is a rain barrel, half filled with foul-smelling water. Four rats, a squirrel, and a possum have all drowned in that barrel.

But never a cat.

A feeling of warmth grows within Alex, extinguishing the fear.

"Let's go for a swim, kitty."

Stroking its yellow and orange fur, Alex carries the cat over to the barrel.

CHAPTER 1

BUSINESS WAS SLOW, which made me extremely happy.

I sat in my office, the omnipresent paperwork mountain on my desk down to a few small mounds. I could actually see the wood through the files in some places. It was brown, as I'd always guessed it to be.

There hadn't been a homicide in Chicago for four days, which had to be some kind of record. We consistently ranked as one of the top murder cities in America, often hitting the number one spot. Whenever that happened, cops from my district would get *We're #1* T-shirts printed up. I had seven, from previous years.

I whittled away the free time with busywork: filing, reviewing cold cases, cleaning out my desk drawers. I even entertained the notion of painting my nails—something I hadn't done since joining the force over twenty years ago.

All play and no work makes Jack a bit flighty.

My partner, Sergeant Herb Benedict, had been using the free time to catch up on his eating. He wandered into my office, lugging a gallon of chocolate milk. He set the jug on my desk.

"I didn't have anything to do, so I brought your mail."

"Someone mailed me dairy products?"

Herb scowled, his walrus mustache drooping. He had a few years on me, which put him past the fifty mark, but his face was plump enough to retard wrinkles.

"This isn't dairy. It's GoLYTELY. I've got to drink this entire bottle to clear out my digestive tract for my colonoscopy tomorrow."

"Sounds like fun. Shall I come by, take some pictures?"

"Funny, Jack. Be happy you're not a man and don't have to deal with this stuff."

"I'm thankful for that every day."

Herb removed the bundle of mail he'd tucked under his armpit and dropped it on my desk.

Among the bills and junk was a small padded envelope. It had *Lt. Jacqueline Daniels, Chicago Police Department, Violent Crimes Division* typed on the label. No postmark, no return address.

"This was in the mail?"

"No. Someone dropped it off downstairs for you."

I frowned. Times being as they were, unknown packages were scary things. But hand delivery meant it must have gone through the metal detector and X-ray machine downstairs; standard delivery procedure. I teased open the flap and peeked inside.

Something thin and black.

I threw caution to the wind and shook it out onto my desk. A VHS videotape. No labels or markings.

My apprehension went up a notch.

"Did the desk sergeant get a look at the person who left this?"

"I didn't ask. You weren't expecting anything?"

I shook my head.

The VCR sat in the corner of my office, on a cart with a TV. I hit a few buttons and put the tape in.

Herb rested his butt against my desk and patted his expansive belly. He'd lost a lot of weight, but had found it again. His stomach growled, perhaps in response to his patting.

"You know what the worst part of a colonoscopy is?"

"You're going to tell me whether I want to know or not."

"I can't eat anything for twenty-four hours."

I considered it. "That's worse than having a long probe stuck up your un-happy place?"

"I'm under anesthetic for that." He took a swig of GoLYTELY and made a Mr. Yuck face.

"I'm guessing GoLYTELY isn't a taste sensation."

"They claim it's chocolate-flavored. More like chalk-flavored. I'd rather drink a gallon of paint."

I pressed Play. After some snow, the TV screen went black. In the upper right-hand corner the date flashed. Eight days ago.

The scene abruptly changed to a wide shot of a two-story house. Midday, the sun casting shadows straight down. The house was nondescript, a Realtor's sign stuck in the lawn. It could have been any house in Chicago. But it wasn't.

I knew this house.

"Is that—?"

I shushed Herb, nodding.

The cameraperson approached the front door at a brisk pace. A hand, wear-ing a large black leather glove, came into frame from the left of the screen and turned the doorknob.

The camera sailed through the foyer, the living room, and over to the base-ment door. The hand flipped on the light switch by the staircase and the descent began.

My heart accelerated, the scene before me playing out just as it had so many times in my memories. I held my breath, hoping this was just a prank, hoping the basement wouldn't contain what I feared.

The cameraperson reached the lower level and panned to the right. The auto-focus blurred, then sharpened, revealing a naked white female tied to a chair with twine, a burlap bag over her head. Her whimpering hit me like a blow.

"Jesus." Herb folded his arms across his chest.

I had to fight to keep my eyes open, watching as the camera approached her, watching as the gloved hand picked up a hunting knife from the floor, watching as the knife rose up to her throat . . .

Herb gagged. I turned away.

When I looked back, she was still alive, arterial blood squirting and splashing down her bare chest. There was a wet coughing sound, and it took me a moment to understand what I was hearing; the woman was struggling to scream through the large slash in her neck.

She didn't die right away. The writhing and twisting and coughing went on for almost a minute. When her body finally stopped moving, the camera faded to black.

I spent a few seconds trying to rally my thoughts.

"I need a Crime Scene Unit ready to go in three minutes, photos, vids, ALS, the works. I'll contact the EPD and clear it with them."

Herb headed for the door, his GoLYTELY forgotten. I hit Eject on the VCR and grabbed a latex glove from my desk. The tape went into one evidence bag, its envelope into another.

Then I called the Evanston Police Department and asked them to meet us at the address. It was one they knew well.

The morning was beautiful for April, sixty degrees, crisp and sunny. I wore a beige Anne Klein pantsuit that I paid too much money for because it slimmed my hips, and a new pair of black low-heeled Jimmy Choo boots. Herb had on an ancient gray suit, designed by Montgomery Ward, and a blue tie already stained with GoLYTELY.

As befitting the weather, the streets and sidewalks were packed with people of all races, ages, and socioeconomic backgrounds. Panhandlers and executives, students and sightseers, all commingling in a giant diverse human stew. We worked out of the 26th District, in the heart of downtown, our building a speck among the skyscrapers. Parked on the sidewalk was a churros cart, which Benedict eyed. After viewing the video, the cinnamon smell repulsed me. We walked around back to the parking lot and climbed into his new Chrysler Sebring—both of us hated my 1986 Nova. Herb rolled down the windows and slowed as he passed the churros, sniffing the air.

"Why can't they make GoLYTELY in a churros flavor?"

"I'll make a few calls."

"Bacon flavor would be good too. Tell your people."

"I'll do that."

"And chili-cheese dog. I'd drink a gallon of chili-cheese dog in a heartbeat."

"I'm sure you would."

Evanston bordered Chicago on the west side, blending into it seamlessly. It was a fifteen-minute drive that we made in ten.

"Maybe the tape was one of Kork's old collection."

Herb referred to the homemade snuff films discovered in Charles Kork's house after his killing spree ended. A task force had been formed to match victims with missing persons, and they'd done a remarkable job, gaining enough accolades to get featured on a *Law and Justice* cable TV special. Having been the ones who tracked down the Gingerbread Man, which is what Kork called himself, Benedict and I were asked to head the task force.

After viewing one of Kork's videos, we declined.

"The date could have been faked." But I didn't buy it. "Did you notice the front door? It had a security plate on it. That's new."

I called Information and got the number of the Realtor whose sign sat in front of the house. After being put on hold for a few minutes, I talked to an agent who confirmed that the house was for sale.

"Can you meet us there?"

"I'm sorry, Officer. I'm in the middle of something."

"I understand. And I hope you understand that we'll have to break the door down."

"I'll see you in five."

I hung up and tried to prepare myself. Several deep breaths couldn't help me control my racing heart, my sweating palms.

The house looked exactly as it had in the video. We pulled alongside the driveway. The CSU had already arrived. I played conductor and set my people into motion.

One officer took samples of motor oil on the driveway near the garage. Another dusted the front door for prints. Two more walked the perimeter, going over every inch of property like a giant grid, bagging cigarette butts and old soda cans.

I cordoned off the route the cameraperson had taken over the lawn to the front door, but the grass didn't hold any footprints. There were several friction ridges lifted from the knob and steel security plate, but I didn't have much hope for them. The person with the camera wore gloves.

The real estate agent showed up, a plump woman with a hairspray helmet that looked like it could withstand a three-story fall. She was clearly flustered, and it took her three different keys before she could open the door.

I went in first, my .38 an extension of my hand. The shades were drawn and the house was dark, save for streaks of sunlight peeking through cracks.

All of the previous furniture had been removed, and our footsteps echoed on the hardwood floor. A pleasant lemon scent hung in the air, even more revolting than the churros smell. We had the Realtor wait outside, and Herb trailed me through the foyer, the hallway, and over to the basement door.

I experienced a serious feeling of déjà vu, except that it wasn't déjà vu; I actually *had* been here a few years prior, doing this exact same thing.

It was just as scary the second time.

The basement light had been left on. We took the stairs slowly, stopping every few steps to listen. When I finally reached the bottom I steeled myself, turned the corner, and stared over at the place where the woman's throat had been cut.

The basement was empty. No body, no chair, not a drop of blood on the floor. I gave the all-clear and the team came in, lugging gear.

I holstered my gun under my jacket and frowned, looking around the basement. It had been finished since my last visit, the bare concrete floor replaced with linoleum tile, the walls paneled in faux wood.

"I got blood."

Officer Scott Hajek, a short, stout guy with large glasses and a spray bottle of luminol on his belt, pointed a UV light at the ceiling, revealing several glowing droplets. Before I had a chance to postulate if it was left over from Kork's activities, more droplets were found on the newly tiled floor.

"Lieutenant! We got something upstairs!"

I followed the voice, relieved to be out of the claustrophobic confines of the basement. Benedict kept on my heels, huffing as I took the stairs two at a time.

"In the kitchen!"

Sitting on the kitchen counter, next to a mason jar full of peanuts, was a gingerbread man cookie.

I got a closer look. It was different from the ones Kork had left with his victims, taunting the CPD in notes that he'd never be caught. This one was larger, with eyes made out of raisins and peppermint candy buttons.

Under the cookie was a handwritten note.

Its good to BE BacK

The crime scene photographer snapped some shots.

"Why a jar of peanuts?" I asked Herb.

Benedict squinted at the jar. "Those aren't peanuts, Jack."

My breath caught in my throat when I realized what the mason jar contained.

It was filled, to the brim, with dozens of severed human toes.

CHAPTER 2

T ECHNICALLY, NO CRIME has been committed in our district."

Herb and I exchanged a glance.

"We realize that, Captain."

Captain Bains sat behind his desk, rubbing his thumb and index finger over his gray mustache—a mustache that didn't match the deep black of his hairpiece.

"There's not even a body."

"The Kork case is ours," I said.

"This isn't the Kork case. Charles Kork isn't going to commit any more crimes. This could all be a prank or a hoax."

I folded my arms, then unfolded them so I didn't look defensive. "The jar of toes isn't a hoax."

Bains leaned forward. "That's for the Evanston PD to pursue, not us."

"They asked us to come in on this. And we've got nothing else going on."

The captain indicated some paper on his desk. "There was a body discovered in a transient motel an hour ago, on Webster. Stabbing death of a homeless guy named Steve Jensen."

"I'll put Check and Mason on it. I want this one, Captain."

Herb's stomach made an unpleasant noise. Bains stood up and gave us his back. He stared out of his window, which offered a lovely view of the garbage in the alley.

"You've got forty-eight hours. If you can't turn up any evidence by then, I'm pulling you."

More strange sounds from Herb's stomach. Bains glanced over his shoulder and eyed him.

"Hungry, Sergeant?"

"That's not my stomach. I think the GoLYTELY is kicking in."

"Go attend to that."

Benedict about-faced and waddled to the door, knees pressed together.

After Herb left, I locked eyes with my boss.

"What's going on, Captain? I usually enjoy some leeway when it comes to picking cases."

Chicago had five Detective Areas, and I worked as a floater. My reputation allowed it.

Bains didn't seem swayed by my reputation. He pursed his lips. Not a good sign.

"What aren't you telling me, Captain?"

"The superintendent has been getting some flack lately about that TV show."

"TV show?"

"That series with the PI and that fat woman who plays you."

I mentally groaned. The show, called *Fatal Autonomy*, featured a supporting character based on me. I never watched it, but from what I heard, the series didn't display the CPD in a good light. Or me either.

"I explained this before, I let them use my name because one of the show's producers helped out with the Kork case."

Which had been a mistake. Anything to do with Harry McGlade wound up being a mistake.

"The super doesn't care. Chicago is buried in crime, and that show makes us look like a bunch of idiots."

"So what are you saying? The super is pissed at me, so he's gunning for my job?"

"I'm saying I don't want you on anything that might make you look foolish, or anything high-profile. This will all go away, but laying low won't hurt."

I leaned closer to Bains and dropped my voice an octave.

"How angry is he?"

"If you see him on the street, turn around and run."

Ouch.

"You have two days to come up with something solid, Jack. And keep the media out of it."

Bains dismissed me, dispersing the wind I'd had in my sails. Having to worry about job security at my age was a stressor I just didn't need.

I looked for Herb, heard scary sounds coming from the bathroom, and chose to leave him alone for a while.

Evidence was located on the first floor. I took the elevator. The day guy, Bill, greeted me with a grin. He was old enough to have milked Mrs. O'Leary's cow. Bill rescued a previous mayor's family member decades ago, and was allowed to stay on without being forced into retirement. It was a good thing too, because he was the only person who could find anything in the cluttered, unorganized Evidence Room.

"You're like a shot of Viagra, Miss Jack Daniels. I love the boots. Can I lick your heel?"

"No. I thought men lost interest in sex after turning a hundred."

Bill winked. "I'm only ninety-eight. But I make love like a man of seventy-five. What are your plans for later?"

"I'm visiting my mother."

"How is she doing?"

I thought of Mom, the tube in her throat.

"No change."

"How about afterward? Maybe a little midnight rendezvous? You look like you could use a little TLC."

Bill hit the nail on the head with that one. It had been months since I'd been with a man. But even though I'd passed my prime, I wasn't desperate enough to date someone so old he farted dust. Not yet, anyway. Give me another few months and I might consider it.

"I appreciate the offer, Bill, but right now I'm interested in a closed case—333871-5."

Bill nodded, tapping his pointy chin. "The Gingerbread Man. Eleven boxes. Anything in particular?"

"I need everything. Sorry. You want some help?"

"Nope. I keep in shape."

Bill held up his right arm and pulled back the short sleeve, flexing his biceps. There was enough extra skin hanging from that arm to upholster a couch. In a liver spot pattern. I kept that to myself.

Bill scuttled off and lugged the boxes out of storage one at a time. I signed the tags and dug in.

The first two boxes were mostly paperwork, much of it mine. I glanced at a few reports, the memories of the case returning full force. Charles Kork had been a very bad man, torturing women in his basement in Evanston, prolonging their deaths for hours and lovingly capturing it all on videotape.

The third, fourth, and fifth boxes contained personal belongings from his last three victims.

In the sixth box, wrapped in tin foil and sealed in a plastic evidence bag, was the first gingerbread man cookie we'd found. Parts of it were stained black with blood. It had candy hearts for eyes and mouth, three gum drop buttons on the front, and had been lacquered. The one we'd recently found was almost an inch larger, had peppermint swirl buttons and raisin eyes, no mouth. Not the same source.

There were other cookies in other bags, but I didn't bother opening them. In the seventh box I found what I'd been looking for.

Twelve videotapes.

The chain of evidence tags noted how often they'd been viewed and duplicated, which was often. Each tape had a label, done in Kork's distinctive handwriting.

Tape #1, "Jerry Dies Slowly." Tape #6, "Kids Say the Funniest Things When They're Bleeding." Tape #11, "T. Metcalf Gets a Surprise." Tape #12, "Slipping the Knife to the Wife."

The videos contained graphic footage of Kork murdering his victims. There had been ten of them in all, six women and four children. The task force had identified all but one of the kids.

Seeing the tapes filled me with a dread I normally felt in life or death situations. Herb and I had watched part of #4, "Making Little Belinda Cry." We could only stand it for two minutes, even with the sound turned off.

I hadn't been able to forget it, much as I had tried.

After only a small hesitation, I sucked up my courage and pulled out the tapes.

"Would you like a bag?"

I nodded, and Bill produced a plastic Jewel Foods bag from under the counter. I poked through the remaining boxes, taking a handwriting analysis report and some autopsy reports.

In the last box, all by itself, was the murder weapon. A large hunting knife with a jagged edge on the back of the blade. Through the plastic evidence bag, I could see some of Diane Kork's blood dried on the edge.

I put the knife in the bag with the other things. Then I signed everything out, parried another seduction attempt from Bill, and walked up a few flights of stairs to my office.

Benedict was leaning on my desk, looking deflated.

I patted his shoulder. "Everything come out okay?"

He grimaced. "They should put a warning label on the GoLYTELY, something about violent explosions. I think I just lost ten pounds."

I gestured at the jug on my desk, still half full of liquid.

"Looks like you have a little bit more to finish."

Benedict glared at the bottle. "I can't do it. If I finish that, I'll have to attach a seat belt to the toilet."

"Maybe an airbag too."

I sat down and reached for the door-to-door reports on the top of my inbox. A quick scan gave me the gist.

"Neighbors didn't see anything." I tossed the reports onto my desk, annoyed. "Why doesn't someone ever commit a homicide next to a nosy busybody with some binoculars who spies on people all the time?"

Benedict didn't answer. He was staring at the bottle of GoLYTELY.

I left him to face his nemesis, and dove into the Realtor's statement. She'd shown the house to over a hundred people since it went on the market last year. Apparently, the stigma of the previous owner had prevented any sales. No one wanted to dwell where a serial killer once had.

There had been talk of bulldozing it, but Diane Kork had insisted on selling. She inherited it from her ex-husband, shortly after he'd tried to murder her.

Herb's stomach made a noise. He said, "Gotta go," and ran for the door.

"You forgot your jug!" I called after him.

I checked my watch, saw it was creeping up on five, and I decided to call it a day. The reports went into my Jewel bag, which I lugged down to my car.

The engine coughed twice, then turned over. The lion's share of my paycheck went to supporting my aging mother. When Mom had lived in Florida, her condo had cost slightly more than the gross national product of New Zealand.

She'd sold the condo last year, to move in with me. That should have freed up some of my financial obligations, but Mom's current condition cost even more than her condo had.

Mary Streng was in a coma, and her insurance only covered partial treatment. The condo money was almost gone, and soon the debt monster would come a-calling.

It was a burden I gladly accepted. My father died when I was a kid, but Mom had showered me with enough love to make up for the loss. A former Chicago cop herself, she was more than a mother to me; she was a hero.

And now my hero lay in a coma.

And it was all my fault.

CHAPTER 3

MOM RESIDED IN a long-term acute-care facility called Henderson House, on Chicago's north side, not too far from my apartment. She was classified PVS—permanent vegetative state, and received artificial hydration and nutrition, though she could breathe without assistance.

I stopped by on the way home.

"Good evening, Ms. Daniels. Would you like to visit your mother?"

The secretary, Julie something or other, already had the phone in her hand to call the nurse station. Normal procedure meant for me to schedule my visits, or to phone ahead of time. That gave the staff time to clean my mother up before I saw her. For what this place cost, relatives tended to get angry if the loved ones they were visiting had a dirty diaper.

"Any change?" I asked when she hung up the phone.

Julie flipped through a chart. "Still Level One on RLA Cognitive functioning. But her Glasgow went up two points. She spontaneously opened her eyes today."

That got my attention.

"When?"

"Chart says this morning. There's a notation that we called you at home."

"Why didn't you call my cell phone?"

"I'm sorry, Ms. Daniels. Would you like me to put down your cell phone as your primary contact number?"

"My cell phone should already be the primary contact number." My voice got louder. "I don't understand why you wouldn't have tried it since you couldn't reach me at home. Or you could have tried work. I do work for a living."

I set my jaw and felt my ears burn.

"I understand, Ms. Daniels. I'll make sure we use the cell next time. Did you want a glass of water? It will be a few minutes before your mother is ready."

I declined, and sat in a relentlessly cheery waiting room, walls painted bright yellow and adorned with framed prints of rainbows and sunrises. I thought about the Glasgow Coma Score. Mom's Glasgow scores fluctuated all the time. While she hadn't spoken since her injuries, her response to stimulus and her eye-opening were on-again off-again. Her doctors told me that a PVS patient might have a low score one day, and then the next day she could suddenly be awake and aware. So much for Glasgow.

I spent a few minutes sitting and staring at a dusty silk flower arrangement on the magazine table and a man I recognized walked in.

"Hi, Tony."

He brightened when he saw me. Tony Coglioso was tall, in his forties, and had classic Italian good looks. His father had been in a coma for three years.

"Hello, Lieutenant. Any change?"

"Up two points. How about yours?"

"Down a point." He smiled, but it seemed forced. "It sounds like we're talking about the stock market, and not our parents."

Tony and I had seen each other many times over the past few months, exchanging little snatches of conversation in hallways and waiting rooms. Like me, he was divorced, but unlike me he had two adult children. I enjoyed his company, and he wasn't hard to look at. I wondered why he never asked me out. I still fit comfortably into a size eight, and just last week, on the street in front of my apartment, a homeless man told me I had a nice ass.

"How are the kids?"

"Too busy to visit Papa. My oldest says it doesn't matter, that Papa doesn't hear anything anyway."

"He hears," I promised him. "He hears every word."

"Yeah. Well. You on your way up?"

I glanced at Julie, who'd been watching our conversation. Julie nodded.

"Go ahead, Ms. Daniels."

I smiled at Tony. "I guess I am."

"Would you like to share an elevator with an old paisan?"

"I'd be honored."

We didn't talk during the elevator ride. Though some of the cops in my district would label me as aggressive, I wasn't that way with men. It didn't make sense. I could bust down a door and handcuff a murderer, but I've never asked a guy on a date. Not once. In all of my romantic encounters, I'd been a follower rather than a leader.

Even worse, I was crummy at dropping hints. Perhaps if I said something like, "Gosh, it's been a really long time since I got laid." Would a guy pick up on that?

I didn't have a chance to find out. The elevator stopped, and Tony went left, without a word or a wave.

Of course, he was off to visit his PVS parent, so I couldn't really fault his manners.

My own PVS parent was lying peacefully on her bed. A cotton bandage covered the hole in her neck, where the feeding tube went in. Her eyes remained closed, even when I shut the door extra loudly, as I always did.

"Hi, Mom. Still napping, I see."

I sat in the rocking chair next to her, held her withered hand, and told her about my day.

We talked for an hour or so. I tried to remain cheery and upbeat. Regardless of what I'd told Tony, I had doubts that Mom even knew I was there. But on the slight chance she did know, I didn't want to depress her.

When I was all talked out, I stood up, stretched, and then did my poking and prodding. I checked her diaper. Examined her for bed sores. Tickled her feet and pinched her arm, hoping to provoke some kind of response.

"You know, Mom, you're only supposed to sleep for one-third of your life. You're using up your allotment here."

After a pillow fluff and a kiss on the cheek, my attention drifted and I wondered if Tony was still here. A kind, good-looking, single man my age was a rarity.

How hard could it be to ask a guy out for a cup of coffee? What's the worst that can happen? He tells me no? On several different occasions, men have tried to kill me. Getting rejected had to be easier than that.

"See you tomorrow, Mom." I leaned down, whispered in her ear. "I think I'm gonna ask him out."

I closed the door behind me, gently this time, and wandered down the hallway.

Tony had left his door open, and when I poked my head in I saw him holding his father close, his face buried in the older man's chest.

He was sobbing. Great heaving sobs that shook his whole body.

Before I could back away, he noticed me, his face a mask of rage and tears.

"Leave me alone, for crissakes!"

"I . . . uh . . . sorry."

I backpedaled, not able to get to the elevator quick enough.

In the car ride home I second, third, and fourth-guessed myself. My conclusion: A coma clinic isn't a smart place to pick up men.

I lived in an apartment in Wrigleyville, a stone's throw from where the Cubs played. The rent was outrageous and the neighborhood younger than me by two decades. I parked next to a hydrant on the street and lugged the evidence bag up the stairs and to my door.

After disarming the alarm, I went into my kitchen and discovered the cat had been playing his favorite game—toss the kitty litter out of the litter box.

I hated that game, but preferred it to his second-favorite, crap on Jack's bed.

I decided to leave the mess until tomorrow. There was a lump of solidifying cat food in the bowl, and I couldn't remember if it was from this morning or yesterday. I scraped it into the garbage and opened a fresh can.

Mr. Friskers leaped onto the counter upon hearing the can opener.

"You don't greet me when I come home, but you come running when I give you food."

He didn't reply. I dumped the food into his dish and he sauntered over and sniffed it. Then he looked at me, his face the picture of utter disappointment.

"How about a thank-you?"

The cat ate without thanking me.

I plodded into the bedroom, took off my outfit and judged it unsmelly enough to hang up, and washed off my makeup in the bathroom sink. I followed that up with a careful mirror examination of my face, studying the wrinkles and deciding I needed nothing short of spackle to fill them in. My roots were showing too. No wonder Tony wanted me to get away from him.

After dunking my head into a bucket of Oil of Olay, I put on one of Latham's old T-shirts and crawled into bed.

Latham was my ex-boyfriend. I loved him, but messed up the relationship by being me.

I reached across my blanket for the remote, and made an unpleasant discovery: Mr. Friskers had indulged in his second-favorite game after all.

"Dammit, cat!"

I curbed a desire to toss him out the window, a desire I often had but never seriously considered because Mom loved the damn cat. Ten minutes later I'd cleaned up Mr. Friskers's gift, microwaved a chicken parm Lean Cuisine for myself, and got under the covers to watch TV.

The videotapes from the Kork case called to me from their bag.

I ignored them, sticking with sit-com reruns and zany late-night talk show antics. But the jokes weren't funny, and my mind wouldn't let me relax. I brought those tapes home to watch them. And I only had forty-eight hours to find some kind of lead.

But I didn't want to watch videos of people being tortured to death.

But this was my job.

But they might not even help the case.

But they might.

But, but, but.

Finally, when the only thing on was infomercials and pay-per-view porn, I crawled out of bed and went for the Jewel bag.

I told myself I could handle it. I told myself that the people on those tapes had been dead a long time. They were beyond my control. They weren't in pain anymore. I was strong. I could handle it.

I could handle it.

I picked out a tape at random and shoved it into my VCR.

Snow. Then an image.

A teenaged girl. Tied to a chair. Crying.

"Hi, Betsy." Charles Kork's voice, low and straining to be seductive. *"We're going to play a game. It's called 'Please God Make It Stop.' You see all of these nails? I'm going to hammer them into you, one at a time, and you're going to beg God for it to stop. Are you ready?"*

This happened in the past. I could handle it. I was a police lieutenant.

"Look at how big this nail is, Betsy. I bet it's really going to hurt."

I could handle it.

"Here it comes!"

Kork put the nail on the girl's knee.

I forced myself to watch.

CHAPTER 4

M Y FATHER WOULD . . . do things. To himself. To us."

"What kind of things, Alex?"

Alex shifts on the shrink's couch, stares at a small water stain on the ceiling. The office is too bright for Alex to get comfortable. It's like being scrutinized under a microscope.

"Father's a very religious man. A member of Los Hermanos Penitentes. Are you familiar with the group?"

"Flagellants. They lash themselves to atone for their sins."

"They're a Christian sect dating back to the sixteenth century, extremely strict, focusing on redemption through pain. They kneel on tacks. Rub salt and vinegar into their wounds. Mutilate themselves to absolve their sins. They also whip their children. Or make their children whip them."

"Your father would whip you?"

Alex's eyes close, memories flooding in. "Among other things."

"How often did this occur?"

"Sometimes a few times a month. Sometimes every day."

"And where was your mother during all of this?"

"Dead. When I was just a kid."

Alex wonders if revealing the next part is wise. But what good is therapy without a little disclosure?

"My mother died of cancer, after I was born. Father took up with different women after that. Bad women. I remember one of them who wasn't so bad. Father killed her. He beat her to death and buried her in the basement."

Alex turns to assess Dr. Morton's reaction. The good doctor remains composed, sitting in his high-back leather chair. Probably fancies himself Sigmund Freud.

"Were the police ever involved?"

"No. Father claimed she ran away, and ordered us never to speak about her."

Dr. Morton leans forward. "Sometimes, when something traumatic happens to small children, they create events to help them deal with the trauma."

"You mean maybe I imagined her death, and blamed my father for it? Because he abused me and she was missing?"

Dr. Morton makes a noncommittal gesture.

Alex considers. "That's interesting. But not true in my case. I watched Father murder her. He tied her to a beam and flayed all of the skin off her body with a cat-o'-nine-tails."

"And you saw this?"

"Father made me help."

Dr. Morton jots something down on his notepad.

Alex smiles. "You don't believe me."

"I believe this is what you believe, Alex. In our last session, you mentioned your father is still alive."

Alex thinks of Father. "Yes. He is. If you can call it living."

"It's difficult to believe he was never arrested."

"Isn't it? I wonder about that sometimes. How different I'd be if someone had stopped him. How many cats would be alive."

Dr. Morton's pen stops on the paper. "Cats?"

Alex yawns. It's been a long week. Not much sleep.

"I kill cats. I get them from animal shelters, and drown them in a bucket of water."

"Why do you do this, Alex?"

"It makes me feel better."

"How often?"

"When the need arises. Does that shock you, Doctor?"

Alex meets Dr. Morton's gaze. The man doesn't bat an eyelash.

"No. I don't judge, Alex. I listen, and try to help. When was the last time you killed a cat?"

"A few days ago."

"Do you think that hurting animals is a way to release some of the pain you endured as a child?"

"Yes. Plus . . ."

"Plus?"

Alex grins. "It's funny to watch them struggle."

Dr. Morton stands up, walks to the window, his hands clasped behind his back.

"You're in control of your own fate, Alex, not a victim to it. At an early age, we all create unique ways to deal with life. With determination and effort, we can change. I don't think you believe that killing cats is therapeutic, or beneficial, and the pleasure you gain from the act isn't substantive." The doctor turns around, raising an eyebrow. "We've talked about setting goals before."

Alex knows where this is headed.

"You think I should quit killing cats?"

"What do you think?"

"Yeah. I could probably do that."

Dr. Morton nods, playing the mentor role to the hilt.

"How are your other goals? You seem more at ease since last we spoke."

"I'm getting all of my ducks lined up," Alex says.

"Any ducks in particular?"

"Tying up loose ends from my past. Working to get over it. Taking small steps, instead of large ones, like you said."

"Glad to hear it. How about that person you've fallen in love with?"

Dr. Morton flips through his notebook, but Alex mentions the name and saves him the trouble.

"Everything is going perfectly. Exactly according to plan."

"And this love—it's reciprocated, right?"

Alex wonders about this often.

"That's an interesting question, Doctor. Can you ever truly know if love is being returned? You wear a wedding ring, so I assume you're married, and I assume you love your wife. But even if she says she loves you, you can't crawl around in her head and feel it for yourself. You can't ever truly know."

"I feel loved, and that's reassurance enough. Do you feel loved, Alex?"

Alex thinks, really thinks hard.

"Sometimes. Sometimes I do."

A gentle beeping sound comes from Dr. Morton's desk. The doctor walks over and presses a button on the alarm, silencing it.

"That's our time today, Alex. See you tomorrow."

Alex stands up, stretches. "Absolutely. This is really helping me a lot. I appreciate you fitting me in."

"That's good to hear. And remember your goal."

"Don't kill any cats. Got it."

They shake hands, and Dr. Morton shows Alex to the door.

Outside the office, Alex smiles big. Leaving cats alone for a week will not be a problem. Not at all.

The next thing Alex plans on killing isn't a cat.

CHAPTER 5

I DIDN'T SLEEP.

Slumber and I were old adversaries, and on an average night I spent six hours doing the toss and turn, with only one or two hours of actual REM.

But last night I had trouble even closing my eyes.

I managed to get through the Kork tape, right up to the sad, sickening end. I kept the sound on, so I heard all the begging, all the screams. All the laughing and grunting.

Cops tended to be more cynical than the average citizen, but I tried to err on the side of neutrality when it came to human nature. I'd seen good, and I'd seen evil, and mankind exhibited both.

Watching the tape changed that for me. I showered, slapped on some makeup, dressed quickly in generic flats, some black Kenneth Cole pants, and a beige turtleneck sweater from the Gap, and drove to work with absolute tunnel vision. There were no depths to human cruelty. The knowledge burned in my stomach like a hot coal.

We were told to be careful of the *us against them* mentality, but when I finally got to my office, fighting rush hour traffic, watching the honking and the swearing as humans cut each other off, I truly hated my fellow man. I tried to bury my feelings in work. After a cup of vending machine coffee that tasted slightly worse than it smelled, I began going through reports.

The CSU had lifted several dozen prints from the Kork house, which were being run through the database. No prints on the toe jar, or the note. The video that had been dropped off was a Sony brand, available everywhere. The envelope manufacturer still wasn't known, but it looked like an average padded mailer, and was probably sold at thousands of stores.

The desk sergeant had used an Identikit to put together a composite of the man who dropped off the video. He was average height, thin, in his thirties, with a full blond beard. He wore reflective sunglasses, a Cubs baseball cap, and a hooded sweatshirt. The picture had an eerie similarity to the much-circulated artist's sketch of the Unabomber.

No prints on the tape. Prints from Herb and the desk sergeant were lifted from the envelope, along with a white powder residue that smelled like cleanser, such as Ajax or Comet. It was an old burglar trick. Scrubbing your hands with detergent will temporarily strip your hands of their natural oils, making it impossible to leave prints.

I called 411, looking for a last known address of Diane Kork, the Gingerbread Man's ex-wife. Couldn't hurt to question her again, if someone had picked up where her husband had left off. I found her in Bucktown, unlisted. I gave the operator my badge number and a minute later he called me back with her address and phone number.

I called, got a machine, and left a message. Then I called the county morgue.

"Hughes."

"Morning, Max. Jack Daniels."

"Hi, Jack. Here's what I got so far. Sixty-eight toes, from nine different bodies. They've been preserved, and I'm guessing they might be anywhere from twenty to fifty years old."

Max was an assistant medical examiner, and he considered small talk a mark of unprofessionalism.

"Preserved?"

"Packed in salt. There are still some grains left. The skin is completely dehydrated, no biological activity present."

"Is that why some of them are so small? They shrunk?"

"There's been some shrinkage, yes, but many of the toes are tiny because they came from children."

My mind catapulted me back to the video.

Hughes went on. "I've got a forensic anthropologist friend named Coran who's taking a look at the X-rays—she'll be more specific. I'm a soft tissue guy, not a bone guy."

"Could they have come from corpses?"

"You thinking a grave robber?"

"Or an undertaker who keeps souvenirs."

"Possibly. But several of the toes have slices along the toenails, and along the underside."

"Hesitation marks?"

"They're more consistent with defense marks. If someone were trying to cut off your toes, you'd struggle. Wouldn't be easy to do, even to a child. I don't think I can test for histamine in a dried specimen, but I'd bet my house they were removed while these people were still alive."

Pleasant thought. I concentrated on the age. If the toes were twenty years old, they could have come from some of Kork's early victims. But anything older would have been impossible.

"One more strange thing, Jack—each of the toes has a tiny hole running through them, through the bones."

"Any idea what that means?"

"None."

"Thanks, Max. Call me when you know more."

I hit the computer, searching for missing persons reports going back to 1950.

The number was in the millions.

I added restrictions to my search, confining it to the Midwest, sticking to the years 1970–1996.

Millions became tens of thousands. Still too many to conceivably go through. I back-burnered the idea for later and spun through my Rolodex, looking for an old number at the UIC.

"You've reached the office of graphologist Dr. Francis Mulrooney. Please leave a message at the beep."

"Dr. Mulrooney, this is Lieutenant Jack Daniels of the—"

A click. "Lieutenant Daniels? How delightful to hear from you! I apologize for not picking up. I've been forced to screen my calls lately due to some unpleasantness. How can I be of service?"

"Do you still have those handwriting samples from the Gingerbread Man case?"

"Of course."

"I've got another note. It looks similar, but I'm not the expert. Any chance of you coming by sometime this week?"

"I've got some things coming up at the university. Let me check my schedule."

I could picture him, reaching a delicately manicured hand into his tailored vest pocket for his appointment book. Mulrooney was short, thin, with a slight blond mustache, comically thick glasses, and a fetish for bow ties. Academics normally intimidated me, but this one I liked. He was both helpful and unpretentious, two traits most professors lacked.

"I'm free tomorrow, late afternoon. But if you'd like a fast and dirty opinion, you can fax it to me."

"If you wouldn't mind."

Mulrooney read off his fax number. I had a photocopy of the recent Evanston note, and managed to feed that into my fax machine on my third try.

"It's coming through now. Will you pardon me for a moment, Lieutenant?"

"Take your time."

I trimmed my thumbnail with my teeth, imagining the petite man going over the writing sample with a magnifying glass.

"Very interesting. Very interesting indeed. Is the original in marker?"

"Yes."

"Clever."

"It's clever to write in marker?"

"One of the things graphologists look at is pressure. Felt-tip pens disguise that. Tell me, the fax you sent, is this the original size, or did you enlarge it?"

"The real sample is half the size."

"I see. I look forward to seeing the actual note. This is a very interesting sample. We don't see this too often."

"See what, Doctor?"

"It appears to be a forgery. Someone who has seen Kork's original handwriting and has done their best to imitate it. The descending *t*-bars. The slant. The capitalization. But there are some obvious differences. First of all, Kork's writing is heaviest in the lower zone. This person is an upper zone writer, an indicator of high intelligence. Also, there are some feminine characteristics at work here."

I blinked. "A woman wrote this?"

"It's impossible to determine sex from a handwriting sample, and men can have feminine qualities in their script, just as women can have masculine qualities."

Mulrooney went into a lecture about the differences between male and female traits in handwriting, but my attention was drawn away by a very unpleasant surprise standing in my doorway.

"Dr. Mulrooney?" I interrupted. "Something just came up. I look forward to seeing you tomorrow."

"Hmm? Oh, yes, of course. Until then, Lieutenant."

I replaced the receiver on the cradle and turned to face my demons.

CHAPTER 6

HELLO AGAIN, LIEUTENANT. I hope you remember us. I'm Special Agent Dailey, this is Special Agent Coursey." He leaned forward a fraction. "From the Bureau."

They had matching crew cuts. Special Agent Jim Coursey wore a gray suit. Special Agent George Dailey, the same height and build as Coursey, also sported a gray suit, but his buttons were squarish compared to Coursey's roundish buttons. That must be how their handler could tell them apart.

"Can I see some ID?" I asked.

Dailey reached for his pocket, but Coursey stopped him with a look.

"She's kidding. She does that."

"Didn't you read my profile?" I asked Dailey.

He dropped his hand back to his side and concentrated on looking Federal. Dailey and Coursey were ViCAT operatives from the FBI's Behavioral Science Unit. ViCAT stood for Violent Criminal Apprehension Team, which used high-tech suspect profiling techniques and state-of-the-art crime detecting computers to waste the time of local cops like me.

"We have some exciting news," said Coursey.

I couldn't pass that up. "You're quitting the Bureau and joining the traveling cast of *Riverdance?*"

"No. The Evanston Police Department has invited us in on the new Gingerbread Man murder."

Here was proof that God hated me.

"We've obtained a copy of the video. It contains some similarities to the previous Kork murders."

"Gentlemen," I began, "while it makes me feel all warm and fuzzy inside that you're—"

"We've had Vicky do a profile." Coursey talked over me while Dailey removed a thick packet of paper from his briefcase and plunked it on my desk.

"Vicky is what we call the ViCAT computer," Dailey added. "She's a comprehensive compiled database of criminal activity committed throughout the United States."

Every time they dropped by, they explained Vicky to me. Perhaps I had a sign around my neck that said: "Tell me again, I'm an idiot."

"Though we haven't had enough time to fully analyze the videotape of the murder, Vicky postulates that this is the work of a copycat," said Coursey.

"A copycat," said Dailey.

"A copycat," said I. "Was your first clue the note, or the fact that it took place in the same house as Kork's murders?"

Sarcasm was wasted on these guys, but that didn't stop me from making an effort.

"If you'll look over the profile, you'll notice that this crime took an extraordinary amount of planning and organization," said Coursey.

"So much so, that Vicky doesn't believe this is the work of a single individual," said Dailey.

"The facts point to the perpetrator being a group of individuals," said Coursey.

"A group?" said I.

"An organized group of at least three people. Perhaps members of a club or organization."

I took a stab. "Like the PTA?"

"Actually," Coursey lowered his voice an octave, "we've been informed by Homeland Security that three members of a subversive Brazilian band went through Customs at O'Hare Airport eleven days ago."

I held up a palm. "Guys, while being sent a videotape may have been meant to inspire terror, I really don't think this was a terrorist act."

"They're not terrorists," said Dailey. "They call themselves the Samba Kings."

Coursey added, "They're musicians."

I took a moment before saying, "You think the murderer is a Brazilian samba trio."

Dailey held up his right hand and ticked off fingers. "They're organized. Focused. Motivated. And are in excellent physical condition, by the looks of the pictures on their CD."

I checked my neck for the *I'm an idiot* sign. I didn't have one. But I was considering getting two of them made, with matching gray letters.

"Gentlemen—" I began.

"There's more," Dailey interrupted. "According to Interpol, both the drummer and the lead singer have priors. And there have been several dozen instances of mutilation in Brazil recently."

Coursey leaned in. "Cattle mutilation," he said.

"Maybe their maraca player is a chupacabra," I offered.

Dailey and Coursey exchanged a glance. "You don't seem to be taking this seriously, Lieutenant."

I sighed. "Sorry, guys. It's been a rough day. Why don't you let me memorize this report you gave me, and I'll get back to you, say, next week?"

Another look passed between them. I wondered if they had some kind of telepathy thing going. Probably not, as that would require a brain.

"How about tomorrow?" said Coursey.

"How about November?" I countered.

"How about on Thursday?" said Dailey.

"How about the first of never?" I returned volley.

"Next week it is," Coursey said. "We'll see ourselves out."

"Please do. And I'll put out an all-points bulletin, asking my people to pay special attention to anyone speaking Portuguese."

The special agents gave me a blank stare.

"That's what they speak in Brazil," I said.

"We knew that," said Dailey.

"We went to Harvard," said Coursey.

"Thanks for stopping by, gentlemen." I held up their report. "I'll get started on this right away."

They left, and I placed the report in the circular file, on top of my empty coffee cup. A quick check of my watch—a Movado that Latham had given me—showed me it was nearing lunchtime, and Herb was probably done with his procedure. I gave him a call.

"Hello?" His voice was groggy.

"How'd the colonoscopy go? You eating a big plate of nachos yet?"

Long pause. I heard hospital sounds in the background. A nurse talking. A doctor being paged.

"They found something. A tumor."

I momentarily ran out of words.

"Jesus, Herb."

"Took a biopsy. Won't know until later."

"Are you okay?"

"No. I gotta go."

He clicked off.

I stared at the phone, unsure of what to do. Go visit him? Herb, though cuddly on the outside, was a classic stoic. Dropping by would cause embarrassment, and possibly anger. But still, a tumor was a serious thing.

I closed my eyes. I'd had partners prior to Herb, but never one I'd cared about. Benedict was like a big brother. If Herb died . . .

The phone rang. I screwed a cap over my feelings and answered, hoping it was Herb.

"Did the Feebies just drop by?"

Bains.

"Yes, Captain. Evanston brought them in."

"I want you off this."

"You gave me forty-eight hours."

"I said to keep a low profile. With those two involved, it's only a matter of time before the *Weekly World News* is camped outside the station. You're off."

"Captain—"

"Off."

I hung up the phone and took a deep breath. That didn't do a damn thing, so I took another, and another.

Something inside of me, some little internal switch, had been flipped, and I wasn't sure who I was. I thought about Herb, and my mom, and my ex-husband, Alan, and Latham, and my job, and my life, and where I'd been and where I was headed.

I thought about how hard I tried to remain in control, and what little good it did. Control didn't matter. Fate didn't care about how hard you tried, or how well planned you were, or how much you wanted something.

Fate had its own agenda.

I was forty-six years old. My job, the thing I devoted my life to, was in trouble. My best friend might be dying. My mother was in a coma. And I had screwed up the one thing that I did have some control over; I loved a great guy, and I blew it. And if I wanted to admit it, to take the hard inward glance that made me ask why, I knew the answer.

Deep down, I wanted to be miserable. I wanted to be miserable, because that's what I deserved, because I hated myself.

Which was a pretty crummy way to live. And not something I wanted to continue.

I picked up the phone, dialing from memory.

"Hello?"

"Hi Latham, it's Jack. I'm sorry. I'm sorry for hurting you. I know a lot of time has passed, and I'm sure you've moved on, but I haven't. I still love you. Can I come over?"

"Who is this? Do I know you?"

The voice wasn't Latham's.

"Ah, hell." I disconnected and tried again, dialing more carefully.

"You've reached Latham Conger, I can't come to the phone, please leave a name and number and I'll get back to you."

I opened my mouth, but nothing came out.

Say something, Jack.

The silence stretched.

Open your mouth.

Dead air, each passing second like a kick in the gut.

Dammit, woman, do you want to be miserable your whole life?

"Latham, it's Jack. I'm sorry for everything. I love you. I'd like to see you again. Please call."

There. I did it. I actually did something for myself. It brought a small smile to my face.

But my shoulders bunched up again when I realized I'd be up all night, waiting for him to call.

Once again, control was out of my hands.

CHAPTER 7

I STOPPED BY Henderson House on the way home from work, but there had been no change. Mom hadn't opened her eyes again. I sat with her for an hour. No talking this time, just holding her hand.

Twice I checked my cell phone, to make sure it was on. It was.

After a pillow fluff, I turned to leave and had a good startle seeing Tony Coglioso standing in the doorway. His eyes seemed glazed, far away.

"Tony?"

"Hi, Jack. How's she doing?"

"The same. How about your dad?"

"The same."

I wondered if I should apologize for barging in on him yesterday, and then thought that maybe he was the one who should apologize for being so rude, and finally accepted that neither of us needed to say the *s* word because, hey, our parents were dying.

"You look nice," Tony said, not quite focusing on me.

I figured I looked like hell, but thanked him anyway.

Tony smiled. "See you soon." Then he walked off.

Strange. Maybe he was drunk, or high on something. Or maybe he stopped by to ask me out, checked the merchandise, and decided to pass.

I fluffed Mom's pillow again, gave her a kiss on the cheek, and headed to the elevator. No Tony in the hall, no Tony in the lobby, and no Tony in the parking lot. It didn't matter. My mind was on Latham, not Tony, so I didn't dwell.

After a quick check to make sure my cell phone hadn't accidentally switched off during my walk to the car, I headed home.

Mr. Friskers gave me a warm welcome, howling and running away when I walked through the door. I reset the alarm and turned the dead bolt. Time to plan my big evening.

I made dinner, maxing out my culinary skills with a BLT. Then I fed the feral cat, plugged my cell into the charger, set my .38 next to my bed, swapped my outfit for a T-shirt and fresh panties, scrubbed my face, ate my BLT, brushed my teeth, and switched on the TV. Network drivel was better than brainwashing when it came to clearing a woman's mind. I hopped on the bed, content to play station roulette.

Next to the TV, still in the Jewel bag, were the Kork videotapes.

They might as well have been blinking like a beacon.

You were pulled from the case, Jack. You don't need to watch more people being tortured. You've got enough on your plate as it is.

I put on a game show, but stared at the bag. I switched to a cooking show, but kept looking at the bag. I tried a sit-com starring the stand-up comedian du jour.

That damn bag kept demanding my attention.

I crawled out of bed. Picked up the bag and carried it into the kitchen.

Mr. Friskers had his face crammed in his bowl. He hissed at my interruption of his gluttony. I hissed back and set the bag on the counter, next to the sink. The cat ran up and swiped a claw at my leg.

I jumped back, knocking the bag over and spilling files onto the floor. My ankle sprouted three shallow cuts, not too far from the other set of shallow cuts that had already healed, but lower than the fresh cuts a few inches higher.

"Dammit, cat!"

It was always my left leg too. He'd clawed me a dozen times, but never on the right leg. Sadism, with an agenda.

I tore off a paper towel, dabbing it at the blood while picking up papers with my free hand. My fist closed around the Diane Kork file, and I paused.

An image, unbidden, flashed into my head, of the first time I'd seen Diane Kork, half naked and bleeding in Charles Kork's basement. I remembered her pleading, crying face. Her ugly wounds, weeping blood. And something else. Something familiar.

I paged through the file, but there weren't any pictures of her wounds. Made sense; the case was closed, and evidence was no longer needed.

But I did have images of Diane. Videotape #12, "Slipping the Knife to the Wife."

"You're off the case, Jack," I said aloud.

I didn't listen to myself.

I found tape #12 and took it into the bedroom. I hit Play and then Fast-forward, cycling through Diane being tied up, up to the scene where he sliced off her clothes.

I paused the tape.

The image jittered, two lines of snow framing the edges of the screen, but I could clearly see what I'd been looking for: a heart-shaped tattoo, the size of a dime, on Diane's hip bone just below the bikini line.

I stared for a moment, then went back to the kitchen and dug out the copy of the tape of the latest murder—the original was still at the lab.

I swapped cassettes and again viewed the slow approach to the Kork house, the walk into the basement, and the zoom in on the naked victim.

I couldn't see any tattoos because the woman was sitting, and the crease in her lap obscured her bikini line.

I let the tape play in slow motion, watching her struggle and die frame by frame, and five minutes into her pain she arched her back and her pelvis came briefly into view.

Pause.

The heart tattoo was the same.

I felt my breath catch, and hashed out the possibilities. Either the killer had put a fake tattoo there to make it look like Diane Kork, or else the victim was indeed Diane Kork.

I had Diane's phone number in my jacket pocket, from when I'd called Information earlier. When I dialed it, I got her answering machine for the second time.

"Shit."

Two options. I could call the station, have them send a car over to check out Diane's place. Or I could go myself, even though Bains had ordered me off the case.

Diane lived on Hamilton, and I was more than a mile closer to her than anyone at the 26th District.

I slid into some Levi's, shrugged on a sweater, strapped on my .38, and was out the door before I gave it any more thought.

CHAPTER 8

ALEX CHECKS THE caller ID. It's Jack Daniels.

Alex knows the number.

Alex knows a lot about Jack. Jack has been part of the plan from the very beginning.

It's a little after ten p.m. and the lights are off in Diane's house. This has been a good base of operations, but Alex knows it can't last. Jack will come by eventually. She might even be on her way now.

What to do, what to do?

"An ounce of prevention," Alex says, and smiles. In the bedroom are a suitcase and a trunk. Alex begins to pack—clothes, shoes, gear, the video recorder, all of the equipment. Alex takes it through the back door, through the yard, and into the tiny, unattached garage adjacent to the alley.

The trunk goes into the backseat of the rental car, and Alex finds a tire iron and a length of garden hose in the garage.

The car has a safety device in the gas tank that prevents siphoning, but Alex breaks through it with the crowbar. The hose snakes down the tank, and a few foul-tasting sucks on the other end brings forth the gas.

Alex fills two old buckets and a washtub, then removes the hose.

It takes two trips to carry the gas back to the house. *Slosh–slosh–slosh.* First the bedroom. Then the kitchen. Then the den. The place is filthy with Alex's fingerprints, and this is much faster than wiping it all down.

When the gas has been poured, Alex begins to search Diane's cabinets for matches. There's a box on top of the refrigerator. Alex takes a deep breath, tastes gasoline fumes, and smiles.

The doorbell rings.

Jack.

Alex selects a matchstick and drags it along the side of the box, annoyed at the interruption.

Arson should be savored.

The match is dropped, igniting the linoleum floor with a soft *whoomp.*

Next to the sink is a semiautomatic pistol. Alex picks it up and walks into the living room, through a path in the flames, and waits patiently for Jack.

CHAPTER 9

RANG DIANE Kork's doorbell again, not expecting an answer. The tattoo match in both videos was enough to suggest a crime had been committed, giving me probable cause to enter her house without a warrant. The front door was heavy wood, dead-bolted, and I doubted even my best tae kwon do spin-kick would open it.

The neighborhood was dark, quiet, parked cars lining the unlit street. Kork's house was typical for Chicago, a two-story red brick duplex with a black iron fence encircling a postage-stamp-sized lot. Similar buildings bookended this one, less than two yards between them. I walked down the porch stairs and took the narrow walkway to the rear of the house, looking for a basement window to break.

The windows along the side had decorative bars on them. I followed the perimeter, advancing into the backyard, my eyes slowly adjusting to the darkness. We were in the heart of downtown, but with the lack of any lights it might as well have been the woods.

The backyard also had a porch, with two small windows framing the back door. I climbed the wooden stairs, tugging my .38 from my holster, keeping my elbow bent and the barrel pointed up.

Two things hit me at once: the smell of smoke, and the orange light flickering through a crack in the drapes.

Fire.

I tried the door. Locked, but the knob was cool. Switching the grip on my revolver, I tapped the glass out of the left-hand window and yanked the curtains through, smoothing them over the ragged shards.

"Police! Is there anyone in here?"

No answer. I tasted hot, foul air, shoved my gun back in my holster, yanked out my cell, and dialed 911. Then I pulled myself through the window.

I fell into the kitchen hands first, palming the linoleum floor and dragging myself along until my feet followed. Two countertops, and the floor in front of me, were ablaze, and the flames seemed to notice my arrival and launched themselves at me.

Smart move, Jack, breaking a window and feeding the flames with O_2.

I reached behind me in a panic, pulling the heavy drapes over my head, feeling bits of glass caress my hair, just as the fire surrounded me.

It got stifling hot, like I'd crawled into an oven. My fingers singed, and I released the burning drapes and rolled toward the door, becoming tangled in flaming, smoking fabric.

My head popped through the front, and a patch of my hair stuck to the melting floor. I peeked through one eye, noting I'd rolled through the worst of it, but the curtains cocooning me were sporting some serious flames of their own. Plus, whatever the curtains were made of, it didn't burn cleanly, and choking brown fumes clouded my eyes and provoked a coughing fit.

First things first. I freed my left arm and tried to unwind the curtains, grabbing for the patches of fabric that weren't on fire yet.

A wave of heat turned my attention to the right, and I witnessed the flames lick up the wall, enveloping the window I'd gone through. No exit there.

My eyes were useless now, my nose running like I'd turned on a faucet, and my coughs racked with phlegm. What kind of material were these curtains made from? Arsenic? I knew I'd choke to death before I burned to death, so I tore away the fabric, kicking and clawing, getting singed over and over until I was finally free.

I coughed, and spit, and crawled through the doorway. My left hand screamed at me, and I squinted at it but couldn't make out the burns from the soot. I made a fist. It hurt, but was still functional.

Still on my knees, I took a quick look around and figured out I was in the living room. The ceiling was obscured by a thick cloud of gray smoke, and the walls looked like reverse waterfalls; flames flowing upward rather than water coming down. And the noise—a sort of low roaring sound, mixed in with the crackle of a billion dry leaves. Loud enough to mask my coughing. The sound of raging fire.

Twenty feet away, I saw the lower half of a doorway. I scrambled toward it on all fours, ignoring the pain in my burned hand, getting within fifteen feet . . . ten feet . . .

Two legs cut through the smoke and appeared in the doorway, obscured from the knees up. They wore loose jeans and construction boots, unlaced.

"Police!" I croaked, fumbling for my holster.

I heard the shot at the same moment I felt it, an explosive *BOOM* passing the right side of my head. I cleared leather and drew a bead, firing three shots at the center mass of the shooter just as the legs darted back.

My head rang with a deep resonation that shut out the sounds of the flames. I rolled right, on my stomach, keeping my gun on the doorway. I waited fifteen seconds. Thirty seconds.

My feet got hot, and I chanced a quick look and saw the fire creeping up behind me. I was about to be engulfed.

I crawled forward, using my legs and my burned hand, my .38 still trained ahead of me. The smoke had filled the room, hovering so low, it was in my face. I fired once more through the doorway, and then got on my feet and ran through it in a crouch.

A quick glance around showed me my mistake.

I'd run right into hell.

CHAPTER 10

ALEX FROWNS AT the miscalculation. The front door, the escape route, is an inferno, a giant wall of flame that is impossible to get through. The other two windows facing the street are also blazing.

There is no way out.

Alex thinks for a moment, then dashes through the haze and up the stairs. Visibility is poor, and it's hard to breathe, but Alex remembers that the master bedroom has a window facing the street. A window that opens onto the roof.

A gunshot, from downstairs. Jack is still alive. Doubtful she will be for long, though.

Eyes burning and teary, Alex squeezes them closed and feels along the wall, eventually arriving at the bedroom. The latch opens easily, and Alex pulls up the window with enough force to crack the frame.

The cool Chicago air is like honey. Alex sucks down a breath, wiping away soot from stinging eyes. Walking onto the roof is ridiculously easy, and Alex follows the gutter around to the rear of the house.

Sirens pierce the night, closing in from all directions. Alex gets down on all fours and scoots to the edge of the roof. The drop is about twenty feet, onto grass, but the gutter looks sturdy.

Gripping the aluminum, Alex swings over the side and hangs for a moment before falling to the ground.

Ankles tight together, knees bent, Alex hits the earth hard but unharmed. Alex ponders for a moment—the suitcase is still in the house, but there's nothing in it that can't be replaced.

Jack is also still in the house.

Not the way Alex had intended for Jack to die, but a fitting way to end the lieutenant's life. Choking, burning, and panicked. What more could a gal ask for?

Digging keys from a front pocket, Alex enters the garage, opens the garage door, and hops into the rental car. The sirens are deafening now. Alex starts the car and guns the engine.

A quick left down the alley proves to be a mistake; there's an enormous fire engine blocking the exit. Alex checks the rearview and sees another truck, also crammed onto the narrow alley.

Leaving on foot isn't an option. There are things in the trunk. Incriminating things.

Alex jams the accelerator to the floor and the tires screech. Between the fire engine and the building is a small gap. It doesn't look wide enough to get a car through, but Alex has to try.

Twenty.

Thirty.

At forty miles an hour the car reaches the gap and Alex grips the steering wheel in iron hands. There's some yelling—firefighters pointing at the car—and a clunking noise as both the driver's-side and passenger's-side mirrors tear from the chassis, but Alex makes it through the hole, clips a fireman and sends him spinning into his truck, and then speeds down Hamilton, grinning like the devil himself.

CHAPTER 11

Like all curious teenagers, I'd tried cigarettes. I decided early on that a nicotine buzz wasn't worth holding hot smoke in my lungs.

That popped into my head as I crawled across the smoldering carpet, my head pressed to the floor in an attempt to suck the last bit of oxygen floating at the bottom of the living room.

The ringing in my head was subsiding, the fire sound coming back. I squinted through the thick smoke, which felt like sandpaper on my eyes, and wondered where I was crawling to. Disorientation had dug its claws in, and I might have been crawling around in circles. I tried to go where there weren't flames, but there were more flames than not, and they danced and jumped around, igniting more things.

The heat had officially become unbearable. One time many years ago, in an effort to bake away my clammy white pallor, I'd visited Oak Street beach in July and had forsaken the sunscreen in order to minimize my tan time. I'd fallen asleep, and wound up with a nice case of sun poisoning, my skin so red, it had blistered.

This hurt worse. Though I wasn't actually on fire, it was so hot, I *felt* like I was on fire. The sweat poured out of me in rivulets, but evaporated almost as soon as my pores squeezed it out.

My knuckles hit something ahead of me. A scorched wall. I followed it, blind and hacking, and it fell away into an opening.

Stairs.

Going up is never a smart idea in an emergency situation, but I couldn't stay where I was. I climbed the stairs on my hands and knees, my .38 still gripped in my fist. Soon it would be too hot to hold. I wondered how stable the rounds were—on top of everything, I didn't need my bullets exploding in my gun.

The higher I climbed, the smokier it got, which made sense because smoke rises. When I reached the top of the stairs, I couldn't see and I couldn't breathe. My lungs felt like two ashy lumps of charcoal, and I was light-headed and in surround-sound pain. I'd begun to cry between coughing fits.

The fire was right behind me.

Not knowing which way to go, I continued on my present course and felt tile under my hands. A bathroom. I got on my knees, felt up the wall, and hit the switch, hoping to turn on the fan to suck away some of the smoke.

No electricity.

Frantic and blind, I closed the door behind me and swung my hands wildly around, bumping the sink. I turned on the water, cupping some in my hands, splashing it onto my face to clear my eyes.

It helped a little, and I could make out the window opposite the sink. A ventilation window. Too small to crawl through, but I sure could use some ventilation right about now.

I fumbled with the latch, tugged it open, and took big, greedy gulps of cool night air.

Above the din of the flames, I heard sirens.

"Help!" I tried to yell. But it only came out as a croak.

I holstered my gun and felt around for a towel. Holding it tight, I stuck my arm out the window and wagged the towel frantically, like I was signaling to surrender. The window faced one of the narrow spaces between buildings, and all I could see was the side of the duplex next to me.

Then the heat suddenly kicked up, and I noted with displeasure that the bathroom door I closed moments ago was ablaze.

I hung the towel on the window latch and then backed away from the door, almost tripping against the bathtub.

Not a bad idea, a bath.

Climbing into the tub, I tugged on the faucet and yanked up the little handle to turn on the shower.

The water came out hot, but it felt wonderful on my face and hands. I stood in the spray, opening my mouth, letting it bathe my scratched throat. Then I bent down and pulled the lever to plug up the bathtub drain, letting the tub fill with water.

Though the window was open, the flaming door was creating smoke faster than it left the room. I sat down, hugging my knees, watching death descend from the ceiling, inch by inch.

The firefighters had to be hosing down the building, right?

It was a brick construction, and that helped, didn't it?

Didn't they see my towel hanging out the window and know I was in here?

Though it had to be over 110 in that bathroom, my whole body was shivering.

I was soaked, so I probably wouldn't burn to death. The smoke would get me. Or maybe the water would heat up to the point that I'd boil. It felt like it was getting close. I had turned the handle to Cold, but there wasn't any cold; the fire was heating the water as it came through the pipes.

It was just a matter of time until they figured out I was in here and rescued me. Two minutes, tops. I could last another two minutes. One hundred and twenty seconds. Then I'd be safe.

I began to count.

One . . . two . . . three . . .

I stopped counting at 160.

The flames leaped from the door to the ceiling, and bits of burning plaster flaked down and sizzled in my tub, a rain of fire. I picked up the bath mat, dunked it in the sooty water, and wound it around my head. The shower slowed to a trickle, and then stopped, with my tub only half filled.

A calm came over me, possibly induced by oxygen deprivation. I was going to die. I didn't have a choice in the matter. I knew that I should be fighting somehow, trying to prevent it. But there was nothing else I could do.

I'd been beaten.

A small part of me didn't want to accept it and screamed for me to act. Maybe I could wrap myself in wet towels and charge down the stairs. Maybe I could bust the bathroom window and scream until I was noticed, even though that wall was on fire now too.

But the larger part of me recognized those options as futile. I'd live a little bit longer if I waited for death, rather than rushed to meet it.

Once I accepted my fate, I accepted everything that went with it.

I wouldn't ever know if Herb had cancer or not.

I wouldn't ever know if my mom came out of her coma.

I wouldn't ever know if Latham would have called me back.

I wouldn't ever know who it was that shot at me downstairs, which seemed like hours ago.

Lifetimes ago.

It made me sad.

The bathroom door burst inward, and the last thing I remembered was a large man in a firefighter uniform reaching out for me.

CHAPTER 12

*S*OME FIRST-DEGREE burns on your left hand, smoke inhalation, and you'll need stitches in your ear."

I took another hit from the oxygen mask, my lungs feeling like they'd been scoured with steel wool. I went on another coughing jag, and spit something black and gross into my tissue.

"Stitches?" My voice was low and raspy.

The doctor, whose name tag said *Williams,* prodded my ear with a wet cotton ball.

"You're missing a tiny piece on the top. You probably nicked it on something."

I stayed silent. I hadn't nicked my ear on anything. That bastard in Diane Kork's house had shot the top of my ear off.

"Nothing to worry about," the doctor said. "It won't even be noticeable after it heals. Well, maybe a bit noticeable. Are you good with makeup?"

While the doc stitched me up, I used his rubbing alcohol and some cotton pads to clean the soot off of my face. My clothes were a disaster, soaked and scorched and garbage. I currently wore a hospital gown, but one of the shift nurses promised she'd find me some pants and a top.

"Are you sure you don't want a local?"

"I'm fine."

The Darvocet I'd been given for the pain in my hand had kicked in, and all I felt in my ear was a slight tugging while he sutured.

He knotted it off, and I had to fill out some forms before being discharged— against the hospital's recommendation. A cute male nurse came in and flushed my eyes with something that helped stop the itching, and while he held my head in his strong and capable hands the shift nurse returned with some clothes.

"Do you think you can squeeze into a size twelve?" she asked.

"Maybe if I suck in my stomach," I told her.

The male nurse offered me a towel and left, and I dressed in a large pair of khakis and a Bulls sweatshirt. The khakis were so large, I had to keep one hand on the waist to hold them up.

Finally, when I was forcing on my wet shoes, the fireman who'd rescued me poked his head through the curtain.

"Just wanted to check how you're doing, ma'am."

He was probably half my age, and his boyish face made him look even younger.

"I'm fine. Thanks again, Peter. You saved my life."

"Just doing my job. Smart thing you did, hanging the towel out the window."

He looked pleased with himself, and had a right to be. Saving a person's life is the best natural high there is.

"Did you find anyone else in the house?"

"No. You were the only one in there."

"No bodies?"

"Nothing."

"You check the basement?"

"We checked everywhere. House was empty, thank God."

I thought about that. I would have bet good money that Diane Kork's body was somewhere in the house.

"Did you see anyone running from the house before me? Someone in jeans and work boots?"

"I didn't. But someone was in a hurry to get away from there. Tommy got clipped by a car in the alley out back."

"Tommy?"

"Tommy Thurston, guy from my unit. He's just a couple beds down. Broken leg. Want to meet him?"

"Yeah, I would." I squeezed on my second shoe and stood, one hand holding my pants.

Peter led me down the hall. Tommy lay on his cot, his calf wrapped in a fiberglass cast. His eyes were closed. He looked too young to shave. Where were they getting firemen these days, out of grammar school?

"Mr. Thurston?"

"What? Oh, hey. You're the one we pulled out."

I offered a hand. "Lieutenant Jack Daniels. How's the leg?"

"Tibia fracture. Not bad."

"I heard you were hit by a car."

"Damnedest thing. He came screeching out of the alley like Dale Earnhardt. Clipped engine number twelve and the side of a building, and gave me a love tap like I wasn't even there. Probably didn't see me."

"Did you see the driver?"

"No. Too dark. Happened too fast."

"How about the car?"

"Dark color. Looked new. Could have been anything. Lots of cars look alike these days, don't you think? Shouldn't be hard to find, though."

"Why is that?"

"Guy lost both his side mirrors driving through the gap."

I nodded. "Any chance you noticed the license plate?"

"Actually, right before it hit me, I did notice the plate. Started with *D* one."

"*D* one? You're sure?"

"Uh-huh. I remember because when it was coming right at me I thought, *I'm the Dead One.* D one. Get it?"

"I got it. You don't remember any other numbers?"

"Nope. There were six or seven of them. Looked like an Illinois plate." His eyes lit up. "Hey, your name is Jack Daniels?"

"That's me. Lightly braised, but in the flesh."

"I like that show on TV that you're in, that *Fatal Autonomy*. You're pretty funny. I loved the one where you were screaming and screaming and screaming for help and that private eye guy took off his dirty sock and crammed it in your mouth."

I gave him a weak smile. "Yeah. Good episode."

Peter chimed in. "My favorite is the one where you tracked down that killer and went to shoot him but you forgot to load your gun." He slapped his thigh, grinning. "Classic."

"That didn't really happen."

"Sure was funny, though." Peter eyed my outfit. "I think it's great you're losing weight. Made my job a lot easier, carrying you."

I considered telling him that I wasn't fat, that was only the actress who played me, but I let discretion be the better part of valor.

"Excuse me." I slid past. "Gotta get home and drink my Slim-Fast shake. Thanks again, guys."

"Nice to meet you, Mrs. Daniels."

Since the paramedics had taken me to the hospital, I had to take a cab to my car, still parked on Hamilton. A single fire engine remained on the scene, hosing down Diane Kork's house. The flames had long since been extinguished, but the heat remained. When the water hit certain spots, it hissed and steamed fiercely.

I wanted to poke around inside, but now didn't seem like a good time. Plus, I was exhausted. I did drive around to the back alley, and was rewarded with a nice surprise: two rearview mirrors, broken and lying on the asphalt.

Evidence. I hoped it would be enough.

CHAPTER 13

I MANAGED TO sleep for six whole hours, which was wonderful, but waking up was a Spanish Inquisition interrogation.

My eyes were glued shut with crust, my nose and throat were raw, my hand felt like I was holding it over a stove burner, and my ear throbbed with my heartbeat. A bad headache was the cherry on top of the pain sundae.

Good freaking morning.

I sat up and stared into the indifferent eyes of Mr. Friskers, who perched at the foot of my bed like a gargoyle.

"What do you want, cat? Food?"

He meowed.

I almost did a double take. Mr. Friskers never meowed. His normal method of communication was hissing or yowling.

"What, are you actually trying to be friendly?"

The cat meowed again.

Though my heart was carved from glacier ice, I felt it melt a bit.

"That's sweet." I reached out to pat him on the head, and he hissed and clawed my hand, drawing blood.

He ran off before I could find my gun and shoot him.

I glanced at the clock. A little after nine a.m. I had a lot to do, plus that handwriting expert was stopping by the office this afternoon, but I couldn't comprehend going to work feeling as crummy as I did. The very thought of explaining to Captain Bains what happened last night made my head hurt worse than it already did.

Screw it. I needed a day off.

I peeled myself out of bed, found my way to the bathroom, coughed and hacked and spit black mucus into the toilet for ten minutes, changed into some old Lee jeans and the Bulls sweatshirt I inherited last night, and then lurched into the kitchen. Checked my answering machine. No calls. Plodded back into the bedroom and checked my cell phone. No calls. Found some aspirin, made quick work of three, then forced myself back into the kitchen, where I liberated a tray of ice from the freezer.

I chewed on the cubes, which helped my sore throat. Then I called the graphologist, Dr. Francis Mulrooney, to cancel our appointment. He wasn't in. I left a message.

I spent the next thirty minutes cleaning and oiling my .38. I carry a Colt Detective Special, blue finish, black grips, with a two-inch barrel. It weighs twenty-one ounces, and is seven inches from butt to front sights. I preferred revolvers to semiautomatics for several reasons. They had fewer moving parts, which meant less could go wrong in terms of jamming and misfiring. At any time, I could visually check how many rounds were left. And they were easier to clean.

I threw away the two remaining bullets still in the cylinder, not knowing how the heat and the water from yesterday had affected them, and was loading six fresh rounds when I heard someone at my door.

It wasn't a knock. It was someone trying to turn the knob.

I slapped the cylinder closed and walked silently up to my door, keeping to the right of the frame.

The knob continued to turn, and I heard the jangle of keys.

Latham? He had a key to my apartment. I disengaged the burglar alarm and almost turned the dead bolt and threw the door open, but thought better of it and checked the peephole first.

Good thing I did. The woman outside my door was someone I'd never seen before. She looked to be in her late thirties, short brown hair, with a jagged scar reaching from her left eye to the corner of her mouth.

I wondered how I should play it. Announce myself as a cop through the door? Ask who is it? Surprise her with a snub nose in her face?

"Who's there?" I said.

My voice seemed to startle her. She backpedaled away from my door and walked quickly down the hall.

I flipped back the dead bolt and swung the door open, my .38 locking on her back.

"Stop! Police!"

She turned and froze, her face going from white to whiter.

"Hands in the air!"

Her hands shot up. "I just moved in! I thought that was my apartment!"

"Palms on the wall, feet apart."

The woman hugged the plaster like she knew the drill. She wore some kind of work overalls, brown and grubby, and the odor she gave off wasn't pleasant.

I did a quick but thorough pat down, and found a butterfly knife in her boot.

"That's for work."

"Where do you work?"

"Department of Sanitation. The sewers."

"You need a martial arts weapon for sewer work?"

"It's under four fingers. It's legal."

I opened the butterfly knife, and it had a short blade. Short but thick. Any blade longer than a handspan was against the law, and this one looked like it could go either way.

"Why were you trying to break into my apartment?"

"I told you, cop." She said the word *cop* as if it hurt her. "I thought it was mine. It was an honest mistake. Quit hassling me."

I fished out a wallet, which wasn't the most pleasant thing to do because she had gunk—presumably sewer gunk—on her pockets. Her driver's license told me she was Lucy Walnut. Address in Oak Park.

"Says here you're in the suburbs."

"I just moved in last week. Haven't got the license changed."

"Okay, Ms. Walnut. Let's see if you're telling the truth. Which door is yours?"

"I'm in 304. The doors don't have numbers on them."

Three-oh-four was right next to mine.

"Keys. And stay put."

She handed over the keys and I kept a bead on her while trying the lock. It turned.

"Told you so. Can I go now?"

"Where'd you do time, Ms. Walnut?"

She stayed quiet.

"I can find out easy enough."

"Did a nickel at Joliet."

"What for?"

Silence again.

"I asked, what for?"

"I don't need to tell you nothing."

"No, you don't. But if you're on parole, I can find out who your PO is and explain how you were trying to break into a cop's apartment."

"That was an accident."

"My word against yours. Who do you think the judge will believe? Now, what were you in for?"

"Battery. I answered your damn questions. Can I go now?"

I tossed her keys on the floor by her feet.

"Keep your nose clean, Ms. Walnut. I'm going to hold on to your knife, because I wouldn't want you hurting yourself with it."

"Whatever."

We both went into our respective abodes, and I took a big breath and let it out slow. My hands were quaking from adrenaline, just like they always did after I shook down a suspect.

I set my gun on the counter, tossed the knife in the garbage, closed my eyes, and let my body return to calm.

The calm was shattered two minutes later, by a knock on my door. Ms. Walnut again, back to take revenge against the cop who stole her knife?

I picked up my gun and peered through the peephole.

It wasn't Ms. Walnut. It was someone a lot worse.

CHAPTER 14

WHAT DO YOU want?" I said through the door.

"Can't an old friend drop by and say hello?"

"An old friend, yes. You, no."

"Come on, Jackie. Open the door."

"No."

He knocked again, harder.

"Hurry! Open up! It's my heart! I feel a blockage in my pituitary artery! My left arm has gone numb! Jackie, for the love of God!"

I thought about going into my bedroom and watching TV, but I knew he'd just keep bugging me until I let him in.

"I'm dying, Jackie! Everything's getting dark! So dark! I'm too young and too pretty to die like this!"

I wistfully eyed the .38 I'd set on my counter, then unlocked my door.

Harry McGlade, private investigator sub-par and namesake to the lead character in the TV series *Fatal Autonomy,* came into my apartment without being invited.

He wore the typical Harry outfit: a wrinkled brown suit, a stained tie, a chubby face in need of a shave, and enough cologne to make my nose hurt.

"Hiya, Jackie. What's shaking?"

"I see you're still allergic to ironing."

McGlade tugged on his lapels like a wise guy. "This is Armani. Armani doesn't wrinkle."

"Then what are all of the crinkles and creases?"

"Those are style lines."

He smiled at me, the smile becoming a wince as he took in my condition.

"Damn, what happened to you? Looks like you got into a fight with an ugly stick, and the ugly stick kicked your ass."

I held my thumb and forefinger an inch apart. "This is the amount of patience I have left, McGlade. What do you want?"

"I need a favor."

"No."

"It's important."

"No."

"It's not work-related. It's personal."

"Hell no."

"I'm getting married."

"My sympathies to your fiancée."

"I'd like you to stand up."

I was about to say no again, but I wasn't sure I heard him correctly.

"What did you just ask me?"

McGlade spent a moment studying his shoes. Brown leather, Italian. Probably worth a fortune.

"I need a, uh, best man. I want you to be my best man."

I considered all of the hurtful put-downs I could sling at him, and gave him my best.

"Let me guess. You don't have any friends because you're an obnoxious bottom-feeding creep, so I'm the only person you can ask."

Harry shrugged. "Yeah. That pretty much covers it."

I rubbed my eyes, a bad move because they hurt like hell. Millennia ago, McGlade worked for the CPD and was my partner. He screwed that up, and screwed me over, which should have been the end of our relationship. But

Harry kept reappearing in my life, like an antibiotic-resistant rash. He was the reason why that stupid character on that stupid TV show was named after stupid me.

"Will you do it?"

"I'd rather eat a box of tacks."

"Please?"

"No."

"I'll pay you. I'm rich."

"Pay someone else."

"I would, but my betrothed wants it to be you."

"She knows me?"

"She loves the TV show."

That damn show. "I'm close to losing my job because of that show."

"Aren't you knocking on retirement anyway, Jackie? Pretty soon you'll be chasing bad guys with a walker."

It was my fault. I let him in.

"You want me to be your best man?" I gave him a sharp poke in his chest, feeling my finger sink into pudge.

"I'm begging you, Jackie. I'll do anything."

"Kill me."

He raised an eyebrow. "Say what?"

"On the show. Kill my character. You're the executive producer, right?"

"Yeah. But an executive producer doesn't do anything, other than collect a fat paycheck."

"Then find some other moron to stand up for you."

McGlade chewed his lower lip, and I could practically see the two gears turning in his head. I was pretty sure there were only two.

"We haven't filmed the season finale yet, and it has a big surprise in it."

"Great. Gun me down."

"Actually, your character professes love for me and we have sex in an alley."

"There's your surprise. After sex, I eat my gun. A perfectly natural reaction."

"I have to talk to the producer. And the writers. And the network."

"Yes or no, McGlade?"

He grinned. "It's a deal. The network has always pushed to replace you with someone sexy. Here's their chance."

"Good. Now you can leave."

Harry headed for the door.

"The rehearsal is in two days."

"Two days?"

"Wedding is in four days. Why wait?"

"Indeed . . ."

"I'll call you tomorrow. And you need to bring a date."

"Why?"

"Holly doesn't have anyone to stand up either."

"Great."

"Toodles, Jackie. And try to wear something nice, not any of that Home Shopping crap."

I may have smacked him in the ass with the door as he left.

After regaining my composure, I hit the bathroom and took a few more aspirin—standard procedure after a visit from Harry—and then attempted to shower.

The water hurt, but I scrubbed until the last of the soot swirled down the drain. After the shower I rubbed some burn salve on my hand, bandaged it up, dressed in a T-shirt and jogging pants, and jogged into the kitchen to eat.

I microwaved a potato and stuffed it with cheddar cheese and some pan-seared broccoli. Swallowing brought tears to my eyes, and the tears in my eyes made them hurt. I was squirting myself in the face with Visine when the phone rang.

Latham? I hurried to answer.

"Hughes at county. Got some results."

I sighed. If I couldn't speak to my ex-boyfriend, I suppose the next best thing was speaking to an assistant medical examiner about a jar of severed toes.

"I'm all ears, Max."

"My bone girl, Jess Coran, confirmed the toes are all about thirty years old. We also did some tests, found saliva."

Yuck.

"Is it from a secretor?"

"It'll take a few days to know. Sample is tiny, it will be tough to pull."

"If anyone can do it, you can."

"I wouldn't need the flattery if I made more money."

"Flattery costs the taxpayers less. What about those holes you found in the toes?"

"I've got a hypothesis. We dissected one, found minute fibers. Could be thread."

"Meaning?"

Hughes clucked his tongue. "I arranged the toes in a circle. There were just enough to make an adult-sized necklace."

CHAPTER 15

ALEX SHIFTS ON the couch and mentally replays the shrink's question.

"What are some of the things your father did to you?"

There are so many, Alex sometimes wonders if they were all real. The punishment box, the size of a coffin, locked inside for days without food or water. Wetting the bed and being forced to lick up the mess. Kneeling on thumbtacks. Being hung from the rafters and lashed until you went hoarse from screaming. Having to help Father kill people. Even other children, friends from school.

"He did many things," Alex says. "If there was an award for child abuse, he'd have won."

"You know it's abuse as an adult. How about as a child? Did you understand your father was unfit?"

"I knew Father was different, but I didn't understand he was crazy until years later. I didn't question the abuse. I just tried to cope."

"By killing cats?"

Alex smiles. Dr. Morton has probably been waiting to slip that in.

"Among other things. We lived in constant fear, and did things to help with the fear."

"What things?"

"I would cut myself, sometimes, on my legs. Isn't that strange? Here I was, a kid, being horribly abused, and I abused myself even more."

"Perhaps you were doing it to express the pain you were feeling inside."

Alex digested this.

"Or perhaps I began to like the pain."

"Do you enjoy pain, Alex?"

Alex sneaks a glance at Dr. Morton. The good doctor is calm and composed, as usual.

"I'm not sure. I was always terrified of being hurt. But after a while, it was kind of like a challenge. Sort of like, *I can handle this, what else have you got?* I don't think I enjoy the pain so much as I enjoy mastery over it."

"How about the pain of others?"

Alex grins, full wattage.

"Oh, now *that* I love."

"Hence the cats."

"Yeah. Hence the cats."

"But you know now that it's not beneficial for you to harm animals."

Alex nods. "Right. No more animals. I'm clear on that."

Dr. Morton makes a grunting sound, perhaps trying to convey approval.

"What are some of the other things you did to cope, Alex?"

"Sex. I had sex."

"Were you sexually abused by your father?"

"No. Never. For Father, sex was something perverted. Unnatural. The devil's work."

"Is that how you feel about sex?"

"No. I think sex between two people who love each other can be a beautiful thing."

"How old were you at the time?"

Alex thought about it. "Fourteen."

"And the person you had sex with?"

"Fifteen."

"Were you in love?"

Alex's eyes close, and the memories seep in. Stolen kisses. Sideways glances. Shameful caresses that felt so good, they couldn't be the devil's doing.

"Yes. Yes, I was in love."

The timer on the desk beeps.

"We've come to the end of another session." Dr. Morton stands up, smiles benevolently.

"Same time tomorrow?" Alex asks.

"Unfortunately, no. I'm booked for the day."

Alex's mood darkens. "You told me we could have daily sessions. I'll only be in town for a short time, and I have a lot to figure out."

Dr. Morton pats Alex on the shoulder. "I'm sorry, but it can't be helped. I can see you the next day, same time."

"I'd really like to see you tomorrow."

"Impossible. But if it matters, I think you're coming along wonderfully."

Alex blinks. "I am?"

"You are. You're well on the road to recovery, Alex. The progress you've made in these last few sessions is tremendous. Take a day off. Do something fun. Enjoy yourself."

Alex stands, extends a hand.

"I'll do that. Thank you, Doctor. See you tomorrow."

Dr. Morton smiles. "The day after tomorrow, Alex. You'll be fine. Trust me."

Alex walks outside, to the rear of the rental car. Looks carefully up the street. Down the street. No one is around. Alex opens the trunk.

Dr. Francis Mulrooney stares up, eyes wide with terror. Clothesline binds his wrists and ankles, tight enough to be cutting off the circulation. It's probably excruciating, Alex thinks. The graphologist's hands are an ugly blue. Deprived of blood, necrosis is already setting in. Like dead fruit, rotting on the vine.

It doesn't matter. He won't be needing his hands ever again.

Mulrooney tries to scream, but the gag muffles it. Alex shushes him.

"It's okay. My psychiatrist says I'm making a lot of progress."

Mulrooney had been incredibly easy to locate; a quick call to the university did the trick. And kidnapping is child's play. All a person needs is some Rohypnol, available over the Internet, and a used wheelchair. Jab a man on the street, sit him down as the drug takes immediate effect, and take him anywhere. He won't even complain.

Alex opens the kit bag by Mulrooney's feet and removes a syringe.

"Nighty-night time. When you wake up again, we'll be at my new place. I'm going to see how much of your skin I can peel off before you die."

Another muffled scream. Alex jams the needle into his biceps and injects the drug.

It will be a pleasant warm-up for Jack. Alex is pleased that the lieutenant survived. It would have been a shame for her to die without getting to know her.

Mulrooney's eyes begin to flutter. Alex pats him on the cheek.

"I have to enjoy myself. Doctor's orders. But first, we need to stop at the hardware store and get some tools. Can't skin you without tools."

Mulrooney continues to scream as the trunk is closed.

CHAPTER 16

WHAT HAPPENED TO your hair?" The stylist frowned at me. "Did you have the hair dryer on too long?"

"Something like that."

I disliked getting my hair done, which is why I kept it long and dyed it at home. Sitting still while someone fussed over me made me nervous.

Unfortunately, the fire had done some major damage, making it impossible to get a comb through it. So I sought professional help. This particular stylist was named Barb. Her own hair was pink, and she had enough facial piercings to set off a metal detector.

"The ends are melted here. You see that?" She held up my bangs and frowned at my reflection in the mirror.

I shrugged. "Cheap shampoo."

"You get what you pay for. We only carry Vertex hair care products. The shampoo is seventy dollars for a thirty-two-ounce bottle."

"Seventy dollars? Is it made out of caviar?"

"Kelp. And biotin."

"Can I pay on installments?"

Barb smacked her gum. She didn't find me funny.

"When I finish cutting, should we do something about these gray roots?"

I didn't find that funny.

An hour later I'd lost six inches of hair, gained some auburn highlights, and was out almost three hundred bucks—but that included the tip and a bottle of Vertex, with biotin and kelp.

While vanity wasn't one of my hobbies, I really liked the new cut. It softened up my appearance, and I daresay, made me look a little younger.

My next stop was an auto supply warehouse. I brought in the two side mirrors I'd picked up in the alley behind Diane Kork's house, and a helpful guy named Mitch found the parts number.

"They're from a Dodge Stratus, a Mitsubishi Eclipse, or a Chrysler Sebring. Coupes and sedans, going back a few years."

"It could be from any of those?"

"It fits any of those. Parts manufacturers sell to different car companies."

"Any way to narrow it down?"

"I could try to match the paint. There's some flakes from where this one broke off." He used his thumbnail to scrape some paint chips onto the white counter, then hauled out a book of colors. "I'm not sure if that's Magnesium or Graphite Metallic."

"Looks like plain old dark gray to me."

Mitch rolled his eyes. "Gray is boring. No one would buy a gray car."

He went back to his book. I neglected to tell him that I had a gray car. Or perhaps it wasn't really gray. Perhaps it was Silver Dusk. Or Sissy Black.

"No to Graphite Metallic. And Magnesium doesn't match either. Which means it has to be Titanium Pearl."

"Naturally," I said. "I'm surprised it took you so long."

I got another eye roll. "Graphite Metallic and Magnesium are colors used by Dodge and Chrysler. If it isn't one of those, it has to be Mitsubishi. They call their gray Titanium Pearl."

"Are you sure?"

"Check for yourself."

He found the appropriate page in the color book and placed the paint flakes on the swatch. Looked like a match to me.

"Thanks, Mitch."

I used my cell to call the station. Herb hadn't come in today, so I gave instructions to Detective Maggie Mason, who was a comer in Violent Crimes due to good instincts and a lack of any sort of social life. Like me.

"Late model Mitsubishi Eclipse, color gray, first two plate numbers Delta one. Call me when you get the search results."

If there turned out to be too many to track down, I could get a team to start calling repair shops, to see if anyone came in to replace their side mirrors.

My next stop was Diane Kork's house. It was in much better shape than I would have guessed, considering the inferno of the night before. The only evidence a fire had occurred were some black scorch marks on the brick, and plywood sheets nailed over the windows and doors to discourage looting.

I stood staring for a moment, wondering how the hell I'd get inside, when luck winked at me and a woman in an OSFM Windbreaker appeared from the backyard, walking a German shepherd.

I flashed my badge.

"Lieutenant Daniels, Violent Crimes. You with the office?"

The woman nodded, offering a hand. She was pear-shaped, short, with large blue eyes.

I hesitated, keeping one eye on the dog, which was the size of a small bear.

"Jeanna Davidson, arson investigator. Don't mind Kevlar. He's a sweetheart."

The sweetheart yawned, showing me enough teeth to swallow a Volkswagen. I shook Jeanna's hand slowly, to avoid getting mauled.

"I'm guessing this was arson."

Jeanna nodded. "Kevlar sniffed out the accelerant. Burn pattern suggests gasoline. Were you the one we rescued?"

"Yeah. Thanks for that. Do you mind if I poke around inside?"

"Sure. Structure's stable. Want a tour?"

"If it's okay with Kevlar."

We went around back and Jeanna walked up the porch. The rear entry had a makeshift door nailed to it, with a standard latch and padlock. Jeanna opened it and switched on a Maglite.

Unlike the exterior, the inside was an unholy mess. What wasn't burned black had been soaked with water. Gray puddles (closer to Magnesium than Titanium Pearl) spread across the kitchen floor, each pool several inches deep. Jeanna led me into the dining room, and I knelt in the doorway and searched the charred floor.

"Looking for anything in particular?"

"Bullet casings. Someone shot at me from here."

"Do you have any bullets on you?"

"In my gun."

"Show one to Kevlar."

I unholstered my .38 and removed a round, passing it over to Jeanna. She held it before the dog's nose.

"Kevlar, scent."

The German shepherd sniffed the bullet, which easily could have fit into one of his huge nostrils.

"Kevlar, find."

She unclipped his leash and the dog shuffled off, snorting here and there.

"Kevlar is one of four dogs in the state's canine arson unit. I've been handling him since he was a puppy."

Jeanna spoke with the inflection of a proud mother. Since she was helping me, I made with the small talk.

"How long have you worked for the Office of the State Fire Marshal?"

"Seven years. I bring Kev in on maybe thirty investigations a year."

"Are there many deliberate cases?"

"Last year the office investigated over a thousand. About four hundred confirmed arson. Usually we don't need the dogs—the signs are obvious, like in here. See how this patch of carpet burned away hotter than that patch? Gas spill."

"So why bring Kevlar along if you already know it's arson?"

"He hates being left out."

Kevlar whined, and Jeanna focused the flashlight on the floor in front of him. I gave the dog a pat on the head and found what he'd been sniffing: a shell casing.

"Good boy, Kevlar."

Jeanna hugged the bear, and I dug a plastic bag from my jeans and coaxed in the cartridge.

"There might be others," I said. "Do you mind if I borrow the flashlight?"

Jeanna handed it over and pulled a smaller, slimmer model out of her jacket. Then she commanded the dog to find more bullets. Useful dog. Much more useful than a cat.

I wandered back into the kitchen, tripping over the curtains that had almost been my shroud the night before. I played the Maglite over the entire room. Nothing jumped out at me.

I crept into the living room, and then the dining room, my Nikes quickly becoming waterlogged. The house had gone from Dante's Inferno to the Addams family, dark and damp and creepy, filled with long shadows and unpleasant odors. Near the wall in the dining room stood a strange-looking pile, and I nudged it with a wet toe and saw part of a handle.

A suitcase.

I squatted and picked through the cinders. Everything was burned pretty good, but two things stood out. The first was a five-inch flat wire, curved into a half-moon shape. The second was a congealed knot that I recognized immediately by its distinctive smell.

Human hair.

"Did you find something?"

"Maybe. Can you check the cabinets in the kitchen, see if any garbage bags survived the fire?"

"Sure. Watch Kevlar for me."

More poking produced nothing but ash and melted globs. I'd take it back for the lab guys to interpret.

Jeanna found a bag, Kevlar didn't find any more shells, and I spent another half an hour bumping around in the dark before calling it quits and heading out into the fresh air.

I placed the wet bag in my trunk and called Mason.

"How's the search for the car going?"

"Narrowed it down to six gray Mitsubishi Eclipses with Illinois plates be-

ginning with D one. Ran priors on five of the registered owners, came up clean
except for traffic violations."

"Send out some squads to visually check the cars for missing mirrors. What
about the sixth?"

"Owned by a car rental place."

She gave me the address, on Irving Park. It wasn't too far, so I decided to
check it out.

The office was typical for Chicago; a tiny building next to a cramped parking lot crammed with vehicles. The lobby was the size of my closet. A stained
coffeemaker with a quarter-full carafe sat next to the unoccupied counter. A
floor plant, brown and shriveled up, sat in an oversized plastic pot, next to a
magazine rack that contained a single copy of *Car and Driver* and nothing else.
I rang the bell.

"Just a second."

He took his time. I stared at the coffee, cooking away on the warmer, probably since the morning. Against my better judgment I poured myself a Styro-
foam cupful. It had the consistency of mud, which was pretty much how it
tasted.

Should have trusted my better judgment.

I dumped it on the dead plant. Probably wasn't the first to do it. Probably
was the reason the plant had died.

"Help you?"

The guy was older, several days' growth of beard on his face, grease embedded in his wrinkles and fingernails. He wore equally stained overalls, and a
sewn-on name tag that said *Al.*

I flashed my star.

"Have you rented out a gray Mitsubishi Eclipse lately?"

He stared, then shook his head.

"Nope." Then he said, "I did rent out a Titanium Pearl Eclipse, though."

I bit back my first response.

"We have reason to believe it was involved in an accident. Can you show me
who rented it?"

"Lemme get the book."

Al plodded off, and eventually plodded back, nose pressed into a cracked binder. This time he had on a pair of bifocals thicker than ice cubes.

"Rented it out last week to a fella named Mayer. Mike Mayer."

"You get a copy of his driver's license?"

He handed me the book. "That's the law, ain't it?"

I checked out the info on Mr. Mayer. White, thirty-seven years old, had an Indiana license that said he lived in Indianapolis. The car was rented for the next two weeks. There wasn't a credit card receipt. I wondered why.

"Paid cash. I've got the card number, though. In case of damage."

"Where's that?"

Al frowned, and disappeared again. I spent the time counting the cigarette butts in the dead plant. Nine, plus a cigar stub, a lottery ticket, and something that looked like a Tootsie Roll. I hoped it was a Tootsie Roll.

"We keep the card numbers on file in here." He set a metal lock box down on the counter and fumbled with the combination.

Three eternities later, squinting through his glasses, Al had found the slip.

"Were you here when Mr. Mayer rented the car?"

"I'm the only one works the counter."

"A testament to your efficiency. Can you describe Mr. Mayer?"

"Looked like his driver's license picture, I reckon."

"I'd like to hear it from your own mouth."

"Thin. My height. Blond beard. Sunglasses, those kind that look like mirrors. Curly hair."

He sounded like a dead ringer for the guy who dropped off the videotape at the station. I had a Xerox in the car, and asked Al to wait for a moment. He grunted.

When I returned with the picture, Al was gone. I rang the bell. He took his time.

"Busy day," he said. "Lots of work."

I made a show of looking around. "Yeah. They're lining up out the door for rentals."

"Rentals are just a side business. We're part of Manny's Car Repair Shop. Mostly use the rentals for loaners. Insurance reimburses us."

"Is Mr. Mayer getting his car repaired here?"

"Nope. Just the rental."

"Do you get a lot of people who rent cars without leaving one to be fixed?"

"Some. Not a lot."

I handed Al a copy of the Identikit picture, the one that looked like the Unabomber.

"Looks like the Unabomber," Al said.

"Is that Mr. Mayer?"

"I thought Ted Kaczynski was the Unabomber."

He had to be putting me on. No one was this slow outside of *HEE HAW*.

"Does this resemble Mr. Mayer?"

He squinted. "Yeah. Could be."

"Anything else you remember about Mr. Mayer?"

"He had a cold. Talked quiet. Did some coughing."

I thought about it. I could have called in a Crime Scene Unit, dusted the place, but a hundred people have probably left their prints in the last week.

"I'll need copies of all these papers."

Al grunted. "I figured."

While Sling Blade loped off to figure out the copy machine, I called Mason back and gave her Mayer's info. She put me on hold and called Indianapolis PD.

Mason got back to me before Al did.

"No record. Guy's clean."

"How about the phone number he left?"

"Disconnected. Didn't pay his bill."

I waited another five minutes, and Al finally returned with my copies. I gave him my card.

"Thanks. When Mr. Mayer comes back, please try to detain him and give me a call."

"Detain him how? Like tie him up?"

"Tell him there was a problem with his credit card. Then call me."

"Might not stop in. Might just park the car in the lot and drop the keys in the slot."

"If he does that, call me as well."

"Might drop it off when I'm not here."

"You said you're always here."

"Might get sick."

"Do you get sick a lot, Al?"

"Might have caught Mr. Mayer's cold."

I drilled Al with a cop stare.

"Are you enjoying yourself, Al?"

He smiled, revealing three missing teeth. "Gotta have fun where you can get it, Lieutenant."

After leaving Al, I really needed a beer.

And I knew just the place to get one.

CHAPTER 17

ALEX OPENS THE bottled water, takes a greedy sip, then pours some on the pliers. The handles are supposed to have no-slip grips, but Alex's gloved hands have already slipped off them half a dozen times.

It's hard. Much harder than expected.

"Want some water? I've got an extra bottle."

No answer.

Alex takes another deep gulp, picks up the pliers, and gets back to work.

Again, it's a strain. Teeth clenching. Muscles bunching. But Alex manages to pull an unbroken fifteen-inch strip of skin from Dr. Francis Mulrooney's bare chest. The longest one yet.

Mulrooney screams his approval.

Almost done with the front, Alex thinks. *Have to start on the back next. Lots of skin there.*

CHAPTER 18

BEFORE I ALLOWED myself any alcohol, I dropped off the bag and the shell casing at the Illinois Forensic Science Center. It used to be called the Chicago Crime Lab, up until it merged with the Staties in '96. One of the officers who worked there, Scott Hajek, had helped me on a few cases, and promised he'd do a rush job on the ballistics and burn analysis.

A rush job meant at least a week. More than enough time to have a beer.

Joe's Pool Hall was kitty-corner to my apartment in Wrigleyville. The after-work crowd hadn't converged yet, and I managed to snag a table near the rear and a cue that still had a tip.

I drank a Sam Adams and settled in, running a rack and trying to relax. It wasn't easy. I had a lot on my mind, plus shooting stick with a burned hand threw me off my game.

A waitress brought me another beer, and when I pulled out a buck to tip her, I noticed she had tears in her eyes.

"Asshole customer," she said without me asking.

I tipped her an extra buck.

Halfway through the next set, a guy I knew came over and stood by the table, watching.

"Came to watch a pro?" I asked.

"No. Came to watch you."

His name was Phineas Troutt. Younger than me by a decade. Blue eyes set in a hard face. Tall, with the type of muscles one got from working rather than working out. Last I'd seen him, he was bald from the chemotherapy. I took the blond fuzz growing on his head to be a good sign.

I ran the table, Phin racked the next set, and we lagged for the break. He won.

"Hair looks nice." Phin executed a sledgehammer break that sunk two solids and a stripe. He chose solids.

"Thanks. It's the shampoo. You should pick some up."

He touched his head.

"Maybe when it grows out a little more."

"It's called Vertex. Only seventy bucks a bottle."

"How big is the bottle? Two gallons?"

"Thirty-two ounces."

Phin grinned. "For seventy bucks, it should clean my hair and then straighten up my apartment and make me dinner."

He pocketed the four ball. I took a pull from my Sammy and scanned the bar for the server. She was two tables over, her face shiny with tears. She tried to move forward, but the man standing next to her moved his body in her path, not letting her pass. The man was grinning.

"Excuse me a second," I told Phin. As I approached I heard the waitress saying, "Stop it, stop it," as the guy pawed at her.

"There a problem?" I used my best commanding tone, the one that scared suspects into confessing to crimes they didn't commit.

The man was young, early twenties, dressed in a golf shirt, shorts, and flip-flops. He looked like he just came from the beach, though I couldn't imagine which one, it being April.

"This is a private conversation, skank."

He said it with a dismissive sneer, and then turned back to the waitress.

"Are you okay?" I asked her.

"She's fine. Mind your own damn business, bitch."

With my left hand, I liberated my badge case from my back pocket. With my right hand, I set the tip of the pool cue down on his bare big toe and leaned on it.

He yelped, jerking his chin left to face me, the perfect picture of fury and pain.

Some of the fury disappeared when he saw my star. But the pain stayed.

"Kind of early in the season for flip-flops, don't you think so, Romeo?"

I leaned harder on the stick. He squealed.

"Let me see some ID."

I put my badge away and took the wallet he eagerly offered. I gave his license a quick glance.

"Okay, Carl Johnson, here's how I see it. Threatening a police officer is a felony. Plus, it pisses me off."

I twisted the cue to indicate my displeasure.

"Shit! You're hurting me."

"Oh, don't be a baby, Carl. I'm not even pushing hard. See how much worse it could get?"

I put some serious weight on the cue, for just a second, and he screamed like I was killing him. Now he had a teary face too, to match the one he gave the waitress.

"Here's the deal, Carl. This is my bar. I never want to see you in here again. Understand?"

He nodded.

"And this lady is a personal friend of mine. If she tells me you've been bothering her, I'm going to pay a visit to 3355 Summit Lane and break both of your knees because you resisted arrest. Are we clear?"

I twisted hard. He moaned, "Yes."

"Now tip your waitress and leave."

Carl pulled out a twenty and handed it to the girl, his hand shaking. I lifted the pool cue and he ran out of there as fast as he could, bumping several customers on the way.

The waitress grasped my hands.

"Thanks so much. He's been coming in here for a month, making comments, pinching my ass, not leaving me alone."

I gave her a card. "I don't think he'll come back. Call me if he does."

"Thanks. Really."

I smiled. "When you've got a chance, we need two beers."

"You got it. Thanks so much."

When I came back to the table, Phin was racking the balls.

"What happened to the last game?" I asked.

"I won. You owe me a beer. You better take this next break, or you might not have a chance to play."

I managed to sink a stripe on the break, and the waitress brought beer for me and Phin.

"On me," she told us.

Being a hero had its perks.

We played for two hours, Phin beating me five games to one. I blamed the losses on my burned hand, though the beer went a long way to easing the pain.

I met Phin several years ago, before he had cancer. It was an odd friendship, because I was a cop, and Phin was a criminal, though I wasn't entirely clear on what kind of criminal he was. I think he operated as some kind of unlicensed private investigator, and considered laws optional.

Thinking of private eyes made me think of Harry, and the wedding rehearsal. McGlade had told me to bring a date, and I got the impression if I showed up solo our deal would be off and my fat alter ego would continue to embarrass the CPD on a new season of *Fatal Autonomy*.

I wasn't the type to call in markers, but desperate times and all that. Occasionally, Phin called me up, needing some bit of info that only cops were privy to, such as a plate trace or a criminal record search. Occasionally, I helped him. That put the karma debt in his corner.

"I need a favor," I said to Phin when he came back from the bathroom. "What are you doing on Saturday?"

"Apparently, I'm doing you a favor."

"It's easy. A guy I know is getting married, and he needs some people to stand up."

"You want me to stand up at a wedding for some guy I don't know?"

"Yeah. But this isn't the wedding. It's the rehearsal dinner."

Phin shrugged. "Sure."

"Thanks. I don't know the time yet. Can I call you?"

"No phone. I'll call you, day of."

We played one more game, he won, and then we said our good-byes and I headed home. It turned out asking guys on dates wasn't so hard after all.

I entered my building and passed my new neighbor walking down my hall. She wore the same dirty uniform she had on that morning, and carried a large leather satchel.

Though she didn't look at me, I heard her whisper "Bitch" as she passed. I let it go. I'd already gone Rambo on her once today. Besides, the woman was entitled to her opinion.

Back at my apartment, Mr. Friskers surprised me by leaving no surprises. No mess. No destruction. Everything was exactly as I'd left it.

This bothered me. Perhaps he was sick. Or perhaps he'd spent the day deep in thought, plotting the annihilation of the human race.

"Mr. Friskers? Where are you?"

I made a kissing sound.

There was an unbearable screech that shook my core foundations, and the cat launched himself at me from atop the refrigerator. He landed on my chest, claws digging in, and I had to clench to avoid soiling myself.

My sweatshirt protected me from any scarring, but my heart was beating so hard I could feel it thump against the inside of my rib cage.

I unhooked the cat from the fabric and placed him on the floor. He sat and stared up at me, apparently pleased.

"You're under arrest," I told him.

He yawned, then walked over to the litter box and began kicking litter onto the floor.

I checked my answering machine. Nothing. Then I searched for edibles and found a can of potato soup that I made easy work of. I also had some vanilla wafers, but only after promising myself I'd exercise in the morning.

My evening's entertainment consisted of the new Robert B. Parker book, which Herb had bought me for Christmas. Why couldn't I meet a guy like Spenser? To make it work I'd have to get rid of his shrink girlfriend, but I figured that was no big loss.

When I was getting too tired to read I turned off the light and tried to sleep.

Sleep didn't come. I had a zillion things running through my head, and my mind refused to shut off. I thought about my mom. About Latham. About the case. About Herb. My hand hurt, and I couldn't get comfortable, and I finally just gave up and flipped on the TV.

Big mistake. The Home Shopping Club was selling designer shoes. I bought some black Prada sling-backs, some brown Miu Miu sandals, and thankfully they were out of my size in Dolce & Gabbana, because my credit card wouldn't have been able to handle the shock.

Two a.m. crept by. Then three. Then four. Then five. I tossed and turned, and finally dozed off trying to picture a woman stupid enough to marry Harry McGlade.

CHAPTER 19

THE PHONE WOKE me up, which was a blessing. I'd been in the middle of a dream where I had to warn some children that danger was coming, but no matter how hard I screamed, no sound came out.

After shaking away the disorientation, I picked up the receiver.

"Daniels."

"Morning, Jack."

I sat up. "Hi, Herb. How are you doing?"

"Okay. Didn't mean to be a jerk the other day."

"You've got a lot on your mind. Any results yet?"

"We should find out today. I heard about the fire. You coming in to work? I've got something."

I looked at the clock. Nine twenty. I'd gotten about four hours of sleep. Not too bad.

"What is it?"

"I got in early, went through the old Gingerbread Man files. Something was missing. I remember searching Kork's house and finding an address book. Wasn't there."

"Misfiled?"

"Signed out. Bill checked the sheet, and the last person to go through the Kork stuff was our old friend Barry Fuller, right after the case ended. So I had Bill pull Barry's things, and found the address book."

"You wouldn't be telling me this unless you found something."

"Book was mostly empty, except for some scribbles. They look like the letter *L*, except some of them were upside down and backwards."

That got me fully awake. "Is it a code?"

"I'll tell you when you get here."

I showered, and dressed in a gray Shin Choi A-line skirt, a white Barbara Graffeo blouse, and some Dior flats, no hose. The shoes were acquired at an outlet store and had been mispriced. I got them for eight bucks. I remember holding my breath when the cashier rang them up, figuring she'd notice. She didn't. That's been the high point of my year so far.

The day was dark, cool. Looked like rain. I stopped at the churros cart before going to my office, and bought Herb two with extra cinnamon.

"Churros?" Benedict lit up like a hundred-watt bulb. "Jack, my stomach thanks you. Both for me?"

"Both for you."

He bit a sizeable portion out of the first. "Mmmm. I'm taking you to dinner on your birthday."

Benedict had been saying that for years. By my count, he owed me 108 dinners.

"What have you got, Herb?"

He handed me the address book, open to the page with the scribbles on it.

⊔ ⅃ ⌐ ⌐⅂ ⊡ ⅃⌐⅂·

"I thought it was a doodle at first. But then I realized it had ten characters."

"A phone number with an area code."

Herb nodded, his mouth full of fried Mexican dough. While he chewed, I stared at the symbols.

"Pigpen code."

My partner frowned. "That took me an hour to figure out."

"We learned it in Girl Scouts." I drew a quick tic-tac-toe board and filled it in with numbers. "Each symbol represents the number inside it. So the first number is a two."

$$\begin{array}{c|c|c} 1 & 2 & 3 \\ \hline 4 & 5 & 6 \\ \hline 7 & 8 & 9 \end{array}$$

Herb stared at me as if I'd grown a tail. "You were a Girl Scout?"

"My mother thought it would build character."

"Can you get cookies at a discount?"

I quickly deciphered the first nine numbers. The dot on the end had to stand for a zero.

I clucked my tongue. "Two-one-nine area code. Indiana."

"I already looked up the number. It's in Gary. Unlisted. And you won't believe who it belongs to."

Herb waited for me to ask, so I did.

"Tell me if this name sounds familiar, Jack. The owner of that phone number is Bud Kork."

"The Gingerbread Man's father?"

We'd tried to locate him after the murders, but he never turned up.

"The one and only."

I thought about the jar of severed toes, all of them at least thirty years old. Too old for Charles Kork to have done it, but not too old for his father.

"Insanity runs in families." Herb shoved the remainder of the churros in his mouth.

I rolled it around in my head. Could our perp be the father, taking over where his son left off?

Only one way to find out for sure.

"Want to go for a ride?"

CHAPTER 20

Gary, indiana, lies forty minutes east of Chicago. I filled Herb in while he drove, covering everything I'd done over the last few days. Rather than praise my heroics, Benedict latched on to the mundane.

"I can't believe that asshole McGlade is getting married. She a hooker?"

"Haven't met her yet. That sounds about right."

"Currency must be changing hands. There's no other way. Unless the woman has some serious mental problems."

"I told you about the fire, right?"

"Twice. Hey, if Bud Kork's our man, how does the rental car fit in?"

I shrugged. The other five Eclipses on my list had been found, their side mirrors intact.

"He could be working with an accomplice. Or Bud Kork might not be our man. Or maybe the fireman ID'ed the wrong car. Or maybe the car that lost the mirrors wasn't driven by the killer—maybe it was just a citizen who panicked."

He drummed his fingers on the steering wheel. "Lots of maybes."

"Someone killed Diane Kork and burned down her house. Someone familiar with the Gingerbread Man case."

"Could be a copycat."

I made a face. "In the thirty years you've been a cop, have you ever encountered a copycat killer?"

"Not once. But it happens all the time on *CSI.*"

Herb took a box of orange Tic Tacs out of his ashtray and offered them to me. I declined, and he emptied the whole box into his mouth.

"Maybe," he said, the candy clicking against his molars, "Diane Kork is the killer. She put a fake tattoo on the woman in the video, making us think she's dead."

"I don't think so. The tattoo was hard to see in the video."

"Still, we can't rule it out. We haven't found her body, and after what she lived through, maybe it pushed her over the edge."

"Diane Kork was a schoolteacher. Whoever shot me missed my head by less than an inch."

"Could have had lessons. Or could have gotten lucky."

Herb called Dispatch on his cell, and had them check if Diane Kork had a FOID card. Illinois required all gun owners to have one. The info came back quickly.

"No firearm owner ID for Diane. But she could still have a gun."

"Doesn't feel right to me. It's someone else. I told you about the suitcase."

He frowned. "The guy's keeping trophies."

Thrill killers liked to keep little reminders of their deeds. The burned human hair probably came from a scalp. And I knew the curved piece of metal was the underwire from a bra, having been poked by enough of them in my time.

"If Diane Kork were the killer, I don't think she'd keep a victim's bra."

"Could have been Diane's bra."

"Was it her hair too? We can call the Feebies, get a lecture about how rare female serial killers are, and how none have ever been found that take trophies from their victims. No, Herb, it's someone else. Someone picking up where Charles Kork left off. Someone who knows the case."

"That could be twenty million people, Jack. Maybe more. Is the movie out on video yet?"

"I hope not."

Before *Fatal Autonomy* became a crummy series, it was a crummy made-for-TV movie about the Kork case. I'd been forced to watch some of it; Harry had conned me into being a technical advisor.

"For verisrealityitude," he'd said.

My input had been ignored, and the movie turned out to be a travesty. But it still had a lot of real facts in it. And after the case ended, there were the inevitable quickie true crime paperbacks, and that TV documentary.

Much of the world knew about the Gingerbread Man. It made me reconsider the copycat angle.

Herb slowed for the toll. We were about to get on the Skyway, Chicago's largest bridge. It ran about eight miles long, and high enough to see deep into Indiana. Our view proffered a smattering of factories, their gigantic chimneys spitting copious amounts of smoke and filth, staining the overcast sky. Industry wasn't pretty.

We drove in silence for a few minutes before Herb finally spoke.

"I'm scared."

I reached over and touched his arm.

"You'll be fine, Herb. Even if it is cancer, you'll get through it."

"That's what Bernice says."

"Smart lady."

"I'm the homicide cop, and she's stronger than I am."

"People deal with death in different ways, Herb."

Drizzle accumulated on the windshield. Herb hit the wipers, causing a dirty rainbow smear.

"Do you ever think about death, Jack?"

"Sometimes. I almost died yesterday, in the fire."

"Were you afraid?"

"At first. Then I accepted it, and I was just sad."

Herb's voice, normally rock solid, had a quaver in it. "My father died of cancer. Strongest man I ever knew. By the end he weighed ninety pounds, had to be spoon-fed."

I thought of my mother, steadily losing weight despite the feeding tube. I pushed away the image and tried to be jovial.

"Don't get your hopes up, Herb. You'll never weigh ninety pounds."

My joke fell flat. Herb looked out of his side window. We passed a particularly ugly factory, its smokestack belching flames like the great Oz's palace.

"What scares me the most is no longer existing. Everything I am, everything I think, everything I feel, all of my memories and thoughts and dreams—erased. Like I've never been here at all."

"You've got family, Herb. And friends. They'll remember you."

Herb's face was a mask of sadness. "But when I'm dead, I won't remember them."

We continued down I-90 east for another twenty minutes. The expressway was newer, and the asphalt better, on the Indiana side. It ran parallel to a train track for a while, and then we turned north on Cline and west on Gary Avenue, and we were soon on the plains, no buildings for miles.

I checked the MapQuest directions.

"We're looking for Summit. Should be coming up."

"Nothing's coming up. Except some cows. Hey!"

Herb pointed to the right. I followed his finger to a large bale of hay.

I didn't laugh, but at least he'd snapped out of his funk.

Summit turned out to be a dirt road, and it ended at a 1950s prefab ranch, the front yard overgrown with weeds. Ancient appliances and rusty old farm equipment peppered the property, and an old barn that looked like Godzilla had stepped on it sat behind the house.

"Is this it?" Herb asked.

"Has to be. There's no place else."

"It looks like the shack from *The Beverly Hillbillies*."

"Or *The Texas Chainsaw Massacre*."

Herb parked next to a Ford pickup truck that looked old enough to run on regular gas.

"Ready to meet the monster's father?"

Herb nodded and we got out of the car. The closer we walked, the worse it looked. The roof was missing half its shingles. Several boards on the front porch had rotted away. So much white paint was flaking off the sides, the house looked like a paper birch tree.

I took out my badge, and noticed Benedict already had his in hand.

Wouldn't be smart to surprise the occupant. It was too easy to picture him crouched behind the front door with a shotgun, waiting for strangers to trespass.

Herb hesitated before getting onto the porch, eyeing it dubiously. I went first. The warped wood groaned, but it took my weight. Benedict followed, stepping gingerly.

I knocked, a thin, hollow sound.

"Bud Kork? This is the police."

We waited.

No answer.

I knocked again.

"Mr. Kork? We see your truck outside. We know you're home."

A voice filtered through the closed door. "Come on in. I'm getting dressed."

I looked at Herb, and we both put our hands on our holsters. He pushed the door open, and I went in fast and stepped quickly to the left.

The house was dark and smelled like something had died under the floorboards. A single fly buzzed around in the stuffy, fetid air. I located a switch on the wall and flipped it on, bathing the room in a sickly yellow glow from a bare forty-watt bulb hanging from the ceiling.

The room took the word *mess* to new heights.

There were several stacks of old newspapers, piled high as my shoulder. A dozen broken television sets, some older than me, lined up along the walls. A large box of rusty gears sat atop a cracked aquarium filled with dry grass. The walls were bare, except for a dusty framed portrait of a severe-looking Jesus, staring down from heaven. The caption beneath read: *God is always watching.*

Herb followed me in, pausing to look around. He was humming something softly, which I recognized as the violin riff from the shower scene in *Psycho.*

I stepped over a bushel basket of balled-up Wonder Bread bags, and walked toward the doorway at the end of the room.

"Mr. Kork?"

"In the kitchen."

He had a cracked, broken voice, like he might burst into tears. I navigated more garbage and peeked through the doorway.

A painfully thin old man stood in the tiny kitchen, his entire body twitching and shaking from Parkinson's disease. He wore a stained white undershirt that hung on him like drapes, and a pair of beige slacks, equally stained, with holes in both knees. His face was a skull with a thin layer of age-spotted skin stretched over it. Thin, colorless lips. A hook nose. Bulbous, rheumy eyes. His head was bald, but he had bushy white eyebrows long enough to comb, and enough ear hair to stuff a pillow.

I showed him my star.

"I'm Lieutenant Daniels. This is Sergeant Benedict. We'd like to ask you a few questions."

He nodded, his oversized Adam's apple bobbing up and down. "About the devil. Questions about the devil."

I stepped closer, the stench of his body odor preventing me from getting within touching distance.

"What about the devil, Mr. Kork?"

"Well, you know all about the devil, don't you? You've met him."

"I've met the devil?"

Parroting tends to draw people out, make them more compliant. Even if they weren't making sense.

"The devil. Charles. My son. Terrible boy. Knew it from the day he shot out his mother's cloaca."

"Cloaca?" Herb raised an eyebrow.

"Her dirty bits. Female parts. His mother was a harlot. The whore of Babylon. Bore me the devil for a son, praise Jesus Christ Almighty in heaven above."

Bud made the sign of the cross, then fished a black rosary from his pocket and kissed it with trembling lips.

I frowned. This wasn't our guy. He couldn't have made the video of Diane's death, or shot at me in her house. He was too disconnected, too frail, the Parkinson's too advanced.

"Where is your wife, Mr. Kork?" Herb asked.

"Roasting in the flames of hellfire."

"Do you have other children?"

Kork looked beyond us, into space. "Had a daughter. My blessed little angel.

Helper and defender of mankind. She sits at God's right hand and watches me from heaven, protects me from sin and from myself and from unnatural urges."

"She's deceased?"

His eyes glazed over. "Taken from me. By Charles. The devil took my angel. Matthew 4:1; 'then Jesus was led up by the Spirit into the wilderness to be tempted by the devil.' Corruption of the flesh, of the soul, my poor little girl."

"Do you have any other relatives, Mr. Kork?"

He shook his head. "No flesh of my flesh, no blood of my blood."

"Cousins? Nephews?"

He made fists and pounded on his thighs. "NO FLESH OF MY FLESH AND NO BLOOD OF MY BLOOD!"

This wasn't getting us anywhere.

"Jack . . ." Herb nudged me and pointed with his chin. Behind Kork was a refrigerator, old enough to still be called an icebox. Next to that, an open pantry, the shelf inside loaded with mason jars.

The law was clear when it came to search and seizure. A cop can only search if given permission, or with a warrant. Kork inviting us into his house wasn't the same as permission to search, but if while in the house we saw evidence of anything illegal or suspicious, the evidence was admissible in court.

The mason jars lining the shelf looked to be the same type as the jar full of toes. I sidestepped Kork and peered into the cabinet.

"Mr. Kork, what's this?"

I pointed to a jar full of small round things. Some were tan. Some pink. Some green.

He grunted. "Used gum. Help yourself if you want some, but I chewed all the flavor out."

"This jar is similar to another jar we found, full of human toes. Do you know anything about that?"

Another faraway looked crossed Kork's face.

"Mr. Kork? Did you hear me?"

"Niblets," he breathed.

"Speak up, Mr. Kork."

"Sweet."

"What's sweet?"

His focus came back, and he looked at me, a thin line of drool sliding down the corner of his mouth.

"The toes of babes. Sweet, like corn Niblets."

Alarms went off in my head. I noticed Herb's hand had returned to the butt of his gun.

"Did you own a jar of human toes, Mr. Kork? Some of them from children?"

" 'And they were bringing children to him, that he might touch them.' Mark 10:13."

"Mr. Kork, may we search your premises?"

"Two Peter 2:14. 'They have eyes full of adultery, insatiable for sin. They entice unsteady souls. They have hearts trained in greed. Accursed children!' "

Herb came up to Bud, put a hand on his shoulder.

"Mr. Kork, do we have your permission to search your house?"

Bud blinked, then looked at Herb.

"What did you say?"

"Your house, Mr. Kork. We'd like to search it."

He grunted, nodding. "Go ahead. Help yourself."

I began sorting through the cabinets. Herb tried the drawers.

"You might want to start in the root cellar."

I stopped, stared at the old man. "What's in the cellar, Mr. Kork?"

Bud Kork peered down at his bare feet, then put the rosary against his lips.

"That's where I buried the bodies."

CHAPTER 21

B UD KORK LED us out of the kitchen. He had a slow, bow-legged gait that seemed to cause him pain with every step. He took us past several cluttered, dirty rooms and through a closed door at the end of the hall.

A soiled bare mattress sat on the floor, pointy springs jutting out through the fabric. As in the first room, the walls were bare, save for a giant black crucifix hanging crookedly over the bed.

"This is the devil's room. Unclean."

Kork pointed to the closet, open to reveal a dozen empty wire hangers hanging from a rope nailed lengthwise inside.

"Under the board."

The bottom of the closet had a four-by-four piece of plywood on its floor, three pairs of worn shoes on top. Herb kept watch on Bud, and I knelt by the board and lifted the corner, dragging back the wood to reveal a squarish hole.

The smell rose up like a ghost, catching in my throat and forcing me to gag.

I covered my mouth and nose. "Something dead."

Herb's nostrils curled back. "Many somethings. Call the GPD?"

I glanced at Kork, who was gnawing on a dirty fingernail. I could smell the schizo on him like I could smell his stale sweat. He was completely unreliable. Maybe there were indeed corpses under the house. Or maybe there were dead dogs, or a pig, or he simply used this hole to dump leftover cooking grease.

"We need to confirm first. Got a flashlight in the car?"

Herb told me no.

"I have a lantern," Kork said. "In my room."

I nodded at Benedict, and he whisked Kork away to locate the lantern. Holding my nose, I took another look into the hole.

It seemed to be very deep. Ancient wood was laid into the dirt floor, making a kind of staircase that led down into blackness. The smell was so bad it penetrated my tongue. The smell of decay. The smell of rot. The smell of old death.

Herb returned, Kork in tow. He held an old-fashioned gas lamp, the wick burning bright inside the glass.

He cleared his throat and asked, "You or me?"

I had no idea how big the space was down there, and Herb was almost double my size. I held out my hand for the lamp.

"Want me to hold your shoes?"

Wrong day to wear Dior.

"No. They only cost me eight bucks. But I could use your handkerchief, if it's clean."

He pulled it from his jacket pocket. "Snot free."

I pressed it over my nose and mouth, held the lamp before me like a talisman, and began my descent.

The stairs canted at a steeper angle than normal. I took them slow, careful of my footing. The walls were cut directly into the earth, like the sides of a freshly dug grave, and the black dirt absorbed the lantern light. The dirt also absorbed sound, and my climb was eerily quiet.

I counted thirteen steps before reaching the bottom. It had a dirt floor, bumpy and uneven, and the lamp revealed an area of roughly twenty feet by forty feet. The ceiling was low, brushing the top of my head. This made the space seem small and tight, and I felt a spark of panic that the ceiling would collapse on my head, burying me alive. I controlled my fear and moved on.

Three steps into the room I saw the first mound. A raised pile, no more than six inches higher than the surrounding earth.

The length and width of a child.

"Herb!" I yelled through the handkerchief—the smell was abominable. "I need a shovel!"

"Just a minute!" He sounded very far away.

I went deeper into the room, illuminating more burial mounds.

I counted eighteen.

"Shovel coming down!"

With four clangs and a thud, a spade hit the cellar floor. Long-handled, with a rusty blade. I set down the lantern and was forced to tuck the handkerchief into my pocket—I couldn't dig with only one hand.

I picked the nearest mound. The spade dug easily into the earth, biting deep with each swing.

Every breath provoked a gag.

I badly wanted to spit the taste of rot out of my mouth, or to vomit, but I kept swallowing it back, unwilling to contaminate the scene. The lamp cast wild flickering shadows along the walls and ceiling, and I knew I was getting close to the end of my reserves. I had two minutes, tops, before I wouldn't be able to take it anymore.

I dug faster, my back muscles screaming, my jaw set tight. The smell made my eyes tear up. The ceiling pressed down, as if I were sinking.

That was enough. I couldn't do it. I was going to barf all over, and no force of will could stop it.

My blade hit something.

Hurrying, no longer caring about getting dirty, I dropped to my knees and scooped away handfuls of earth, inch by terrible inch, until the child's head appeared, a pink barrette still clipped in the muddy blond ponytail.

I jerked my hand back, pulling out several strands and part of the scalp. The flesh had taken on the consistency of soap.

Game over. The smell had become a living thing, so potent, so pungent, I could feel it even though I held my breath. It dug into my pores, penetrating my skin, infecting me with its corruption.

I pressed my lips together and made it up the stairs before the vomit burst forth, spewing onto the stained mattress.

Herb approached me, concerned, but stayed back when the stench of me hit him.

"Call the Gary police," I managed to get out between expulsions. "Tell them to bring digging equipment, HazMat suits, the county coroner, and at least twenty body bags."

Herb fussed with his cell phone. "No signal. Where's your phone, Kork?"

Bud Kork eyed Herb, an odd expression on his face. He didn't seem nervous, or upset. More like curious.

"In the kitchen," he answered.

"I'll watch him," I told Herb. He waddled off.

I coughed, spit. The smell was in my clothes, in my hair, on my skin. I knew from experience it would be hell to get rid of. I stared hard at Bud Kork, anger slowly replacing my revulsion.

"How many are down there, Bud? How many kids?"

He spoke softly. "'He must manage his own household well, keeping his children submissive and respectful in every way.' That's 1 Timothy 3:4."

"How many people, Bud? How many children?"

"Sinners. All sinners. I helped them atone."

His palsy became worse, his fists shaking like he was plugged into an electrical outlet.

"Tell me about Diane Kork, Bud. Did you kill her?"

"I'm a sinner too. Lord, I am a sinner!"

Kork dropped to his knees, his eyes filling with tears.

"O my God, I am heartily sorry for having offended You, and I detest all my sins . . ."

He began to rock back and forth, bending down, touching his forehead to the floor.

"Did you kill your son's wife? Or do you know who did?"

". . . because of Your just punishments, but most of all because they offend You . . ."

"Do you have a video camera, Mr. Kork?"

". . . my God, who is all-good and deserving . . ."

"Who brought the jar of toes to Chicago?"

". . . of all my love, I firmly resolve, with the help of Your grace, to sin no more!"

His rocking was violent now, and he snapped his body back and drove his head hard into the wood floor.

"Mr. Kork!"

"Sin no more!"

He smashed his head down even harder. Blood erupted from his face and nose. I made it to him in two steps, reaching for his shoulders, trying to pull him back. He was much stronger than I would have guessed, and he had momentum on his side.

"SIN NO MORE!"

With his final blow I actually heard the sound of his skull cracking. He slumped over onto his side, one eye closed, the other open and fully dilated.

"Herb! We need an ambulance!"

I put two fingers against his grimy neck, feeling for a pulse. It was weak, but there.

Pulling back his collar, I noticed some scar tissue on his breastbone. A sense of uneasiness, of dread, came over me, and without thinking I lifted up his ratty undershirt.

It was one of the most horrible things I've ever seen.

CHAPTER 22

ALEX WAITS FOR Dr. Morton outside the pizzeria, on the sidewalk. The doctor had gone in alone, eighty-five minutes ago. Long enough for a leisurely lunch. This place is known for its deep-dish pizza, baked in a pan with the sauce on top of the cheese. Alex has never tried it.

At the eighty-sixth minute after entering, Dr. Morton exits the restaurant. His face is the picture of shock and surprise when he bumps into Alex at the door. He recovers quickly, but Alex is secretly delighted to have flustered the shrink.

"Alex! Oh, hello. Just in the neighborhood?"

"There are more than three million people in Chicago, Doctor. What's the likelihood we both just happened to pick the same restaurant for lunch?"

Alex watches him puzzle it out.

"So, you followed me. Was there any particular reason?"

"I need to talk to you."

Dr. Morton looks at his watch. Very unprofessional. "I'm sort of pressed for time, Alex. Don't we have an appointment tomorrow?"

"You spent eighty-six minutes eating pizza. You can't spare ten minutes for me?"

"But I'm seeing another patient, Alex."

"I have to talk to you now, Doctor." Alex checks the street, which is clear, and casually pulls the gun out. "I'm having a crisis."

Dr. Morton doesn't look afraid. But that doesn't matter.

He will. Soon.

"Can we talk in my car? Just five minutes. I can even give you a ride back to the office, save you some cab fare."

The doctor lets out a slow breath. "Fine. But I want the gun."

"Don't you trust me, Doctor?"

"You said yourself that you're having a crisis. I wouldn't want you to do anything regrettable."

Alex smiles, hands over the weapon.

Dr. Morton shoves it into his blazer pocket, and Alex leads him to the car. If the good doctor notices the missing side mirrors, he doesn't say anything about it.

After the doctor puts on his seat belt, Alex jabs him with the needle in the upper arm.

"Alex? What are you doing . . . ?"

"Just something to relax you, Doctor."

Dr. Morton's mouth opens. He's shocked. He isn't used to surprises. He's used to being in control. Alex can read it in his face.

The doctor grabs for the door, but Alex has disabled the handle. He pulls four or five times, but it doesn't open.

"Sorry, Doc." Alex grins.

"Let me out of here, Alex."

"I can't do that, Doc. You're a loose end. I told you too much, and now I have to take care of you."

"Take care of me?" His words are beginning to slur.

"I'm going to cut a small slit in your belly, right under your navel. And then I'll stick some tongs in there, and pull your intestines out through the hole. Then you're going to eat them."

Dr. Morton's eyes get comically wide. He gropes for the gun and pulls it out.

"Do you know how to work a semiautomatic, Doctor? That one has a safety on it."

The doctor obviously doesn't know. His hands are shaking, and he's trying to pull the trigger. Alex reaches over, flips off the safety for him.

Dr. Morton doesn't hesitate. He points the gun at Alex's head and fires. There's a clicking sound, and the slide goes back.

No bullets.

"I'm disappointed, Doctor. Is that how you deal with the mentally ill? By trying to shoot them in the head? I'm surprised you have any patients left at all."

The doctor raises the gun, tries to hit Alex with it.

Alex laughs, easily blocking the blow, then pops Dr. Morton in the nose, causing a minor explosion of blood.

"Don't bother trying to fight, Doctor. I'm stronger than you are."

Dr. Morton doesn't listen. He again tries to club Alex with the gun. Alex slips the blow and takes the gun away.

"Enough. It's nighty-night time."

"Please." Dr. Morton's head lolls to the side. He's almost out.

Alex pats him on the head.

"You'll have plenty of time for begging tomorrow, Dr. Morton. I promise."

CHAPTER 23

WHEN THE DOCTOR came into the waiting room to talk to me, he looked ashen. I put him at about my age, five-ten, graying temples, nurturing a pot belly on an otherwise skinny body. His name tag read *Murphy*.

"How's Kork doing?"

"The patient has a linear skull fracture, a third-degree concussion, and a broken nose. I also put six stitches in his scalp. You said this was self-induced?"

"He banged his head into the floor."

He pursed his lips. "That makes sense, considering the overall shape he's in."

"You've obviously seen his chest."

"The chest is child's play compared to some of the other things I found. He has no relatives?"

"None." I stood up, stretching my back, my vertebra popping like a cellophane bag. I'd been cramped in the little plastic chair for over three hours.

For the second time this week I sported the latest borrowed hospital fashion: baggy jeans, a Pacers shirt, and sandals. The clothes I'd put on this morning, including my Dior flats, were double-bagged in plastic. I doubted I'd ever get the stench out of them.

The hospital had been kind enough to let me use the residents' shower, and

I scrubbed myself pink with industrial strength antibacterial soap. It still hadn't been enough to get the stink of rot out of my hair and skin. The stench lingered like a perfume I'd put on. Eau de Decay.

"I'd like to see him, Dr. Murphy."

"He isn't conscious yet. Might not be for a while."

"I want you to show me the other things you just mentioned."

The doctor hesitated. I had no authority there, but I pressed anyway.

"He's a mass murderer. They've pulled eleven bodies out of his basement already, and more are on the way. Let me see him. It may help save some lives."

Dr. Murphy relented, and ushered me down a brightly lit hospital corridor to a room in the ICU. A uniform from the Gary PD stood guard by the doorway, young enough to still have acne.

"Just pulled out number twelve." He tapped his radio and gave me a respectful nod. "You did Indiana a huge favor."

"Let's hope your district attorney thinks so."

Though Herb and I went by the book, there might be prosecution problems because this wasn't our jurisdiction. But I had more immediate concerns.

Bud Kork lay on a hospital cot, handcuffs locking him to the bed frame. White gauze swaddled his head like a turban. Cotton packed his nose, and a piece of tape stretched across the bridge. Two shiners encircled his eyes, and his mouth hung open, revealing decades of dental neglect in muted browns and yellows.

Dr. Murphy pulled back the sheet and the hospital gown, exposing the marks on Kork's pale, sunken chest. The scars were in the shape of three-inch letters, forming the word *sinner*. The word was repeated eight times on his chest and abdomen in raised pink skin.

"I'm guessing this came from branding."

"It was. We found the branding iron back at his house."

That wasn't all we found, so I had an idea of what to expect as the examination continued.

"Help me turn him over, Lieutenant."

He pushed Kork's shoulders, and I pushed at the hip. Kork flounced onto his belly. His back was a road map of pain. There wasn't a single patch of unmarked skin from his collar down to the backs of his knees. It looked like a buffet of chopped, congealed lunch meat, knotted and discolored.

"Most of these marks appear to be self-inflicted." Displeasure bunched up Dr. Murphy's face. "Some kind of many-tailed whip with barbs on the end."

In Kork's bedroom closet we'd found an old toolbox full of implements. These scars would match the cat-o'-nine-tails he owned.

"Down here, along the thighs, the pattern is different."

The rusty wire brush, used for stripping paint.

"These X's here, here, here, and here are burn marks."

Another branding iron, in the shape of a cross.

"And these puncture marks appear to be from nails."

We hadn't found any nails in his mutilation kit, but they'd probably turn up.

"Let's put him on his back again. There's more."

We flipped Kork over and his head lolled to the side. He snored softly.

"Brace yourself for this, Lieutenant. I've been an MD for sixteen years, never saw anything like it."

He pulled down the sheet, exposing Kork's groin. I winced.

Bud Kork had no genitalia. His penis and testicles were missing. A small brownish nub of scar tissue poked out of the nest of gray pubic hair.

The doctor dropped the sheet. "It gets worse. When I saw the mutilation to the genitals, I ordered a pelvic X-ray." He pulled out the chart at the foot of the bed. "Take a look."

I stared at the X-ray of Kork's pelvis and thighs. It appeared to be covered with white scratches.

"See all of those lines? Between two and four centimeters long? There are forty-three of them."

"What are they?"

"Needles."

I stared at Kork in disbelief.

"He's got over forty needles embedded in his groin, rectum, buttocks, and thighs. See the dotted lines here? Those are ones that have been in him for so long, his body is breaking them down. The pain must be unimaginable."

I recalled how Bud Kork walked, like every step hurt.

"Any idea when he'll wake up?"

"Could be in ten minutes. Could be next year."

I gave the doctor my card. "It's very important you call me if there's any change. Or when he regains consciousness. Besides all those dead kids we found in his cellar, he's a prime suspect in a current homicide investigation."

"When he wakes up, he might not remember where he is or what happened. Head injuries are fickle."

I offered a grim smile and shook the man's hand. "I've dealt with something similar before. Thanks, Doctor."

I stepped out of the room and asked the officer to contact the team at Kork's house and put me in touch with Sergeant Herb Benedict. After a burst of static and some chatter, Herb came on.

"Hi, Jack. You're missing a real circus here. Over."

"Perp's out, will be for a while. How's the search? Over."

"No camcorders, no videotapes. Guy didn't even have a TV that worked. No black gloves or hunting knives either, over."

The killer in Diane Kork's murder video wore black leather gloves and used a hunting knife.

"Anything at all, Herb?"

"They're removing the thirteenth body now. Plus, there's some weird stuff."

"On this end too. When you're done, pick me up."

"I'll be there soon. Out."

I'd left Herb on the scene because Gary PD broke the Kork story, and there were now more reporters in this town than residents. So far the hospital had kept them out, which suited me fine. I'm sure Bains was already cultivating an aneurism about the fire last night. If he saw me on TV, his head would explode.

I went back to the waiting room and watched CNN. Two guys in disposable paper suits and air regulators hauled another body bag out of Kork's house. The top graphic read *Horror in Indiana,* and the rolling caption along the bottom of the screen told how this was the home of Bud Kork, supposed father of Charles Kork, the infamous killer known as the Gingerbread Man.

The scene cut away to some footage from two years ago, the day we closed the Gingerbread Man case. My face came on, full screen, and I said something about justice being served.

The graphic flashed my name, Lieutenant Jack Daniels, in large letters, and then went on to explain how the event turned me into a television star on the series *Fatal Autonomy*.

I wondered if the superintendent watched CNN.

Mercifully, my big face was replaced with some awful tragedy happening in the Middle East. I buried my nose in a *Woman's World* magazine and waited patiently for Benedict to arrive.

He did, twenty minutes later.

"There's a horde of reporters out there, Jack. Maybe you want to take a back way out? Or wrap a sheet around your head?"

"Doesn't matter now. I was just a sound bite on CNN, and they'll replay it every forty minutes until this all blows over. Let's just get out of here. It's doubtful anyone will recognize me anyway."

Herb and I stepped outside into a thick sea of reporters, cameras, and crews. Someone yelled, "It's Jack Daniels!" and the mob closed in and swallowed us up, chattering and shoving.

"Lieutenant Daniels, did you make the arrest?"

"Lieutenant Daniels, have you spoken to Bud Kork?"

"Lieutenant Daniels, how does this compare to the Gingerbread Man case?"

"Lieutenant Daniels, you look like you've lost weight. Is it the stress?"

Herb tried to pull me through the throng of bodies, but the throng refused to budge. With no other options, I finally held up a hand and yelled, "I'd like to make a statement."

Everyone shut up.

"I'm not in Gary because of Bud Kork. I was visiting the Blessed Mercy hospital to have elective surgery."

"What kind of surgery?" eight or nine networks shouted.

"I was having my foot removed from a reporter's ass. I don't want to have surgery again so soon, so please let us through."

They let us through. When we finally reached the car, Herb grinned at me.

"I'm guessing they won't air that."

"Who knows? Fox might. I don't really care. My hand hurts, my lungs hurt, and we still have nothing at all on this case. And I smell like dead people. I just want to get home."

Herb motored out of the parking lot and followed the signs to the expressway.

"We just took a very bad man off the streets, Jack. Should be happy about that."

"He's crazy. He'll spend the rest of his life in some cushy institution, being scrutinized by ViCAT chuckleheads. He was doing a fine job punishing himself. We could have left him alone."

"Punishing himself?"

I gave Herb the condensed version. He looked appropriately ill by the end of it.

"He cut off Little Willy?"

"Right at the root."

"And the twins?"

"Lefty and Righty, both."

Benedict shuddered. "Jesus. That's who they belonged to. Cops found a set of genitals wrapped in foil, in the freezer."

I made a mock-serious face. "Herb, you know what that is, don't you?"

"No. What?"

"It's a cocksicle."

He didn't laugh. Maybe my timing was off. Comedy is all about the timing.

"Guys don't find castration funny, Jack."

I nudged him with an elbow. "That's because it's like getting a lobotomy."

"See? Not funny."

But I still had more material.

"In a way, I kind of feel sorry for Bud. I mean, where does he put his hand when he's watching TV?"

"Not all men grab themselves when they're watching TV."

"Or when they're driving?"

Benedict looked down, noticed he was adjusting himself. He turned a shade of red normally seen on valentine cards.

"I wasn't grabbing."

"What were you doing? Frisking yourself?"

He went sheepish. "Just checking to make sure they were still there."

Benedict merged onto the expressway. When his blush faded a bit, he changed the topic.

"We found some seriously awful things at Kork's place. In the barn there was a locked wooden box, with tiny holes punched in it. When we opened it, the inside was covered in scratch marks. He kept people in there."

I shuddered. "Jesus."

"This guy's a monster. Sort of makes sense why his son turned out the way he did. Can you imagine growing up in a house like that?"

"I don't even want to try. It's not my job to understand these kooks. It's just my job to catch them."

"Doesn't understanding them make catching them easier?"

"Sure. Next time I see a guy who has *sinner* branded all over his chest, I'll place him under arrest."

"Want to hear the weirdest thing we found? In the bathroom. The bathtub. Filled to the top."

I bit. "With what?"

"With urine. Kork must have been peeing in that tub for years."

"That's disgusting."

"Gets worse." Herb made the Mr. Yuck face. "Next to the tub was a bar of soap and some piss-soaked towels. Apparently, he's been taking baths."

I massaged my temples. This had officially become too freaky for me to adequately process.

We spent the remainder of the ride trying to gross each other out, and by the time Herb dropped me off at home I'd decided to give up food forever.

Back in my apartment, Mr. Friskers ran away from me when I entered. Must have been the death smell. I checked for messages (none), and drew a bath into which I dumped every oil, salt, and soap I owned. I'd just climbed in, bubbles up to my ears, when the phone rang.

I let the machine get it.

"Jack, it's Latham."

I vaulted out of the tub, almost met my death slipping on the tile floor, and snatched up the phone, out of breath.

"Latham? Hi! I just got in."

"Hi yourself. How are you doing?"

Stinky. Alone. Depressed. Freezing. "Great. I'm great. How about you?"

"Good. Job's going well. I love the new condo. How's your mom?"

"Still in a coma."

"That's awful. I'm sorry."

"Can we get together?" I bit my lower lip. I was so cold, my knees were knocking together.

"Sure. That would be nice. The thing is, though, I'm seeing someone."

If he'd cut my heart out of my chest with a cleaver it would have hurt less. I squeezed my eyes closed and tried to sound upbeat.

"That's great. What's her name?"

"Maria."

"Maria. Great. Great name. Is it serious?"

"We've been dating for a few months, and I just asked her to move in with me."

Latham had asked me that same thing, but I turned him down, because I am the Queen of All Who Are Stupid.

"Well . . . that's great. I'm happy for you."

"I'd still like to see you, though. To catch up. Touch base."

Screw me until I can't stand up? Instead I said, "Yeah, that would be nice."

"I'll give you a call in a few days?"

"Yeah. Sure. Sounds good."

"Bye-bye, Jack. Great talking to you."

"Yeah. Same here."

He hung up.

I stood there a moment, teeth chattering, and then moped back into the bathtub.

It was my fault that he was with Maria. Just like it was my fault my mother was in a coma. She'd been living with me, and a criminal I'd been chasing broke into my apartment and took his wrath for me out on her.

I wondered if Bud Kork had a branding iron that said *fuckup*.

After a long soak, which still didn't get all of the stink out, I crawled into bed and stared at the ceiling, knowing I'd never be able to fall asleep.

So I didn't even try.

CHAPTER 24

D R. MORTON TRIES to scream, but he can't—his mouth is full.

CHAPTER 25

SLEEP NEVER CAME.

I crawled out of bed at six a.m., hacked up some black gunk from my lungs, forced myself through a hundred sit-ups, and showered. I'd spent all night watching the Weather Channel, and there was enough meteorological evidence to suggest that today would be partly cloudy, with a high of seventy-five.

I dressed in a gray Ralph Lauren pantsuit, a black short-sleeved blouse, and some two-inch heels I picked up at Payless. It would take me a while before I wore nice shoes to work again.

I also put on just a small spray of L'Air du Temps. I'm not a perfume kind of gal, but I wanted to cover up the smell of decay that still clung to me. I was supposed to meet up with Harry McGlade tonight. If I stank, he'd be vocal about it.

After feeding the cat, who still avoided me, I searched the pantry for foodstuffs and found some cranberry granola bars. Mom loved them. I hated them. But I was starving, so I forced one down.

I stuck another one in my pocket, disengaged the alarm, and opened my door to leave. As I did, a small package that had been leaning against the door fell inward.

Same brown envelope as the one delivered to me at work.

I tugged out my Colt, looked left, right, then hurried down the hallway to the stairwell.

There wasn't anyone to chase.

I went back into my apartment, nudging the envelope in with my toe. Then I found some rubber gloves under the sink and carried the package over to the kitchen table. I slit it open with a bread knife and dumped out the obligatory unlabeled black VHS tape.

Such a small, harmless, everyday item. Yet it filled me with dread.

The first tape had been wiped clean of prints, but hope springs eternal, so I only held the video by the very edge in my gloved hand. I brought it into the bedroom, put it in the VCR, and let it play.

This one began with a close-up of a man's bare chest. He was sitting on a chair with his hands behind him, probably tied or cuffed.

A black gloved hand, with a long black leather sleeve, used a box cutter to open him up from nipple to nipple. The screams were so loud they distorted the audio. Then the hand came back into frame with some pliers.

The granola bar jumped around in my stomach. I hit the Fast-forward button, watching this poor guy get his chest, then his back, peeled in triple time. When the atrocities finally ended with a deep slash across the carotid artery, the killer stepped behind the camera and zoomed out, revealing the man's head.

No burlap bag this time. The victim's face was clear. And worst of all, identifiable.

Dr. Francis Mulrooney. The eccentric, gentle handwriting expert. A man whom I considered a friend.

The tape ended, reverting to blue screen.

Anger came first. Then sadness. Then, like a slap, fear.

The killer had murdered Diane Kork and Francis Mulrooney, two people involved in the Gingerbread Man case. The killer also knew where I lived.

When I received the first tape, I took it to be a boast by the perp. *Look what I can do, and you can't catch me.*

This second tape was more than a boast. It was an obvious threat. He was saying *You're next.*

I placed the tape and the envelope into a fresh plastic garbage bag, and headed for Mulrooney's office, keeping a careful eye on the rearview mirror. Why did it seem like every looney in Chicago knew where I lived? Did they give out my address at Serial Killer School?

The day was partly cloudy, I'd guess it at seventy-five degrees. Score one for the Weather Channel.

The graphologist's office was on Fifty-ninth Street, at the University of Chicago's Hyde Park campus. I took Lake Shore Drive south, a twenty-minute trip, exiting at the Museum of Science and Industry on Fifty-seventh, following Stony Island to Fifty-ninth. The campus area covered about five square blocks, wooded and peaceful and brimming with coffee shops and used bookstores and academic activity. But south of Stoney, and west of Drexel, the neighborhoods turned very bad very fast, with high crime rates and Emergency Stations every few blocks—phones that linked directly to 911.

I parked next to a hydrant and entered the old brownstone where Mulrooney worked. A fat security guard sat behind a round counter. He had a squashed appearance, with several chins, and resembled a bullfrog perched on a toadstool. I flashed my gold, my earlier anger and fear stored safely behind a cloak of cool professionalism.

"Where's the office of Dr. Francis Mulrooney?"

"Second floor, last door." His voice was high and whiny, ruining the frog motif he had going for himself.

"Is it locked?"

"Probably."

"Can you open it?"

"Sure."

We took the elevator, a small space that could carry five people, four if they were as rotund as my security guard friend. Someone had scratched some swear words into the stainless steel panel next to the buttons. Even our highly praised bastions of education weren't immune from folks who thought "shit-breath" was high comedy. Why didn't vandals ever quote Shakespeare? I'd love to see graffiti in iambic pentameter.

"Has Dr. Mulrooney had any visitors lately?"

"Students."

"Any adults?"

"No."

"Have you seen this guy hanging around?"

I showed him the Unabomber Xerox, which I now carried everywhere.

"No."

"When was the last time you saw Dr. Mulrooney?"

"Yesterday afternoon. Left the building at his usual time, around one."

"Did he seem worried? Scared? Distracted?"

"Seemed normal."

The door opened. The guard went first, leading me down a thinly carpeted hallway to a hollow core door I could have opened by sneezing on it. The first two keys didn't work, but the third was a charm.

I thanked him, and he waddled off. The office wasn't much larger than the elevator, and certainly more crowded. All four walls were lined with crammed bookshelves. A desk sat in the corner, covered with papers and folders and clutter. An older model Dell rested on the desk, the monitor partially obscured by Post-it notes, a screen saver bouncing around a Microsoft logo.

I nudged the mouse, and the Windows desktop appeared, which was almost as cluttered as his real-life desktop. I clicked on Outlook and read a few e-mails. Nothing interesting. Then I clicked on the Start Menu and looked at Recent Documents. Nothing there either.

I searched his real desk next, uncovering a combo phone/answering machine beneath a stack of student reports. A number four blinked in the red LED window. I hit Play and began going through drawers.

The first message was from me, canceling our appointment. The machine beeped, and the next message played.

". . . you're going to die . . ."

The voice was a whisper, barely audible. A few seconds of silence followed, then a beep.

". . . today . . ."

More silence. Another beep. I found the volume control and turned it up.

". . . did you like the video, Jack? You're next . . ."

That seriously weirded me out. I pressed Play and listened again. The sex of the speaker was impossible to determine. I tried to find the Eject button to save the tape, but the machine had no tape—this was a model that recorded digitally. Whispers could be voice-printed, but I didn't know if unplugging the machine would erase the data on the chip. I left it alone for the time being.

The desk yielded no secrets, save for a single key with a round green tag that Mulrooney had carefully labeled *House spare.*

I pocketed the key, closed the door behind me, and took the stairs back to the frog.

"I need Dr. Francis Mulrooney's home address."

He had a large black binder labeled *Faculty Directory,* and I learned Mulrooney conveniently lived a block away, on Fifty-eighth.

The walk was pleasant, though my cheap shoes pinched my toes. Mulrooney's building was an apartment, three stories, two tenants per floor. The single key fit both the security door and his door, on the ground level. I knocked first, in case he had a dog, and when no noise erupted from within I went inside.

His dwelling was the opposite of his office, everything neat and tidy. I gave the place a thorough toss, beginning in the kitchen, then the bedroom, bath, and living room.

Like his office, I couldn't find any signs of a struggle. Unlike his office, there were no messages on his answering machine.

I found an address book, tucked it into my pocket, and locked the door when I left.

Abducting someone isn't very hard. Mulrooney was a slight guy, short and thin. A reasoner, not a fighter. A large man could have muscled him into a car or truck within a few seconds, without attracting much attention. Or he could have been drugged, or tricked, or gone someplace with someone he trusted.

I stood on the curb and called Officer Hajek at the Crime Lab, asking if he had time later to swing by Mulrooney's office to see what could be done with the answering machine. He promised me he would.

"*. . . did you like the video, Jack? You're next . . .*"

I shuddered.

This wasn't the first time I'd been a target, but that didn't mean I was used to it.

I walked back to my car, acutely aware of my surroundings.

CHAPTER 26

HERB WAS WAITING for me in my office. He looked to be in good spirits, and cradled half a large bag of Chee·tos. His walrus mustache had a distinct orange tint. It matched his orange fingers, orange shirt, and orange tie. That's how I knew for sure Herb wasn't the killer; he would have left an easy-to-follow trail.

"Morning, Jack. You look upset. Saw the captain?"

"He looking for me?"

"That's the buzz around the station."

Great. I left the garbage bag containing the latest video on my desk, told Herb I'd be back in five, and headed for the lair of Captain Bains.

As expected, Bains didn't greet me with flowers and a big hug. The large vein in his forehead bulged out when he saw me, and I heard him grind his teeth; not a happy sound.

"Goddammit, Daniels. I recall ordering you off the case. Do you recall that?"

"Yes, Captain."

"And since then you've been involved in an arson, a high-profile arrest outside your jurisdiction, and your face is all over national news telling the media you'll stick your foot up their collective asses."

"They aired that?"

Bains made a face. I made one as well. At least he didn't mention the shots fired at Diane Kork's. When a police officer dischargers her firearm, there's an automatic IA inquest and a mandatory visit to the department shrink. I didn't have time for either.

"You're suspended, Jack. With pay. Report to the commissioner tomorrow at nine a.m."

"What?" That clocked me from left field. "What's the charge?"

"Does it matter? Pick one. How about official misconduct? Insubordination? Acting like an ass on CNN? The superintendent wants your job, and it seems like you want to give it to him. I need your badge and gun."

I was so furious, I could spit. I spoke through my teeth.

"This isn't a good time. He's hunting me."

"Who is?"

"The killer."

"The killer's in Indiana, in a coma. Case closed. Take a week off and let this blow over."

"Bud Kork isn't the guy we're after. The guy we're after came by my apartment last night and gave me another videotape. A videotape of Dr. Francis Mulrooney getting skinned alive."

The anger melted off the captain's face. It was replaced with a tired kind of sadness. When he spoke, the venom was gone.

"He's dead?"

"You remember him?"

"I'm the one who asked him to assist on the Charles Kork case."

"Well, I've got thirty minutes in screaming color of him dying an agonizing, horrible death. And it was dropped off at my house, Captain. I'm a target. You can't pull me off now."

Bains didn't seem to be listening. "Francis was my cousin," he said in a soft voice. "I used to baby-sit him when we were kids."

"I'm sorry." I wasn't sure what else to say. "He never mentioned that."

"Did you bring him in on this?"

"I had an appointment with him, but had to cancel. I think he knew someone was stalking him, but didn't mention it to me. There were some threatening messages on his office phone. The same person also threatened to kill me."

Bains put his hands on his desk and stared at them, spreading out his fingers.

"I know the suspension is bullshit, Jack. It's out of my hands. But the paperwork hasn't been done yet, the official charges haven't been filed."

"How long do I have?"

"Two, maybe three days. You can fight it, of course. Contact the union rep. Request a hearing. But you're being suspended with pay. Doubtful you'd get much sympathy."

"The super can suspend me for a year after I catch this guy."

Bains nodded. He looked smaller than he normally did. "We never had this conversation. Go find this animal. And keep your face off the boob tube, or it will be both our jobs."

I reached into my pocket, placed Mulrooney's address book on the captain's desk.

"Did you want to inform his family?"

"I'm part of his goddamn family."

I waited.

"I'll make the calls." Bains took the book.

Back in my office, I gave Benedict the blow-by-blow.

"Bains is a careerist. He's bucking for commander. He won't go down with you, Jack."

"He's a good cop."

"He's a politician. Shit trickles down. If the super wants you out, you're out."

"I can fight it. Unreasonable termination. Discrimination."

"No you won't. You're not the type." He looked at the garbage bag on my desk. "Couldn't find a purse you liked?"

"I got another video this morning. The graphologist, being skinned."

Herb winced. I didn't want to watch the tape again so soon, but I snapped on a glove and popped it into the VCR.

Three minutes into it, Herb excused himself to go to the men's room.

I made myself be analytical. I freeze-framed on the gloves, to try to read the tag inside the cuff. I freeze-framed on the pliers, to try to see the manufacturer mark. Emotional detachment was impossible, but I owed it to Dr. Mulrooney to do my job as best I could.

By the end of the tape I had no leads, and I was quivering with disgust.

I spent a few minutes trying to calm down, trying to distance myself from the images. The phone rang, scaring the hell out of me.

"Hiya, Jackie. What are you wearing?"

Harry McGlade.

"A frown," I answered.

"We on for later?"

"Unfortunately."

"How's three o'clock?"

"I'm at work."

"Take a day off. You deserve it. Meet us at Mon Ami Gabi, on Lincoln Park West. I've got reservations under the name Buttshitz. You're bringing a date, right?"

"I think so." Phin hadn't called yet.

"Rent a guy if you have to. Or bring that fat partner of yours. Tell him it's free eats; he'll come running."

"Good-bye, Harry."

"Don't be late. You're late, I'll make sure your TV character gets her own spin-off series."

He hung up. I searched my desk for aspirin, finding the bottle just as the Feebies walked in. Well, a single Feeb anyway.

He nodded at me, wearing the same gray suit he had on a few days ago. Or perhaps a completely different gray suit that looked exactly the same.

"Lieutent Daniels. How are you?"

I was tired and bitchy and not in the mood to suffer fools.

"Now's not a good time, Agent Coursey."

"I'm Dailey."

"Where's your partner? Aren't you guys always side by side, holding hands?"

"He's ViCAT's liaison with the Gary Police Department, investigating the Bud Kork murders. And our relationship is purely professional."

"So you don't give each other oily back rubs after a long day of securing our personal freedoms?"

His lips twisted somewhere between a grin and a wince.

"I understand. You're attempting to assert your control over this situation by belittling my masculinity."

I got wide-eyed. "Wow. You BSU guys don't miss a trick."

"Now you're using sarcasm to undermine my professionalism."

"It's like I'm under a microscope. All of those Quantico classes have given you tremendous insight into human nature. What am I doing now?"

"You're giving me the finger."

Herb returned, a bit green around the gills. He surveyed the situation.

"Am I interrupting an intimate moment?"

"Special Agent Dailey was just leaving. He's got a samba band to chase."

Dailey cleared his throat. "We believe the Gingerbread Man wasn't working alone."

That got my attention.

"What do you mean?"

"After careful analysis of the twelve previous Charles Kork murder videos, we've deduced the recordings were made on two different camcorders. Each particular brand leaves a unique signature when laying down an electromagnetic control track on—"

I held up my palm. "Spare us the details. What difference does it make if there were two recorders? So he used one for a while, it broke, then he bought a new one."

"The camcorder recovered at Charles Kork's residence matches six of the videos. The other six were done on a different machine, an RCA DSP3. The recent videotape that you were sent was also done on an RCA DSP3. It's an older model, discontinued years ago."

That was compelling, but not enough to get me excited. "I'm sure they sold thousands of that model. Any way to prove the same camcorder recorded both?"

"Not conclusively. But let me show you something. Do you have a DVD player?"

"Not in the budget this year."

Special Agent Dailey put his briefcase on my desk and opened the clasps. Sure enough, he had a mini DVD player. It took him a minute to attach it to my TV, and then he inserted a disc.

"This is from one of the RCA tapes. Number seven, which Charles Kork titled 'Fresh Meat.' We had it cleaned up and transferred to digital. A videotape is normally an analog signal, so during the transfer—"

"No technospeak. Please."

"Fine. Just watch this and tell me what you notice."

This was one I hadn't seen, and had no desire to see. Dailey retrieved a remote from his attaché, pressed a few buttons, and the image showed Charles Kork brutally slapping a bound woman. The slapping went on and on, the camera zooming in closer and closer, until you could clearly see the marks Kork was making.

Dailey paused the video.

"Did you notice that?"

"I saw a woman getting beaten. It was revolting."

"Of course it was revolting. But what else did you see?"

He began the scene at the same point, and again we witnessed the atrocity, starting with Kork full body and ending with him right in our faces, close enough to see his sweat.

Herb pointed at the screen. "The zoom."

Then I got it. Kork was in front of the camera. If he was in front, who zoomed the lens in?

Now I got excited.

"Was it an automatic zoom?" I asked. "Or a remote control?"

"That RCA model doesn't have one. Not only that, we analyzed this frame by frame. The camera is mounted on a tripod, but at the beginning of the zoom, the picture jars slightly. Consistent with someone behind the camera, pressing the zoom button."

"The Gingerbread Man had a partner."

Dailey nodded, somber.

I sat on my desk. Bud Kork, though a serial killer himself, couldn't have been Charles Kork's accomplice. Bud was in a coma when I received the videotape this morning. And the cameraperson who taped Diane Kork's death had steady hands; Bud's were racked with Parkinson's.

"Who?" Herb asked.

"We've discovered that Bud Kork had a common-law wife for twelve years. She's doing life for manslaughter—she sliced up a girl she believed was sleeping with Bud."

"She's still in prison?"

"Yes. And she had a boy of her own. We know he was one year younger than Charles, and they lived together for a while."

"Remember what Bud Kork said yesterday?" Herb nudged me. "*No flesh of my flesh*. This kid lived in his house, but wasn't Kork's son."

I tried to picture two little boys, growing up in the hell house of Bud Kork. They'd both be majorly screwed up. Chances are they relied on each other. Bonded. Maybe developed the same grotesque appetites.

"Where's this guy now?"

"We haven't been able to locate him. Last known address is in Michigan."

"Record?"

Dailey paused. "Assault and battery. Burglary. Armed robbery. Rape. Did a few stints in prison. But three years ago, the guy just disappeared."

"Have you asked his mother where he is?"

"Not yet. As of today, the special agent in charge of the Chicago office is sending me to Gary to assist Special Agent Coursey."

Now this generous sharing of information made sense.

"You came to us, knowing we'd want go and interview her."

Special Agent Dailey smiled. "We're all on the same side, right?"

"Fine. What's her name and where is she?"

Dailey played coy. I stated the obvious.

"You want something."

"The Behavioral Science Unit is facing cutbacks. Homeland Security is getting all of the funding. We're going to be downsized. A major bust would go a long way to preventing that."

"You want the collar."

Dailey nodded. "We're willing to share. But we'd like to be in on it. If I give you the woman's name, and you find out where her son is, we'd like to assist in the arrest."

"Won't that only matter if state lines have been crossed?"

"We can still be there to smile pretty for the cameras."

I mulled it over. "We could find her on our own."

"Maybe. But it will be tough. You don't have access to all of the information that we do. You'd need subpoenas to obtain records. All of that will take time."

I glanced at Herb. He shrugged.

"Deal." We shook hands on it. "What's her name?"

"Her name is Lorna Hunt Ellison. She's currently in the Indiana Women's Prison in Indianapolis. Son's name is Caleb."

I wrote the info down, then hit the Eject button on my VCR.

"I got another tape this morning. It shows the death of the handwriting expert who helped with the Gingerbread Man case."

Dailey raised an eyebrow. "You believe Diane Kork was killed on the first tape, correct?"

"We don't have a body, but the tattoo matched. And someone burned down her house when I showed up. I find it hard to believe that's coincidental."

"So do we. And it's also not a coincidence that the handwriting expert was killed. It appears that the Gingerbread Man's partner is targeting people involved in that case. Who else had a hand in it?"

"Harry McGlade, obviously. And a guy named Phineas Troutt helped out. Some men from the medical examiner's office, Phil Blasky and Max Hughes. A handful of uniforms from my district, who did legwork. Guys from the Evanston PD."

"And us." Agent Dailey frowned. "We're on his list too."

CHAPTER 27

INDIANAPOLIS WAS A three-hour drive. Herb and I made arrangements with the warden to visit with Lorna tomorrow afternoon. Indianapolis was also the hometown of Mike Mayer, who rented the Eclipse. We could check out his house after visiting Lorna.

I still hadn't heard from Phin. Herb vehemently disliked Harry, and not even a free meal would convince him to sup with the PI. Racking my brain for someone else to bring was an exercise in futility. I didn't have any friends. I hadn't dated anyone in months. My life was police work.

I wondered, ironically, whom I would ask to stand up if I ever got married. I was in the same boat as McGlade in that respect.

Not that I'd ever have to face that situation.

"You gonna eat that?"

Herb pointed at the cranberry granola bar sticking out of my jacket pocket. I flipped him the bar. He took a tiny exploratory bite.

"This is awful."

"I know."

"And so tiny."

He finished it, then traded me a five-dollar bill for singles to go on what he called a Carb Quest—a trip to the vending machines.

"Want anything?"

"No."

"I'll drop by later."

"Herb . . . let me know when you get the biopsy results."

I gave the Detroit PD a call, and asked them to give me whatever they had on Caleb Ellison. They reiterated what Dailey had told me. Ellison was a career dirtbag who dropped off the face of the earth.

"Probably in a shallow grave someplace," said the cop I spoke with. "No big loss."

I asked him to fax over Caleb's record, which turned out to be a Greatest Hits package of felony arrests. Presuming Caleb wasn't in a shallow grave someplace, he was in his late thirties, two hundred pounds, with red hair and lots of tattoos.

I switched gears, and hunted and pecked my way through the reports I'd been neglecting, beginning with the fire from two days ago.

Three hours later I was bleary-eyed and falling asleep. The phone snapped me out of my stupor.

"Hi, Jack. It's Phin."

That was a relief. "Hey. Thanks for calling."

"Where are we meeting?"

"At Mon Ami Gabi, a French steakhouse in Lincoln Park. Three o'clock. Reservations are under the name Buttshitz."

"Unfortunate name."

"It's not real. Harry thinks he's funny."

"See you at three."

He hung up. I yawned, stretched, checked my watch. Twelve thirty. Back to the thrill-a-minute fast lane of report writing.

The writing was so white-knuckle exhilarating that I actually did fall asleep. Someone nudged me out of slumber an undetermined time later.

"Jack. You asleep?"

I peeled my eyes open, focused on Herb. "Not anymore."

"Sorry. Didn't mean to disturb you. I'm heading home."

I felt a brief flash of panic and checked my watch. Ten after three.

"Shit. I'm late." I focused on Herb. "Why are you heading home so early?"

"I got my biopsy results." His face split into a broad grin. "Benign. Bernice and I are going to celebrate."

I cracked a huge grin and gave my partner a hug. "That's great, Herb. Congrats. Tomorrow, early, we go to Indiana."

I rushed past Herb, flew down the stairs, hopped in my Nova, stuck the cherry on top, and hit the siren.

Even with traffic parting for me, I didn't get to Mon Ami until a quarter to four. I did a quick once-over in the rearview, threw the valet my keys, and entered the posh Beldon Stratford Hotel.

The restaurant occupied the left of the lobby, up some carpeted stairs. It was an upscale French steakhouse; probably a redundant description, considering there aren't any budget French steakhouses. Small, intimate, with starched tablecloths and a wine cart worth more than a Mercedes. I sheepishly gave the tuxedo-clad hostess the reservation name, and she led me past a dozen or so tables, all occupied.

During the ride over, my mind filled with worst-case scenarios, most of them centered around Phin murdering Harry.

Color me surprised when I spotted their table and heard gales of laughter.

"Jackie!" Harry pointed at me, speaking much too loudly for the venue. "Come! Sit! Meet my beloved."

I eyed Phin, who was looking pretty good in a charcoal jacket and a light-blue button-down shirt, open at the collar. He offered me a pleasant smile.

Harry stood up to greet me, an unprecedented move, and Phin stood as well. McGlade clasped my hand as if I'd just returned from war, his face glowing with happiness. He wore another wrinkled suit, but his shirt was starched, and the handkerchief in his breast pocket matched his tie.

Harry's beloved didn't stand up, but she flashed me a dazzling smile. I practically did a double take.

This woman was actually cute. Great skin, a delicate nose, full lips, high cheekbones, deep blue eyes, thick black hair in a bob cut.

"Jack Daniels, meet my fiancée, Holly Frakes."

Holly offered a hand, her nails to die for. She had a strong, firm grip.

"So this is the famous Jack Daniels. Quite a difference from your TV counterpart. I love the suit."

"Thanks." I wished I'd dressed up a little more. Her cream silk blouse was gorgeous, displaying her figure to good effect. I glanced at her lower body and noted a matching skirt, and a handbag that was unmistakably Prada. A Prada purse cost more than everything I owned put together.

"Nice to meet you, Holly. That's a lovely outfit as well."

Holly's smile blazed brighter. "Emanuel Ungaro. I just love Ungaro, don't you?"

"Only from afar." Emanuel Ungaro hadn't appeared on the Home Shopping Club yet. I wasn't holding my breath.

I sat down between the men, placed the napkin in my lap, and glanced at Phin again.

Phin was staring at Holly.

"Holly was just telling us a skip trace story." McGlade patted her on the hand. "Go ahead, baby."

"You're a bounty hunter?" I asked.

"Private investigator. Like Harry. I occasionally chase bail jumpers to keep things interesting. Where was I, hon?"

"You had him cornered in the alley."

"Right. So the punk didn't want to be brought in, even though I had my gun out. He told me to go ahead and shoot him."

"What was his crime?" Phin had puppy-dog eyes.

"Assault. He liked to hit women. Now, personally, I wouldn't have minded pumping a few rounds into this son of a bitch. He deserved it. But he wasn't armed, and the local police department probably wouldn't have supported such an action. So I fired twice, over his head, to get his attention. Guy just stares at me, not moving."

Holly had a totally engaging way of telling a story, her eyes wide and her hands in constant motion, adding greater impact to her words.

I instantly disliked her. There was a bottle of red wine on the table, and I filled my glass and took a healthy slug.

"So I fire another round, between his legs."

"How far away were you?" Phin asked.

"Twenty feet."

"Holly's an expert marksman." Harry beamed.

"Marksperson," Holly corrected. "I've won a few trophies. No big deal."

"So have I. I'm the Area champ."

Was that me talking? Jesus, Jack, are we that insecure?

"What do you carry?" Holly asked me.

"A .38 Colt."

She wrinkled her nose. "What is that, a two-inch barrel?"

I knew what she was hinting at. A .38 snub nose was no good for sharp-shooting.

"In my job, I've never had to hit anything farther than ten feet away. The shorter barrel means a quicker draw. For handgun competitions I shoot a .22 LR, Smith and Wesson Model 2206."

"Capable weapon. I prefer the Number 41 Rimfire."

"Doesn't that have a shorter barrel?"

"Half inch less than the 2206, and five ounces heavier. But I like the thumb-rest on the grips, and think it's a better balanced weapon."

She knew her firearms. Which made her even more annoying.

"So what happened next?" Phin asked.

Holly grinned. "Well, I probably missed his peter by two inches, and that would have scared the spaghetti out of most men, but this guy still just stands there. Now the only way I can collect from the bondsman is if I bring him in, and he outweighed me by about a hundred pounds and wasn't afraid of guns."

Harry's smile threatened to crack his face. "I love this next part. Tell them what you did, baby."

"I put away my gun, walked up to the prick, and asked him if he was right-handed or left-handed."

"And what did he say?" This from Harry, who had somehow turned into Ed McMahon.

"He called me a bitch, and told me it was none of my business."

"So what did you do?"

I know what I did. I drank more wine.

Holly sipped some wine too. Both Phin and Harry reached for the bottle to pour her more. Phin won.

I set my empty glass on the table.

No one filled it.

"Well, I told the guy that I was originally planning on just breaking his bad arm. But since he wouldn't tell me which that was, I'd have to break them both."

Harry clapped again, and let out an inappropriate whoop.

"So what did he do?"

"He laughed in my face."

"And what did you do?"

Holly's smile was tight-lipped. "I broke both of his arms."

Harry laughed, and Phin joined in. A waitress came by and filled my wine-glass, asking if we'd like another bottle. I gave her a vigorous nod.

Harry nudged me. "Holly's a martial arts expert."

"Really?" I feigned interest. "Which discipline?"

She shrugged. "Tae kwon do. Third dan black belt, but I don't practice much anymore."

I was only a first dan black belt. I drank more wine, then tried the bread. Excellent bread.

"So where did you two meet?" This from Phin.

McGlade puffed out his chest. "Eye-Con. It's the largest private investigator convention of the year. Held in Chicago this year, in February. I sat next to her during a lecture about listening devices, and she recognized my name from the TV series."

"You just met two months ago?" I formed the words around the bread in my mouth. "Isn't it kind of soon to leap into marriage?"

"Why wait?" Holly reached over and held McGlade's hand. "We're not getting any younger."

I went fishing. "That's ridiculous. You're how old, thirty?"

"Thanks so much." Holly patted my forearm. "I'm thirty-eight."

Now I *really* hated her.

The waitress came again, with more wine, and after an elaborate wine presentation she discussed the daily specials. I tuned her out, trying to understand what the hell Holly saw in Harry. He was probably rich because of the series, but all the money in the world didn't make up for the fact that McGlade was one of the most obnoxious, offensive, and annoying people to ever drag his knuckles, and Holly seemed, well, perfect.

We ordered. Holly regaled the boys with more tales of heroics. I drank. After my fourth glass, I came right out and asked.

"Holly, you have to tell me. What in God's name are you doing with McGlade?"

"What do you mean?"

I mutely gestured with both hands, finally saying, "Well, look at him."

Holly placed a hand on Harry's head and ruffled his curly brown hair.

"He makes me laugh."

McGlade wedged a fist-sized hunk of bread into his mouth. "Plus I'm hung like a beluga whale. But I have more hair."

They shared a kiss. I rolled my eyes. I'd fallen for my share of losers too. At least when she divorced him, she'd get a decent settlement.

Dinner arrived, and it was probably excellent, but I had too much of a buzz to notice. I switched from wine to coffee, knowing I'd eventually have to drive, and Holly held Phin's hand and asked him in a breathy Happy-Birthday-Mister-President voice if he'd do her the honor of standing up on her side at the wedding two days from now.

Phin agreed, of course. If she'd asked him to cut off his own legs he would have been racing for the hacksaw.

"And you, Jack, thank you so much for being there on Harry's side."

She said it in such a genuine way that I actually believed her.

"It's my pleasure." I wasn't nearly as genuine.

If Holly noticed, she kept it hidden. "You know, I've got some free time during the afternoon tomorrow. It'll be the first time in days."

Harry grinned and held her hand. "I don't like letting her out of my sight for very long."

Holly grinned back. Love sure was disgusting.

"Anyway, Jack, I haven't been shooting in forever. Would you like to fire off a few rounds?"

"Sure." I didn't know what else to say. "Drop by the station tomorrow, around five. We'll hit the range."

I had no idea why she was making an effort, and an even lesser idea of why I was reciprocating. Because I had no friends? Because I still didn't understand why such an incredible woman was marrying Harry?

Or was it because I'd take an obscene amount of delight in outscoring her ass on the firing range?

We had dessert, more coffee, and then Holly got up to visit the ladies' room.

"Well?" Harry elbowed me in the arm. "What do you think of her? What a filly, right?"

I rolled my eyes. "Yeah, Harry. She's a real filly."

"How about you, Jim?"

"Phin."

"Phin. Pretty prime piece of real estate I'm developing, huh?"

"She's lovely." Phin looked at me, for only the second time of the night, a question in his eyes.

Harry slurped some coffee, spilling it onto his shirt. "I'm the luckiest man who ever lived, that's for sure. She's beautiful, smart, funny, and the sex is mind-blowing. She doesn't wear underwear. Can you believe it? I'm writing a letter to *Penthouse*."

Holly returned, McGlade made a big show of picking up the check, and everyone hugged everyone else, some more enthusiastically than others. The valet got Harry's car first, and he and Holly drove off honking and waving.

"That was surreal," Phin said as we stood in the lobby.

"How so?"

"McGlade. That guy is an idiot. Actually, calling him an idiot isn't fair to all the other idiots. What in God's name is she doing with him?"

"McGlade's rich. She could be gold-digging."

"Maybe that's it. She obviously doesn't love him."

"Why do you say that?"

"Come on, Jack. Who could love that guy? If I had to spend ten minutes alone with him I'd eat my gun. Or make him eat it."

The valet pulled my car up.

"I read somewhere that beautiful women are often lonely because men are afraid to approach them."

That received a snort. "Get real, Jack. Did you look around the restaurant? Everything with a Y chromosome was ogling her. Holly hasn't lacked for companionship a single day of her life."

That made me feel much better.

"You need a ride someplace?"

"No. I'm good. See you Monday, Jack."

"Thanks for coming, Phin. I owe you one."

"It was fun. Hey, you don't like McGlade, right?"

"He's like the brother I never wanted."

"If he met with some kind of fatal accident, would that be a problem?"

I couldn't tell if Phin was joking or not. I tipped the valet, climbed into my beater, and opened my window.

"You can't kill him until I'm off the TV series."

"Got it. You looked nice tonight, Jack."

"I'm glad someone noticed," I said. But I said it after I'd already pulled away.

CHAPTER 28

SERGEANT HERB BENEDICT gives his sleeping wife a pat on the rump and climbs out of bed. It's a hair past midnight, and midnight is the perfect time to have a midnight snack.

He creeps to the door—the house is old and the wooden floors creak like the shrieks of the damned. Bernice is a light sleeper. She made a wonderful rib roast for dinner, and there's very little left. If he wakes her, he'll have to share.

Herb takes the stairs slowly, as if stepping on eggshells. He doesn't put on any lights. He doesn't need to. He's lived in this house for decades, and can navigate entirely by feel.

The kitchen floor is slippery under his bare feet. Bernice waxes the tile once a week, and Herb's soles are dry and calloused. More than once he's almost taken a dive during a late-night refrigerator raid.

He manages to keep his balance this time, pulling the Tupperware bowl of meat and potatoes from the fridge, deciding whether the microwave is necessary, or if straight from the container will suffice.

The kitchen is cold, so he goes with the microwave. He sets it for a minute—just enough to get the chill out of the food—and opens the utensil drawer, feeling for a fork.

A creaking sound comes from the living room.

Herb freezes. Instantly he knows the noise came from a person, and that person can't be Bernice because he would have heard her coming down the stairs. The lights are off, but there's illumination coming through the small window of the microwave. Herb squints across the kitchen and into the dining room, where he sees the drapes ruffling.

The window is open, the wind blowing in. That's why the kitchen is cold. That's how someone got into his house.

Benedict's gun is upstairs, next to the bed. He keeps it there on the off chance someone ever tried to break in. He's aware of the irony. Who knew he should have armed himself to go eat leftovers?

Another squeak. Closer. The person is right around the corner, less than ten feet away. Herb considers his options. Most burglars don't want to be confronted. They run at the very thought of the house being occupied. A loud shout will scare this type of criminal away.

But this might not be a burglar. It might be someone with a grudge. Someone Herb arrested in the past, looking to settle a score.

Or someone else. Someone planning on making a new videotape to give to Jack.

He chances a quick glance at the microwave. Thirty seconds left. Then there will be a loud beep to signal the food is ready. Herb had planned to open the microwave door a few seconds early, so the sound didn't wake Bernice. Now he decides to use the beep to his advantage. When the microwave beeps, the light will go off. Maybe the combination will mask Herb's movement, giving him a chance to strike first.

Silently, Herb reaches back into the utensil drawer and finds a paring knife. Long-bladed weapons aren't good in a fight. They get caught on clothing. The large blade makes penetration more difficult, and easier to defend against. A short blade is easier to control and wield, and can do more than enough damage.

Herb takes one for each hand.

The microwave reaches 15 seconds left . . . 14 . . . 13 . . .

Benedict spreads his feet apart, widening his stance.

12 . . . 11 . . . 10 . . .

The kitchen is dark, but he knows every inch of it. He imagines the three steps he'll have to take before the quick right turn into the living room.

9 . . . 8 . . . 7 . . .

He bends his knees and crouches down. He'll hit low, use his weight to knock the person over.

6 . . . 5 . . . 4 . . .

Herb takes a deep breath, holds it, clenching the knives as hard as he can.

3 . . . 2 . . . 1 . . .

BEEP-BEEP-BEEP!

Benedict is already two steps into his run. Before he can make the turn into the living room he bumps straight into the man standing next to the refrigerator.

Momentum takes Herb forward, but the shock of hitting someone sooner than expected, plus the slippery floor, makes him lose his balance. He falls face-first, trying to break his fall with his knuckles, realizing at the last possible moment that falling on two paring knives is a bad idea.

Herb manages to stretch one knife in front of him.

The other penetrates his chest and slips between two ribs, puncturing his right lung.

The pain is instant and intense. A sharp, searing pain, accompanied by a sudden urge to cough.

Ahead of Herb, the intruder also hits the floor. It's followed by a clanging sound, something metal hitting the tile. A crowbar? A gun?

"Herb?"

Bernice. She heard the sound. Herb tries to warn her, but he can't take a breath. Nothing comes out, only painful wheezing. He pulls at the knife in his chest, and it comes out with a wet sucking sound.

A foot catches Herb in the face. Herb lashes out with the knife, finding a calf, digging the blade in.

There's a scream, low and loud, and the leg is pulled away. Herb hears limping footsteps heading into the living room. And then he hears something that almost stops his heart: the stairs creaking.

Bernice is coming down.

Herb tries to get up. He's struggling to breathe, and there's a wet hissing sound coming from the hole in his chest. He presses his palm to it, pain be damned, and manages to get to his knees.

The light goes on in the hallway.

"Herb!"

Bernice's voice, panicked. There's a grunting sound. Something breaks, sounds like glass.

Not Bernice please God please not my wife . . .

Herb crawls across the tile, desperate. Another light goes on, in the living room. He sees what the intruder dropped. A hunting knife, the blade over ten inches long.

Footsteps, getting closer. Herb raises the paring knife, ready to fight.

Bernice walks into the kitchen. She's holding Herb's gun.

"Oh my God, Herbert!"

Herb tries to speak. Can't. Bernice reads the question on his face.

"He's gone. He saw the gun and broke through the living room window."

Herb coughs, blood bubbling from his lips. He collapses onto the floor and is conscious long enough to notice the note on the floor, next to the hunting knife.

CHAPTER 29

FOR THE SECOND time in twelve hours, the phone woke me up. I squinted at the clock in the darkness. One a.m. I'd been asleep for almost an hour.

The phone rang again. I slapped it to my cheek.

"Daniels."

"Jack? It's Bernice Benedict. Someone just broke into our house."

I went from groggy to alert in record time.

"Are you okay? Where's Herb?"

"He's been stabbed in the chest."

She sounded scared, but in control. Cops' wives were tough.

"Have you called 911?"

"An ambulance is on the way. The man who broke in, he left a handwritten note. It says 'All shall be punished.'"

"I'll be there in ten minutes. If you're already on your way to the hospital, leave the back door open."

I threw on some jeans and a sweatshirt and made it to Herb's place in nine minutes. Scores of squad cars jammed the side streets; cops took care of their own.

I parked on his lawn and caught Benedict being shoved into the rear of an ambulance. His pajama top was open, and an EMT pressed a large piece of gauze to his bloody chest. Herb's face was literally gray, but he was awake.

"How you doing, partner?"

He rolled his eyes, which buoyed me with relief. The dying don't bother with sarcasm. He whispered something, more a gargle than a whisper. I leaned over, my ear to his lips.

". . . stabbed the guy . . . leg . . ."

"Description?"

". . . dark . . . Bernice . . ."

"She saw him?

His eyes said yes.

"I'm going to check out the scene. I'll visit you later."

I patted his cheek, and he whispered something again.

". . . crow wave."

"What?"

". . . microwave . . . don't touch my rib roast."

Bernice stood in the doorway, talking to three cops. She was in her mid-fifties, short and a shade too plump for this era. Her gray hair was in a bun, and she hugged her robe around her, cold or scared or both. I approached, and when Bernice noticed me she grasped my hands.

"Are you okay?"

"I'm fine." Though I didn't see how she could be.

"Did you see his face?"

"Yes. Short red hair. Acne scars. Chubby. I don't know about height—he was limping and hunched over. In his late twenties or early thirties."

"What was he wearing?"

"A black sweatshirt, black jeans, gloves."

"Black leather?"

"White rubber. Like a doctor wears."

"Tell me what happened."

Bernice laid it out for me: waking up when she heard a noise, calling for her husband, hearing a man scream, grabbing the gun and coming downstairs, finding the suspect in the living room. When he saw the gun, he busted out through the window.

"Did you see which way he went?"

"No. I was in a hurry to find Herb."

Something in her tone made me wonder if there was more. "Anything else, Bernice?"

"Yes. He spoke to me, before he ran off."

"What did he say?"

Bernice didn't flinch. "He said, *I'll be back, bitch.*"

I left Bernice in the capable hands of Chicago's finest and entered her house. The Crime Scene Unit hadn't arrived yet, and the first-on-the-scene officer was reluctant to let me in, even though I pulled rank. He was worried about contaminating evidence, which wasn't an unfounded concern. A few recent high-profile court losses due to compromised scenes had made many of the higher-ups unhappy.

I assured him I'd be careful, and wandered through the living room, mindful where I stepped, taking everything in.

The entry point was through a living room window. A hole had been cut in the glass, wide enough to accommodate an arm. Then the latch had been turned and the window raised. Silent and effective. It was an MO I'd seen before—the Gingerbread Man had used it.

The perp had exited through another window, smashing the glass. There was blood on the window frame, on the wood floor trailing up to it. I followed the blood into the kitchen, found the note and the hunting knife. The note seemed to match the first note left for us, and the hunting knife appeared to be the same one used in the Diane Kork video.

There was more blood here, Herb's and the intruder's, smeared around in a pattern that suggested a struggle. Two paring knives were slathered with the stuff.

I looked in the microwave, found the Tupperware bowl full of rib roast. I didn't see how touching it would in any way, shape, or form hurt a conviction, so I put it in the refrigerator.

Careful to avoid the blood, I left the kitchen and followed the blood spatters, through the living room, up to the window. Hanging on a jagged shard of glass were three red hairs.

Caleb Ellison, who lived with Charles Kork for ten years, had red hair.

The CSU arrived. Pictures were taken. Video was shot. Samples were acquired. I left after an hour, heading to St. Vernon to check on Herb. He hadn't come out of surgery yet. I sat with Bernice, holding her hand, trying to get my mind around everything.

It didn't make sense.

The note and the hunting knife looked to be matches, but other than that, this crime didn't seem at all related to the deaths of Diane Kork and Francis Mulrooney. There were too many discrepancies. The MO was all wrong.

Diane and Francis were abductions. No evidence had been left. Their deaths had been videotaped. Their killer wore black leather gloves. Everything pointed to him having a blond beard.

But in this case, the killer was a redhead who wore latex gloves, tried to kill his victims in their homes without recording it on tape, and left a truckload of physical evidence.

Why so many differences? Was the killer escalating? Or getting sloppy? Or was this a hasty attempt, thrown together at the last minute?

By four a.m., Herb was out of surgery, and his doctor came to see us. I didn't like the fact that he appeared grim.

"We repaired the damage to his lung and inserted a tube to reverse the pneumothorax—the collapsed lung—but while on the table your husband suffered a myocardial infarction."

Bernice's only reaction was to blink.

"He had a heart attack?" I asked.

"We were able to resuscitate, and he's in Recovery now. We anticipated this might happen. A chest CT before surgery revealed large amounts of calcium deposits on his arterial walls. So after closing him up I ordered an MRA and found evidence of coronary artery disease. He's going to need angioplasty at the least—I need to run some more tests. There's enough plaque to qualify for bypass surgery."

Bernice began to cry, and I didn't feel so hot myself.

"I want to see my husband."

The doctor nodded. "One visitor only. He's still in critical condition."

Bernice hugged me, and the doctor escorted her out of the waiting room. I sat for another hour, pestered the nurse to visit Herb, got turned down, and went home, worried sick.

CHAPTER 30

SLEEPING WASN'T AN option, so I left for Indianapolis early, the rising sun in my face as I headed southeast. There was a little bite of winter lingering in the air, a frigid breeze that made a jacket necessary. I wore my three-quarter-length London Fog trenchcoat, black Levi's, and a black and red blouse by Kathleen B that I picked up in a small boutique in Aurora. The blouse was made of material called poodle fabric, and had the thickness of a sweater without the bulk. For shoes, I went with Nikes—no woman likes to drive long distances in heels.

I did a lot of thinking during the trip. If I truly was happy being miserable, as I suspected, then I'd just attained a state of euphoria.

My father died when I was young. My mom raised me, but she'd worked full-time as a police officer, and from eleven years old on I spent a lot of time alone, locked in our little apartment. I loved Mom, and appreciated all she'd done for me, but I didn't need a therapist to know I had abandonment issues. Control issues too. Chasing bad guys helped keep the issues at bay. It was easier than dragging them out into the sunlight and dealing with them.

But at times like these, when the world felt like it was falling apart around me, when it didn't look like the bad guys would ever get caught, when I needed more than ever to be strong—I always seemed to come up short.

When I joined the police force out of college, Mom hugged me and told me how proud she was, and then begged me to quit. She was my role model. I wanted to be like her, and didn't understand why she regretted me following in her footsteps.

Now I understood. It took twenty years, but I understood. I did a lot of good things, helped a lot of people. Saved lives. Caught criminals. Made the world a better place.

A better place for everyone but me.

I had a husband. I could have had a family, and pursued some other career that didn't involve death.

Funny thing about regrets. I don't lament what I've done, but rather, what I didn't do.

And now, with my partner hurt, my job in trouble, my love life nonexistent, and my mother in a coma, I couldn't help but wonder if I should have listened to Mom and not have become a cop.

Would I be happy?

I considered the melancholy I felt when I thought I was going to die in the fire. I'd faced death, and met it with apathy.

That spoke volumes.

I arrived at the Indiana Women's Prison a few minutes before nine. From the outside it looked like an old schoolhouse, a two-story building made of reddish brown brick, with a circular driveway and well-tended green landscaping. The assistant superintendent met me inside, a thin reed of a woman named Patricia Pedersen. She had severe black eyebrows that looked like caterpillars and the barest hint of a mustache above thin lips. Her pantsuit matched the mustache.

"Lieutenant Daniels, welcome to our facility. We'll need to check your weapon, of course."

My .38 was locked away, and Ms. Pedersen had me sign in before leading me inside. I knew a little something about the prison. It was the first all-female penal institution in America, having opened in the 1870s. High-medium security, dorm living rather than individual cells.

"We're currently over capacity, with 388 inmates. Most of the latest are juvenile offenders. We just received an eighth grader who beat her mother to death with a baseball bat. Tried as an adult and sent here. Thirteen years old."

The hall we walked down didn't have any doors—just concrete blocks painted gray and a white tile floor that met Ms. Pedersen's square-heeled shoes with a horselike *clip-clop*.

"Tell me about Lorna."

"Admitted twelve years ago. She cut off another woman's breasts. Lots of trouble, for the first few years. Fighting. Attacking guards. Starting fires. She's settled down some recently, since turning sixty. Still a strong woman, though. Don't underestimate her."

"Any visitors lately?"

"I don't think so. I can check the records."

"If you could."

She led me through some heavy steel doors and into the first dormitory. It resembled a military barracks, beds alternating with metal lockers. All were empty.

"Breakfast just began in the mess hall. We'll catch her as she's coming out. Need a private room, or can you talk in the yard?"

"A room."

"I can move some chairs into isolation, post a guard on the door for you."

"If you could take her there first."

"Of course. You can wait in my office."

"Can I read her file?"

"I've already pulled it for you."

Ms. Pedersen took me through more locked doors, another lonely hall, and into a small room with a cluttered desk. An American flag hung limply on a pole in the corner, and a signed picture of a former president adorned the wall. I sat in a wooden chair, the red vinyl cushion cracked and hard.

She brought me the Lorna Hunt Ellison file, and I gave it a quick go-through. Lorna had been born in Indiana, sixty-two years prior. She'd been arrested over a dozen times, mostly violent offenses, and previously served a two-year stint in Rockville Correctional Facility for setting fire to a liquor store.

That was the litmus test for blue-collar crime: liquor store burning.

A psych eval spun a story of antisocial personality disorder, passive-aggressive disorder, impulse disorder, and sadistic tendencies. A recent update added bipolar to the diagnosis. Lorna took a daily cocktail of antipsychotic medication, the dosage high enough to cause stupor in a gorilla. Her IQ was in no danger of reaching the triple digits.

Hardly any mention of her son, Caleb, and no mention at all of Bud Kork.

I wondered if the Feebies were wrong, and Lorna had nothing to do with Kork. Wouldn't be the first time.

Ms. Pedersen came back and told me Lorna was ready. "She's not in a pleasant mood this morning. Just warning you."

"Did you check her visitor list?"

"Yes. Not a single visitor since her incarceration."

"Popular lady. Do you think I might grab a bagel or something? I left early and missed breakfast."

"Sure. Let's swing by the mess."

I wasn't really hungry. I wanted Lorna to stew for a while.

We went through the kitchen entrance, and I had two slices of toast with butter while standing next to two women who were peeling an impossibly large pile of potatoes. They didn't talk to me, I didn't talk to them.

Ms. Pedersen remained silent during my meal; not hurried, but not noticeably pleased to have to watch me eat. After a good ten minutes had passed, I asked to be taken to Lorna.

The isolation area was clean, brightly lit. The doors were solid metal, with a sliding panel covering the eyehole slot. A male guard with a pot belly sat outside the door.

"Half an hour long enough?" Ms. Pedersen asked.

I nodded. "It should be."

"I promised Lorna extra dessert if she cooperates with you. Years ago, she stabbed another inmate with a fork to get her cobbler."

"Thanks."

"We've heard about the corpses at the Kork house, of course. Terrible."

"Does Lorna know about it?"

"Everyone knows about it. See you in a half."

Ms. Pedersen walked off, her footsteps echoing after her.

The guard stood up and offered a lazy smile. "If she gets frisky, just pound on the door or yell or something. Then I'll come in and save you."

Save me? I figured it would have taken me all of four seconds to blind him, break both of his knees, and leave him singing castrato. But since he had the key, I kept that to myself. He opened the cell door.

The smell hit me first, the pungent reek of old body odor. I crinkled my nose and stepped inside. The door clanged shut behind me.

The room was small, perhaps fifteen feet by fifteen, with stark white walls and harsh fluorescent lighting recessed into the ceiling. A stainless steel toilet jutted from the corner, next to a one-valve sink that resembled a drinking fountain.

Lorna Hunt Ellison sat in a lightweight plastic chair, facing me. Her hair was white and Einstein wild, like she'd just French-kissed an electric outlet. Her face looked worn, eroded, but the eyes sparkled like oily blue marbles.

She wore jeans, perhaps a size sixteen, her belly hanging over the waistband. Her shirt was light blue, big enough to be a painter's smock. Armpit stains spread down her sides, past her ribs, her small breasts hidden in the folds of the fabric.

"Good morning, Lorna. Sorry to keep you waiting."

"Pig." Her voice came out cracked and squeaky. A witch's voice.

I sat in the second chair, facing her, our knees almost touching. Lorna scooted her chair backward.

"Got nothing to say to you, pig."

Charm to match her beauty.

"I just saw Bud. He says hello."

She hocked up something from deep in her lungs and spat it onto the floor. "He's not saying dick. He's unconscious."

"That's what the papers say. The truth is, he's talking up a storm. He's telling us all kinds of things. Things about you. About your victims."

Lorna squinted, her oily eyes focusing.

"I didn't kill none of those folks. You can't prove nothing."

I kept quiet. We both knew she had a hand in the killings. But that wasn't why I came.

The silence stretched. Lorna scratched an armpit and left her hand tucked beneath it. She broke first.

"What's your name, pig?"

"Lieutenant Daniels. And if you call me a pig again, Grandma, I'm going to grab you by your chicken neck and make you lick the toilet clean."

Lorna cackled, her eyes crinkling in amusement. "Daniels! I know you! You the one that got little Charles."

"You did a good job raising that one. He was a real piece of work."

"Charles was already ruined, 'fore I moved in. Bud thought he was the devil hisself."

"Is that what you thought?"

She shrugged. "Boy had some problems."

Which might have been the understatement of the century.

"How about your boy? Caleb? Did he have problems?"

"Caleb was a good boy. Listened to his mama."

"Where's Caleb now?"

She didn't answer, but her eyes stayed on mine. I didn't see any intelligence there, but I saw cunning. Animal cunning, as if I were staring at a snake, or a rat.

"Did you once have red hair?" I asked.

"No. Used to be brown. Been white since my forties."

"So Caleb got his red hair from his father?"

"Damn Irish deadbeat. Wasn't worth his weight in shit."

"Where's his father now?"

She smiled, like a naughty child caught in a lie. "Caleb didn't like his daddy much."

"Are you telling me Caleb killed his father?"

"I'm not telling you nothing . . ." Her lips were about to form the word pig, but she read my expression and instead said, "Lieutenant."

"Were you married to his father?"

"Up until his untimely death."

"Caleb keep in touch with you?"

"Writes me, sometimes."

"Do you still have his letters?"

"Maybe."

"Would you like to show them to me?"

"Fuck, no."

Lorna folded her flabby arms. She had an unhealthy-looking brown growth on her elbow.

"I've talked to Ms. Pedersen. She's authorized me to give you certain things if you cooperate."

"She thinks I'm going to give up my son for some extra pie? She can kiss my hairy hole."

A real charmer, this woman. She should send in her application to *Who Wants to Marry a Psycho-Bitch?*

"When did you and Caleb move in with Bud?"

Another hack. Another spit. "Years ago. When Caleb started the junior high."

"Did Caleb get along with Charles?"

"Caleb got along with everyone. Such a good boy."

"For a good boy, he seems to get in trouble a lot."

"He's misunderstood."

"I'm sure he is. Plus, look at the hand he was dealt. Growing up in a house full of psychotic perverts."

Lorna didn't like to be called names. I watched her hands form into fists. I kept up the heat.

"You think that's why he hates you? Because you're a fat, psychotic pervert?"

"Watch what you say, cop."

"I'd hate my mother too, if she was retarded gutter trash."

"I ain't trash."

"Have you looked in a mirror the last couple of years?"

"And I ain't no retard."

"I read your file, Lorna. And if you were able to read, you'd see the word used several times."

Lorna seemed too focused on the older insults to process the newer ones.

"I ain't no retard, and my boy don't hate me. He loves his mama."

I leaned in closer, fighting the stench. "Why hasn't he ever visited you?"

Lorna's face twisted. "He's been busy."

"Busy every day for the last twelve years? Isn't that how long you've been here, Lorna?"

"He sends me letters."

"I don't believe you."

"He does."

"Show me."

"You want me to show you? Then you gotta do something for me."

I waited.

"I want to see Bud."

"No."

"I want to see his beautiful face again."

"I'm sure you'll share the same cauldron in hell."

I stood up, headed for the door. I needed some fresh air, and I knew Lorna wasn't going to give me anything else.

"You don't want Caleb's letters?"

"I don't care about his letters. I want to know where he is."

"I don't know. He doesn't tell me. But I do know something, might interest you."

"All I'm interested in, Lorna, is getting away from you."

I pounded on the door.

"Let me see my Bud again, and I'll show you something."

The door opened. I'd had enough of Lorna for the rest of my life.

"I know where more bodies are buried."

That stopped me.

"What did you say?"

"If you let me see Bud, I'll take you to more bodies." She smiled, showing me tiny sharp teeth. "Lots more."

CHAPTER 31

M s. PEDERSEN WAS painfully clear on prisoners' rights to privacy. "They have none. They're prisoners."

So Lorna Hunt Ellison stayed in isolation, and we raided her footlocker. We found some stinky clothes, a collection of empty candy wrappers, a faded Polaroid of a younger Bud standing in front of his ancient pickup truck, and two letters from Caleb.

I donned a single latex glove and appropriated the picture and the letters. They had no return address on the labels. The postmarks came from Detroit. The first relayed, in some of the worst handwriting ever, that Caleb was sorry he hadn't written before, because he was busy, but he'd write more often from now on. It was dated eight years ago.

Apparently he'd lied, because the second letter was dated three months ago. According to the chicken scratches, Caleb's PO had made him get a job and he was working at a car wash, but wouldn't for very much longer because he was planning on *killing the fat prick who ran it.*

That didn't make sense. I checked with Detroit PD, and according to them, Caleb Ellison didn't currently have a parole officer. So was Caleb lying to his mother? Or did he recently do time under another name? And how could I find that out?

I put thoughts of Caleb on the back burner, threw the letters and the pic into a paper bag that Ms. Pedersen supplied, then used her office phone to call the Indianapolis PD. I talked myself up the chain of command, and eventually got a captain on the other end, a gruff-voiced woman named Carol Mintz.

"Talk fast, I'm busy."

"You're following the story in Gary?"

"The whole state is."

"I'm here at IWP, and just had a heart-to-heart with Lorna Hunt Ellison, who was Bud Kork's common-law wife. They lived together for more than a decade. She claims to know where more victims are buried, but there's a catch. She wants to visit Bud."

"That's doable. The catch will be keeping the media out. I'm surprised they aren't camped outside the prison."

"I don't think they know the link yet."

"You want a piece of this?"

"No. But I'm in bed with the Feds on this one, and they'll be in touch."

"Great." She said it like an expletive.

Ms. Pedersen showed me out, and we exchanged good-byes and I consulted the MapQuest directions I'd printed earlier, which would supposedly lead me from Randolph Street to Kellum Drive and the address of Mike Mayer, who supposedly rented the Titanium Pearl Eclipse supposedly seen fleeing Diane Kork's house.

MapQuest did me proud. I went west on Washington Street, merged onto the expressway, merged off the expressway, and wound up in a pleasant little housing development filled with two-bedroom ranches on green-lawned quarter-acre lots. I parked in Mayer's driveway and knocked on an aluminum front door.

No answer. Not too surprising, considering Mayer just rented a car in Chicago.

I had a few options. I could break into the house, breaking the law in the process. I could call Captain Mintz back, explain the situation, have the IPD obtain a warrant, and die of old age waiting to be allowed entrance. Or I could assume that in a nice neighborhood like this, Mayer had nice neighbors.

I chose the house on the right first, traversing the well-maintained lawn and knocking on their aluminum door. A young girl answered, maybe ten or eleven, long brown hair and a face full of freckles.

"Is your mom or dad home?"

She nodded, eyes big, and then belted out, "Mom!" with all the force of a foghorn.

Mom looked like an older, pudgier version of the little girl, with just as many freckles.

I showed her my badge, hoping she didn't look close enough to notice I was from out of state.

"Ma'am, my name is Lieutenant Daniels. Your name is?"

"Linda. Linda Primmer."

"Linda, can you tell me the last time you saw your neighbor Mike Mayer?"

Her forehead crinkled in thought. "Been two or three weeks, it seems. Is Mike okay?"

"We're not sure. Tell me a little about Mike."

"Single. Keeps to himself. Kind of a loner. Seems nice enough."

Which was the exact description all neighbors gave of the serial killer living next door.

"Is this Mike Mayer?"

I showed her the Identikit photocopy.

"That sort of looks like him."

"This may sound unorthodox, but we're worried Mike might be in some kind of trouble. Did he ever give you a spare key to his house? In case he locked himself out, or to water his plants while on vacation?"

"No. But he did lock himself out once, last year. He came over here to call the locksmith. The locksmith sold both of us a key rock."

"A key rock?"

Linda stepped past me and onto her front stoop. Next to the door was a holly bush, surrounded by stones. She squatted and picked up a four-inch stone and showed it to me.

It wasn't a stone at all. It was a plastic replica, and on the bottom there was a slot, hiding a spare house key.

"Mike uses one of these?"

"He bought one. I don't know if he uses it."

"Thanks, Mrs. Primmer."

I gave her a cop nod, letting her know that I was in control and everything was okay, then walked back over to Mike's house.

Even with a key, it was still unlawful entry. If I found something, and defense counsel knew I'd illegally been in the dwelling, any evidence in the house would be inadmissible.

Or, if Mike Mayer turned out to be innocent, and discovered I entered his house without a warrant, I could be swimming in criminal and civil charges.

Of course, I also had a maniac threatening to kill me, and stopping that from happening was higher on my priority list than avoiding legal action.

Near Mike's front door, in the dirt by a window well, was a key rock identical to Mrs. Primmer's.

I thought about it for less than a second, then picked up the rock and opened the door.

I needn't have worried about illegal entry. Once the smell hit me, probable cause was assured.

There was something dead in the house.

Now I went by the book. I locked the door, returned the key, and dialed 911, explaining that I was a cop following a lead, and I smelled a dead body through the door.

It took four minutes for a squad car to roll up. Two Indy uniforms, a man and a woman, got out of the car. The woman pulled out a notepad and asked me my name.

I showed them ID, explained that the neighbor told me about the key rock, and pointed it out.

They both sniffed the door, and enough residual death odor made entry a no-brainer. They didn't object to my tagging along.

The air was heavy with decay, and several insects buzzed around us. Blowflies. They laid their eggs in dead flesh.

We found the corpse in the kitchen. And it was ugly.

It sat in a chair, and was recognizable as a male, barely, because a few patches of hair clung to its face. The torso was bloated, the skin on the bare chest split as if sliced open. Maggots squirmed in the wounds, and black and yellow carrion beetles scurried over ruined flesh in tiny roadways. They'd devoured much of the face, the lips, the eyes, the nose.

Blue jeans, stained black with putrefying fluid, hugged the thighs. The feet were bound to the chair legs with wire, which cut to the bone.

The male cop went running for the door, hand over mouth. The female cop, her name tag said *Lindy*, also put hand to mouth, but stood firm. I held my breath and walked closer.

Cause of death wasn't easily apparent. I concentrated on the ruin of a face, trying to see past the mottled flesh, past the insect activity, searching for some evidence of trauma. Nothing stood out.

I walked around to the other side of the corpse. The hands were wired together behind the chair. All ten fingers were missing, and a pool of dried blood stained the floor beneath them.

The insects hadn't eaten the fingers; there were defined cuts along the knuckles. I scanned the floor for digits, not finding any.

That made me wonder again about the cause of death. I took a closer look at the face, still holding my breath, my heart beating faster and faster in an attempt to squeeze some extra oxygen from my blood. I peered inside the mouth, partially obscured by blowfly larva and beetles scuttling over stained teeth, and proved my hunch correct.

Outside on the front porch I sucked in clean air and tried to ignore the Indy cop fertilizing the lawn with his breakfast.

Officer Lindy called for a Crime Scene Unit and the coroner using her lapel mike, and then walked up to me.

"How'd he die? The chest wounds?"

I shook my head. "The rents in the chest occurred after death. Gases were released while he decomposed, and they stretched the skin and broke through. This guy died of suffocation."

"How?" Her pallor resembled the sidewalk, but I gave her points for trying to learn from the situation. "Killer put a bag over his head?"

"No. Someone jammed his severed fingers down his throat. Probably tried to make him eat them."

I looked across the lawn, down the street, at all of the middle-class suburban homes. A nice community that would never fully recover from the notoriety once this story got out.

I could have stuck around, kept an eye on the investigation, but there was no point to it. If the killer left evidence, I'd hear about it eventually. I had no doubt the deceased was the unfortunate Mike Mayer. Perhaps he had some connection to the killer, something that provoked his awful death. Or perhaps he was simply murdered for his identity, and tortured just for fun.

Either way, the guy I sought wasn't in Indianapolis. He was in Chicago.

I gave Officer Lindy my card, then hopped in my car and headed north.

CHAPTER 32

I CALLED THE hospital on the way back to Chicago, and Bernice put a very groggy Herb on the phone.

"I had a heart attack, Jack."

I forced a jovial tone.

"Astonishing, considering the peak condition you keep yourself in. Have they scheduled surgery yet?"

"Wednesday. Doctor told me my arteries look like Interstate 90 during rush hour."

"Look on the bright side. At least you're not dying of cancer."

A long pause. My attempts at humor weren't working.

"Jack . . . if I don't make it . . ."

"Don't talk like that, Herb."

"I'm having a triple bypass."

"Everyone has a bypass or three these days. It's like going in for an oil change."

"An oil change only costs twenty bucks."

Herb began to cough, and I heard Bernice yell at him to stop coughing or he'd tear his stitches.

"Look, Jack, if . . . if the oil change goes bad, I want you to know that you're the best cop I know, and I love you like a sister."

Herb began to sing the chorus of "You've Got a Friend" by James Taylor, and Bernice took away the phone.

"He's taking a lot of morphine, Jack. Don't mind him."

"What's the prognosis?"

"He had more tests. They came back bad. That's why they're operating again so soon."

"Why wasn't this diagnosed earlier? He just had a colonoscopy."

"I'm guessing it's hard to diagnose a heart condition by sticking a camera up your ass."

I'd never known Bernice to swear. The strain she was under must have been awful.

"I'll call later."

I made good time, stopping once for a fast food burger and fries and once for gas and some Yellow Bombers, legal amphetamine pills made with caffeine and synepherine and sold in packets of two. Truckers took them to stay awake. My lack of sleep had caught up with me, and mile after mile of nothing but flat, boring plains did nothing to keep me alert.

I arrived at the station at a quarter after four, heart pounding and palms sweating. I called Hajek, and he'd managed to get Mulrooney's answering machine back to the lab without losing the messages. Of course, a voice print would only help with a conviction if we caught the guy, and I was no closer to catching him than I was when this case started.

I called up Al at the car rental place and asked if the Titanium Pearl Eclipse had been returned.

"Not sure. Hold on."

He put me on hold for eight minutes, and by the time he picked up again my blood pressure was so high I could have put out a fire by pricking my finger.

"Uhhhhhhhhhhhhhhhhhhhhhhhhhhhhhh . . . nope."

Justifying manpower in the Chicago Police Department was tricky. We had no evidence of any crime in our district, other than on the videotapes, and no clear-cut connection between those and the rented Titanium Pearl Eclipse. And since the car was rented under an assumed identity, there was a good chance it might not even be returned.

But no stone unturned and all that crap. I scoured the station and threw together six cops and had them meet in my office.

"This is shit detail. Stakeout, teams of two, eight-hour shifts. Can't interfere with your regular assignments, but I'll sign off on overtime."

I explained the target and what to do in case the target was sighted, and let them figure out the details.

Bains would hang me for the overtime, but maybe this would all be over before the paperwork went past his desk. We'd catch the guy, or I'd be killed, and in either case my concerns weren't monetary.

After dismissing the troops, I called the Gary PD and asked for anything they had on Bud Kork, Charles Kork, Caleb Ellison, Lorna Hunt Ellison, and the daughter Bud claimed was dead. The fax machine whirred, and the info came chugging in. Lots of it.

My phone rang, and the desk sergeant told me there was someone in the lobby asking for me. Holly Frakes, Harry's fiancée. I'd forgotten we were going shooting, and wondered how I could blow her off.

Then I decided, why the hell not? Maybe firing off a few rounds would help to release tension.

I met Holly downstairs. She wore a fitted tee that had *VERSACE* embroidered on it, and tight, faded jeans with tears in the knees that were usually bought by women half her age. Red pumps, probably by some obscure designer whom I couldn't afford, rounded out the ensemble.

"Hi, Jack!" She smiled, apparently happy to see me. I endured a quick hug and a kiss on the cheek. "I love your top. Who is it?"

I glanced down at the poodle fabric sweater I wore. "Her name is Kathleen B. Local designer."

"You have to take me there."

I could think of few things I'd prefer less.

Holly must have mistook my silence for confusion. "You're still up for some shooting, right?" She lifted a pink leather satchel. "I brought ordnance."

"Sure. Range is in the basement. Come on back."

The desk sergeant nodded at me behind two inches of bulletproof glass, and buzzed us through the security door. I led Holly past a maze of desks, to the rear staircase, and we descended two flights of metal stairs, her heels echoing like hail on a tin roof.

The shooting range occupied the entire basement. It resembled a four-lane bowling alley, though the lanes went back as far as seventy-five feet, while a bowling alley ended at sixty. The rangemaster, a lanky guy in his sixties whom everyone called Wyatt, flashed tobacco-stained teeth at us as we approached. Wyatt had been here almost as long as Bill in Evidence. He was one of the only cops in the city who shot as well as I did, though I didn't have a cool cowboy nickname.

"Hello, ladies. Qualifying or having fun?"

"Fun." Holly placed her satchel on Wyatt's counter and unzipped the top. I doubted anyone else in the world used Louis Vuitton as a gun bag.

"Whatcha got in here?" Wyatt stuck his beak into the bag, then eyed Holly. "May I?"

"Please."

He removed a pair of impressive automatics; black barrels, slides, and grips, silver butts and trigger guards. Wyatt let out a low whistle.

"McMallin Wolverines. Designed around the classic 1911 Colt. Serious hardware. You compete?"

"Sometimes."

"Quick draw?"

"Sometimes. You spotted the mods."

Wyatt turned the guns around in his hands. "Recessed front and rear sights, burr-style hammer, wider trigger, and it looks like a dehorning job. Nice one too."

"Thanks. The hammer is stock, but I did the sights, trigger, and dehorning myself."

Dehorning involved rounding every sharp angle on a gun, so it didn't catch on holsters or clothing. It could improve a draw by several milliseconds.

Wyatt sighted the gun, worked the slide, and ejected the magazine.

"Chambered for nine mil?"

Holly offered a full-wattage smile. "Forty-fives are too big, and I'm just a girl."

"I noticed. But I'm guessing that doesn't hold you back much."

"Not much."

I unpursed my lips long enough to speak.

"Can we get some headgear, Wyatt, or are you going to fondle her weapons all night?"

My glare cut off any potential wisecracks. Every time I came down here to shoot, Wyatt flirted with me. Every single time, for the last fifteen years. Now he didn't seem to notice I was even there.

Wyatt grabbed some field glasses and ear protectors off the wall, and Holly handed me a weapon. It was slightly large for my hand. The grip was high but the Pachmary rubber made it comfortable. It was wonderfully balanced, though it had to go two pounds—twice the weight of my .38.

"It's the officer's model," Holly told me. "Five-inch barrel instead of six." She winked at Wyatt. "Bigger isn't always better."

"Amen to that," he said, handing out the gear.

Holly took out a plastic bag full of shiny brass rounds. Since they weren't straight from the box, I assumed them to be reloads. Wyatt noticed too.

"You load your own?"

"Lots of gun nuts think the nine-millimeter round lacks the stopping power of a .40 or a .45, but I've found that it's the bullet that makes the difference, not the caliber. I pour my own lead and load my shells to 150 grains. The expansion and penetration can compete with anything out there. Design can make up for weight and velocity."

I respected weapons. I even got a certain degree of satisfaction from them, as I would from any high-performance tool. But this woman was the Martha Stewart of firearms.

Holly popped her clip and loaded it. When she reached ten bullets, she slapped it in, worked the slide to chamber a round, and dropped it back out to add one more shot to the clip. I pressed the oversized release catch and did the same. We each filled a spare clip as well.

"Silhouettes or bull's-eyes?"

Holly asked for silhouettes. Wyatt handed us two 25" × 35" targets, each featuring the life-sized torso and head of a man done in black ink. On the chest was a white area the size of a pineapple, with the number five in it. On the head, an orange-sized circle contained a number ten.

Holly and I donned our gear and each walked to a lane and attached the paper to the overhead metal line with spring clips. I pressed a lever and the target moved backward on a pulley system, traveling down the range.

I watched Holly, and she stopped at fifteen yards. I did the same.

The lane floors were covered in a thick layer of sand, and at the end of the range was a pockmarked metal wall, tilted on a forty-five-degree angle. Rounds went through the targets, hit the wall, and ricocheted into the ground, where they buried themselves.

I started with a two-handed grip to get used to the recoil. The first shot surprised me. Not only was the trigger pull less than I expected—it moved like butter—but the recoil was extremely light and the muzzle rise minimal. Must have had a compensator built in.

I squeezed off two more rounds, both eyes open, knees slightly bent, letting the gun teach me how to hold it. The high grip helped steady the weapon, and I put both shots through the sweet spot in the head.

I tried a one-handed grip, angling my body sideways, sighting along my right arm. Three more shots, through the heart.

To be playful, I put the last five in the groin, then looked over at Holly.

As far as I could tell, all eleven of her shots went through the chest. We brought in our targets and traded papers. Not only were all of hers in the chest area, but they were grouped in a space the size of a silver dollar.

Wyatt brought more targets. He appraised Holly's, then mine, giving us both nods of approval. We gave him our empty clips and he went off to fill them.

This time I sent the silhouette back the full twenty-five yards. I loaded another clip, sighted the target, and fired all ten shots at the head as fast as I could pull the trigger.

When I brought the target back, I saw I'd put all but two rounds through the ten-point circle. The other two went through the neck. It was a damn fine weapon.

I watched Holly fire her last three shots. Her face remained blank, but her eyes were wide and excited. Again, her target had a tight grouping in the chest area. Perhaps even tighter than the previous one.

The woman was good. Very good.

Wyatt returned with two more silhouettes. These were ten-yard targets, half the size of the previous ones. We exchanged our empty clips for full ones and hung the targets.

Holly glanced at me. I wouldn't call her stare hostile, but it was far from friendly, and the ugliest I'd seen her. She pressed the lever, sending her ten-yard target past the ten-yard mark, all the way to the end of the range. Her eyes stayed on me the entire time.

I did the same with my target, squinting at the distance. It appeared to be about three inches tall.

I aimed, and let out a breath. My hand had the slightest tremor; my veins were still processing those Yellow Bombers I'd taken on the road. I placed my left hand under my wrist to steady it, tried to ignore the pain from the burn, then emptied my clip at the target.

Holly had watched me the entire time, her ugly scowl replaced by an equally unattractive smirk. I pulled in my target. Five to the head, two to the neck, and two outside the body. When Holly saw this, her smirk became a superior grin.

I raised my eyebrows, challenging her to do better.

She stuck with the one-handed grip, sighted the target, and fired so quickly, her finger was a blur.

When she brought her target in, I could see she had once again grouped every single shot in the chest.

Wyatt tapped my shoulder, indicating for me to remove my ear gear. Holly did the same.

"Damn nice shooting, ladies. Damn nice. I were the judge, I'd call it a tie."

Holly folded her arms. "You think so? I notice she missed a few, that last turn."

"Jack went for the head. You went for the body. Head is more points. I got the score as even-steven."

He handed us each a fresh ten-yard silhouette and a clip.

"Let's try quick draw. Four rounds. Weapons kept at your sides until I give the signal. Nine extra points to the one who gets them all off first. You game?"

I nodded. Holly flashed a dazzling smile and tossed her hair back, which Wyatt took for acquiescence. I shoved in the clip, chambered a round, and pinned up my target, taking it all the way back to the end of the line.

She's better than I am, I thought. Probably faster too. But the head shot is worth more than the heart shot, and she always goes for the heart. If I can hit three, I'll win even if she hits all four and outdraws me.

So the smart move would be to take my time, let her shoot fast, and win on score.

But I didn't want to play it smart. I wanted to prove I was just as fast.

"Weapons at your sides." Wyatt stood between us, but he was staring at Holly. We each relaxed our arms, barrels pointing at the floor.

"On three. One . . ."

I pushed out a breath, relaxed my shoulder, concentrated on my grip. The gun felt good, natural. But I still had tremors, and I hadn't slept in over thirty hours.

"Two . . ."

I'd have to shoot one-handed. When you speed draw to a two-handed stance, the free hand meets the gun hand so fast, it throws off the aim before it has a chance to stabilize it, wasting valuable milliseconds.

"Three!"

My arm shot up on its own initiative, my trigger finger flexing fast, the four shots gone in an instant. The noise was deafening without the ear protection, but I still heard well enough to know I'd outdrawn Holly; her last shot went off a fraction of a second after mine.

My elation was short-lived when I noticed my target.

One shot through the head. Three misses.

Holly, as expected, placed all four of hers in the silhouette's heart.

"Jack receives the nine points for speed, plus a ten-point shot to the head. Nineteen points. Holly hit the heart four times, five points each, for a winning score of twenty points."

Holly glowed, her face bright as a camera flash.

"Not many people can shoot as fast as I can, Jack. I'm impressed."

"Speed doesn't mean anything if the accuracy is poor."

"I'm sure you're just having an off day." Her tone suggested something contrary.

"Yeah. Well. Nice shooting."

"Nice shooting."

She came over and hugged me. Just two regular girls, celebrating marksmanship.

I endured the hug, which was tight enough to make me lose my breath. Holly had some serious muscles. I gave her a quick pat on the back, and when she released me she stayed within my personal space, her face so close I could smell her mint gum.

"Want to grab a bite to eat? My treat."

"I'm sort of in the middle of a case."

"Really? What kind of case?"

"Homicide."

"Isn't Indiana out of your jurisdiction?"

I wondered how she knew, then remembered I'd been a media darling of late.

"I'm not working on the Kork case. I'm working on something parallel."

"Really? What?"

"Can't. We cops are sworn to secrecy." And I was getting uncomfortable with her being so close.

"Come on. Spill. I've spent every waking hour with Harry these last few days, and all he talks about is the adventures you two had. I always wanted to be a cop."

I leaned back an inch or three. "You're military, right?"

"Semper fi. How did you know?"

"You didn't learn to shoot like that on a farm in Alabama, and you called your guns *ordnance*."

"The lingo is tough to shake. I did a tour, when I was a kid."

"So why didn't you join the force? A lot of cops are ex-military."

She hooded her eyes, as if she was about to share some juicy gossip. "I've got a few boo-boos on my record. Nothing major, but enough to keep me from being a law enforcer."

I took a full step back and met Wyatt at the counter. Holly followed. We returned our gear and I asked for a broom to sweep up our brass.

"I'll get it." Wyatt grinned like a schoolboy. "It was a pleasure to witness such a fine competition."

I felt a buzz in my pocket, and the beeping followed a moment later. I slapped the cell phone to my face.

"Daniels."

"Lieutenant? This is Raider, Gary PD. Bud Kork woke up about an hour ago. He's lucid, and talking up a storm. My chief said you'd like to speak to him on a related subject."

My spirits jumped. "Yes, I would. I appreciate the courtesy call. When can I come?"

"Anytime is fine. You've got full access. Way we see it, you're the one who found the guy."

"I'll be there in about an hour. Thanks."

I pocketed the phone, Holly so close, she was practically wearing my pants. Her eyes shone.

"I heard everything. I want to come with you."

"No."

"I'll stay out of your way. I just want to see him. Come on, I'm a cop junkie."

"No."

"I can help."

"You're a civilian."

"A civilian who just kicked your ass on the firing range."

I was beginning to see why she was with Harry. She was annoying in an eerily similar way.

"No, Holly. Thanks for the offer, but this is police business."

"But that killer, he's a man, right? I'm good with men. I can get him to talk to you."

"Won't work on this one." I pictured Kork's missing male anatomy.

"Please, Jack. Harry's doing some kind of bachelor party thing tonight. Something to do with midgets."

McGlade? That bastard told me he didn't have any other friends.

"His buddies are taking him out?" I kept my tone neutral.

"No. He's alone. Well, alone with the little people." Holly tugged on my arm. "Come on. You have to take me along. I can't spend my last night as a free woman watching infomercials on TV."

I knew how that felt.

"Sorry, Holly. Can't do it."

She was on my heels all the way up the stairs, like a puppy. An irritating, yipping, undaunted puppy.

"Please."

"No."

"I'll just keep you company for the trip. I won't even get out of the car, Jack."

"No."

I walked out of the station and onto the street. The day had cooled down, and the breeze felt nice on my face. I walked around to the back parking lot, Holly still begging me. Perhaps beautiful women didn't understand the word *no*.

"Come on, Jack. I'm a licensed private investigator. I can handle myself, and I've worked with law enforcement before."

"We're not working together, Holly. And this is getting silly."

It was also making me uncomfortable. I didn't want to be rude to her when I was standing up at her wedding the next day, but soon she wouldn't give me much choice.

Holly was quiet for a minute, and I thought I'd finally gotten through. Then I heard the sniffle.

When I turned to look, Holly was all pouty and teary-eyed.

"I don't have any friends, Jack."

"Excuse me?"

Her shoulders began shaking.

"My job. I keep crazy hours. I don't have a single friend. Why do you think I went to that stupid private eye convention? I could give a rat's ass about the latest surveillance technology. I just wanted to meet people. Harry's the first man I've been with in six years."

"I'm sorry." And I meant it from the bottom of my soul.

Holly faced me again, her cheeks glistening.

"Don't you get lonely, Jack? When was the last time you had a girls' night out?"

"Interrogating a multiple murderer isn't a girls' night out."

"But it's better than being alone. I've been alone my whole crummy life. My dad died when I was a kid, and we moved around a lot. I never had friends."

The thought of someone so attractive being without friends was ridiculous, and I almost sneered. Holly read my thoughts.

"I wasn't like this back then. I was very fat, and had some skin problems, and big old buck teeth. It wasn't until my twenties that I lost the weight, went to a dentist, and had some work done. A lot of work done." Holly put her hands on either side of her breasts. "These won't be paid for until I'm too old to appreciate them."

She wiped her hand across her eyes, and I had a surprising thought. If I could put my jealousy aside, I might like this woman. I knew how hard it was to lose a father at a young age. Plus, the fact that she'd had plastic surgery made her seem more human, less Charlie's Angel. Though her taste in men was seriously flawed, Holly was strong, competent, funny, a great dresser, and had an energy that you didn't see very often.

I wondered if I wasn't falling victim to her charisma the same way everyone else seemed to. Then I wondered why I always overanalyzed everything. I hadn't had a female friend since, well, high school. Here was one trying to make an effort. Would it hurt to bend a little? To maybe have someone to talk to?

It's been a long time since I had someone to talk to.

Holly backed up, arms folded across her chest. "I'm sorry, Jack. Overreacting. Pre-wedding jitters, I guess. It's been a tough week. I'll see you tomorrow."

My inner cop told me to shake hands and walk away. But I'll be damned if I didn't say, "You can come."

"I can?" Again she lit up, and again I was subjected to a firm hug.

But this one I didn't mind as much.

When she finally released me, we hopped into my Nova, and for the second time that day I headed for Indiana.

CHAPTER 33

Harry told me about what he did, when you two were partners. He feels bad about it."

I replied with a snort. Holly and I had already talked about fashion (consensus: Fashion is good), guns (consensus: Guns are good), and parents (consensus: Parents are good if you still had them, but hers were dead and I only had my comatose mother), and we'd finally worked our way around to men.

Holly wholeheartedly agreed I'd screwed up my chances with Latham, and I made a heroic effort to convince her to do the same with McGlade.

"He's changed, Jack. Loyalty is actually one of his most endearing qualities."

"It wasn't back then."

"He was younger, ambitious. Now he recognizes that friendship is more important than a career. He considers you a good friend, Jack."

I snorted again. With good friends like McGlade, having serial killers hunting me was almost welcome.

Holly reached for another french fry. We'd stopped at the McDonald's oasis on the Skyway. I'd polished off my burger and fries a while ago. Holly had bought a Happy Meal, and divided her time between picking at her food and playing with the included toy, some kind of movie tie-in figurine.

The fry disappeared in three bites. Holly chewed slowly. "It's been years. Why do you still hate Harry so much?"

"I don't hate him. Let's just say my life hasn't been enriched by his involvement."

"He helped you with the Gingerbread Man case."

"Reluctantly."

"And with the case you had last year, that guy who was killing prostitutes."

"In both cases he wanted something."

"Isn't that why you agreed to stand up at our wedding?"

Oops. "He told you that?"

"He said you wanted to get your character off the TV show, and you wouldn't be his best man until he agreed."

I shifted in my seat. It was getting dark, so I switched on the headlights. The Gary exit was coming up.

"He's the one who got me on that damn TV show. It's jeopardizing my job."

"Maybe he would have gotten you off the show if you just asked."

I made a noncommittal grunt.

"He's really sweet, Jack. I wish you could see that."

"Yeah. He should be a plush toy."

Holly dug back into the bag, and found one of the pickles she'd taken off her burger. She put it into her mouth, a gesture that struck me as odd.

"Why'd you take the pickle off if you like them?"

"I hate them."

"Then why'd you eat it?"

"Waste not, want not. Right?"

"I guess."

Neither of us talked for a moment. I refused to feel guilty about anything to do with McGlade, even if I was starting to like his girlfriend.

"Tell me about this Bill Kork guy."

"Bud. His name's Bud. He was Charles Kork's—the Gingerbread Man's—father. You saw the bodies on the news?"

Holly crinkled up her nose. "Yeah. What kind of sicko would bury people in his basement?"

"The same kind who bathes in his own urine, sticks needles in his groin, and whips himself with a scourge."

Holly made a face and shoved my shoulder. "That's not true."

"It's true. He also emasculated himself."

She mouthed the word *emasculated,* and then said, "He cut his own dick off?"

I nodded. "He lost his luggage, and both carry-ons."

"That's gross."

"Apparently he was punishing himself for his evil deeds. Some kind of warped Christian thing."

"Remind me not to attend *that* church."

I took the Gary exit, trying to remember if the hospital was north or south. I chose north.

Holly liberated her last french fry, sniffed it, and popped it into her mouth. "I don't know anyone that gross, but we had some killer in Detroit a few years ago. He was peeling people."

I tensed. "Really?"

"Some serial killer whack-job. He was cutting people up and pulling off their skin. You didn't see it on the news?"

"I try not to watch the news. Too depressing. They catch the guy?"

"No. Killed three people, then disappeared. Cops called it some kind of organized crime thing. Pretty terrible way to die, don't you think? Getting skinned?"

I thought about the Mulrooney video. "Yeah. Pretty terrible."

I knew I made the correct turn, because there were over a dozen news vans, each with that big antenna/dish thing on its roof, parked along the street. The hospital had cleared the media out of the parking lot. I found a handicapped space and pulled my siren out of the glove compartment, sticking it on the roof so I wouldn't be towed.

Holly got out with me.

"I thought you were waiting in the car."

"Let me see the guy. Please, Jack? I'll stay quiet. I just want to look in his eyes."

"This isn't the zoo, Holly. We're not visiting the monkey house."

"I'm good with men. I really am. If you want him to talk, maybe I can help."

As with Harry, arguing with Holly was an exercise in futility. We went back and forth for thirty seconds, and I realized the only way I'd get her to stay in the car would be if I handcuffed her. Which I considered, but physical restraints weren't a good way to begin a friendship.

"Don't say a word. You can observe, but not interfere."

Holly mimed zipping her mouth closed.

There were cops in the lobby, including the uniform I'd met who'd previously stood guard over Kork. He gave me a passing nod, then glued his eyes to Holly. The other cops did the same, without giving me a passing nod. If this were a cartoon, their tongues would have unrolled out of their mouths and onto the floor, red-carpet style.

The Feebies, Mutt and Jeff, were thankfully nowhere to be found. Perhaps they were grilling Lorna Hunt Ellison. Or perhaps they were engaged in a sweaty ménage à trois with Vicky, the ViCAT computer. Wherever they were, I thanked the universe I didn't have to deal with them along with everything else.

Kork's room was being guarded by two more cops, who'd been expecting me. They weren't expecting Holly, but when she smiled they all talked at once, introducing themselves and pledging their allegiance.

I left them to their flirting and went in to visit the monster.

Bud Kork eyed me when I entered, his eyes saggy and bloodshot, his complexion sallow. If he recognized me, he didn't show it.

Then Holly walked in. Penis be damned, Bud caught a breath and stared wide-eyed.

Perhaps it was the Versace tee. I needed to get one of those.

"Mr. Kork? Do you remember me? I'm Lieutenant Daniels. I dropped by your house the other day, and you showed me your root cellar."

He nodded, his gaze still fixed on Holly. She moved toward the bed, her hand extended, and Kork flinched hard enough to make the frame squeak.

"Holly Frakes. Nice to meet you, Mr. Kork."

Bud reached for her hand as if it were a rattlesnake. He managed a quick, limp handshake, which he retracted immediately.

"How are they treating you?" I asked.

"They . . . they won't give me any lemon for my water. I keep asking, but I don't get any lemon."

He stuck a finger into his mouth and gnawed on a cuticle, his gaze flitting back and forth between me and Holly.

"I'll see what I can do."

As I spoke this, Holly went out into the hallway. I imagined the cops tripping over themselves searching for a lemon.

I pulled up a plastic chair and sat next to the bed.

"Do you know why you're here, Bud?"

"To be punished. Because I've been bad."

He seemed appropriately sad when he said it. Then his face creased in a wicked grin and he began to giggle.

"What's funny, Bud?"

" 'Blessed are you when men hate you, and when they exclude you and revile you, and cast out your name as evil.' Luke 6:22."

His whole body shook, as if he were having a seizure. The Parkinson's. It subsided before I could call the nurse, and Bud again burst into laughter.

"Indiana has the death penalty. They'll kill me by lethal injection."

"That amuses you?"

"I don't deserve it."

"You've killed a lot of people, Bud."

He bit at his hangnail and pulled. Blood smeared across his lips, bringing color to their liverlike pallor.

"I should be tortured to death." He giggled again. "Lethal injection is too good for me."

He sucked on his finger, tongue lapping at the blood. I kept my expression neutral.

"I saw Lorna earlier today."

Bud frowned around his finger. "She never visits me."

"She's in prison, Bud."

"She helped me, with the sinners. Liked to do the flogging. Sweet, sweet Lorna."

He hummed a song, off tune, suckling his bleeding digit.

I had no doubts Bud Kork was insane. But there was more to it than that. Sitting this close to him, I felt a deep sense of revulsion—the same kind of feeling I had when I watched a nature program on TV that showed a spider catching a fly. Bud Kork radiated a very real feeling of harm, of fear and decay and death.

Talking to him made me want to take a hot shower and brush my teeth until my gums hurt.

"Would you like to see Lorna again, Bud?"

"Yes. My sweet love. So good with the repentant. So eager to make them confess their sins."

I lowered my voice, so he had to strain to hear me.

"I can arrange it, Bud. For you to see her." I figured it would happen anyway, once Lorna cut her deal. Bud didn't have to know it didn't come from me. "But I need you to tell me something first."

He stared at me, slurping on his finger, a line of pink drool rolling down his chin.

"I need you to tell me where Caleb is."

Bud began to cackle. "'You are of your father the devil, and your will is to do your father's desires.' John 8:44."

"You treated Caleb as your son?"

"Caleb was the devil, like Charles was the devil. But not the devil of my flesh. A devil conceived in light."

I leaned closer, though I had to force myself to do so.

"Where is Caleb?"

Bud opened his mouth to speak, then his yellow eyes darted behind me, to Holly.

"I found a lemon for you, Bud." She offered him a wedge of the fruit.

Bud snatched it in a gnarled fist, then squeezed it onto his bloody hangnail and rubbed it in, gasping and shuddering.

"Freaky," Holly said, eyes wide.

I reached for the lemon, then thought better of it; Bud was grinding it into his open cut, and the pulp was turning orange with blood. Instead, I tapped his shoulder.

"Where's Caleb, Bud?"

He ignored me, focusing on Holly.

"'How art thou fallen from heaven, O Lucifer, my angel of the morning.' Isaiah 14:12."

Holly found another chair and pulled it over to Kork's bed. She straddled it and leaned on the back, resting her chin on her forearms, her eyes bright and alive.

"I hear you like needles, Bud."

He nodded at her, gasping.

"Look what I found in the gift shop."

She held up an emergency sewing kit: three mini spools of thread, a thimble, and eight sewing needles.

"Holly." I gave her a look. "Remember what we talked about in the car."

She kept her eyes on Bud. "Lieutenant Daniels asked you a question, Bud. Where's Caleb?"

He eyed the needles like a starving man staring at a menu. "I . . . I don't know where Caleb is."

Holly opened the pack, pulled out a needle. Examined it.

"Where does he live?"

"Different places."

"Which places?"

"Indiana. Michigan. Illinois."

Holly parted her lips and placed the needle between them. Bud was panting in a manner that could only be described as sexual. The lemon was dropped, forgotten.

I'd lost control of the interrogation. I shook Bud's shoulder.

"Where is Caleb now?" I asked.

Bud remained transfixed on the needle in Holly's mouth. "Illinois."

"Where in Illinois?"

"I don't know."

"When did you last hear from him?"

"I don't know."

Holly pouted, and slowly pulled the needle out of her mouth, letting it linger on her tongue before she put it back in the kit.

"If you want this, Bud, you have to give us more than that."

Bud swallowed, an audible gulp that the stretching silence amplified.

"Talk to Steve."

"Steve who?"

"Caleb's friend. Steve Jensen. He'd know."

I'd heard that name recently, and couldn't remember where. Steve Jensen. Steve Jensen. Steve . . .

And then I had it. I shook Bud again, harder.

"Do you know where Steve is, Bud?"

"No."

"How does Caleb know Steve?"

"Friends for years. Very close." He looked at Holly, then back at me. "Had the devil in him. Like Caleb. And Charles."

"Have you spoken to Steve lately?"

Bud jackknifed into a sitting position, making me and Holly rear back. He pointed his bloody finger at her.

"'Get behind me, Satan! You are a hindrance to me; for you are not on the side of God, but of men!'"

Holly winked at him. "Matthew 16:23." Then she tossed Bud the sewing kit.

Laughing, hysterical, Bud fumbled with the kit and removed a needle. He pinched it between trembling fingers and hiked up his hospital gown, exposing parts that should have remained unexposed.

I stood up and turned away, anxious to leave.

Holly said, "Freaky! Look at what he's doing, Jack!"

I made the mistake of a backward glance. Bud was causing some real damage, jabbing and poking, tears streaming down his face, little rivulets of blood cascading down his ruined thighs.

I reached back to take the needle away from him, but Holly caught my arm. Her grip was iron.

"Let him do it. He's a child killer."

Bud was sobbing now, mumbling something about angels. Perhaps it was a prayer. I tore my eyes away and pressed the call button for the nurse.

Holly pulled a face, obviously disappointed. I twisted out of her grip and walked past.

"Let's go."

The cops parted for us. I kept my pace brisk enough that Holly was forced to jog to catch up.

"Are you pissed at me, Jack?"

I didn't answer.

"Come on. The guy was scum. Besides, he was doing it to himself."

"He's insane, Holly."

"So?"

I stopped, faced her.

"My job is to protect and serve. Even the ones who don't deserve it."

She put her hands on her hips, oozing attitude.

"Shit, Jack, why so tense? You PMS-ing?"

"Excuse me?"

"Are you trolling for vampires? Riding the dry weave burrito? Red river canoeing?"

I blinked, unsure of how to respond. If Holly were a man, I would have smacked her. Is this how women talked to each other? Were all of those commercials with girls trading tampons in the locker room based on fact?

"No," I managed.

"Is it a postmenopausal thing? Change of life came early?"

Crass. Insensitive. Obnoxious. Ignorant. It was like talking to Harry McGlade. Two peas in a pod. No wonder they found each other.

I spoke through my teeth. "I'm not postmenopausal, Holly. This has nothing to do with my ovaries. What you did in there was wrong."

"Fine. I apologize for coming with you and getting your suspect to spill his guts."

Now she stormed off, and I had to run to catch up. Classic McGlade tactic. Start out abusive, and when resistance is met, act petulant.

I grabbed her arm, which was like grabbing a steel cable.

"Look, Holly, I'm the cop. Got it?"

Something flashed across her face, the same hostility I'd glimpsed on the firing range. The scowl disappeared fast, so fast I wasn't sure if I'd imagined it. She smiled, broad enough to show her dental work.

"You're right, Jack. I'm sorry. I was out of bounds back there. I thought we were doing that good cop/bad cop thing."

In a way, she was right. Though Herb wouldn't have been so ruthless, he and I would have played the situation very much the same way. I didn't like her approach, but she did get results.

"Come on, Jack. Forgive me?"

I didn't see much of a choice. I could stay angry, and the drive home would be uncomfortable, the wedding even more so.

"Fine. But next time, listen to me."

I endured another hug. Who knew friendship was so much damn work?

Back in the car, Holly asked the obvious.

"Who's Caleb?"

"It's a current case I'm working on."

"Want to share details?"

"Can't. Sorry."

"No problem. I understand."

The silence lasted almost ten whole seconds.

"Who's Steve Jensen?"

"Holly . . ."

"Come on, Jack. It's not like I'm going to go flapping my mouth off on CNN."

Ouch.

"Holly, don't take this the wrong way, but you and I aren't partners."

"Where is your partner?"

I hesitated. "He's unavailable at the moment."

"Do you two discuss cases?"

"Of course."

"Two heads are better than one, right? And didn't I do good with Bud?"

"This isn't about that."

Holly furrowed her eyebrows. "Why don't you like me, Jack?"

"I like you, Holly."

"Why don't you trust me?"

"It's not in my nature to trust anyone."

"You trust Harry."

"Not really."

We drove in silence for a few minutes.

"When I got out of the Corps, I was pretty reckless for a few years. Ran with a tough crowd. Got involved in a car theft ring. I did it for the excitement, at first. Then I got in over my head. Cops picked me up and offered me a deal. Do time or rat on my friends."

I was uncomfortable with her opening up like this.

"I squealed, Jack. I squealed long and loud. I don't blame you for not trusting me."

She didn't get all teary-eyed again, but she looked like a kicked puppy.

I knew I was being manipulated. But friendship was a two-way street, right?

"Four days ago a man named Steve Jensen died in a transient hotel in my district. I was busy with this case, so I transferred the call to Mason and Check."

"How does Jensen fit in with this?"

I pressed the gas down, easing the car up past eighty.

"I'm about to find out."

CHAPTER 34

ON THE WAY back to Chicago, Detective Maggie Mason filled me in on the Jensen homicide.

"Stabbed over thirty times. Found in the Benson Hotel for Men on Congress, in a room rented to his name."

"How long had he been living there?"

"Nineteen days. It's a pay-per-week hotel, more rats than tenants. Landlord came by to collect rent, found the corpse."

"Anything?"

"Nothing. Door-to-doored the whole building, wasted three days interviewing Sterno bums and crackheads. No leads."

"Autopsy?"

"Still waiting."

The cell phone got crackly, and Mason asked if I was still there.

"You view the body?" I asked.

"Yeah. Nasty."

"Impressions?"

"Went beyond a crime of opportunity or anger. This was a deliberate attempt to inflict pain."

"Defense wounds?"

"Ligature marks on the wrists. He was tied to a chair."

I thought of Mike Mayer in Indianapolis.

"Did he still have his fingers?"

"I think so. I didn't notice them missing."

"How are the walls at the Benson?"

"Tissue paper. You can read a book through them."

"Why didn't his screaming attract attention?"

"Sorry, Lieut. I forgot to mention the hooks."

"Hooks?"

"The victim had a mouth full of fishhooks. Lips, tongue, throat, all torn to hell and stuck together. Must have been a hundred of them in there. He couldn't have opened his mouth with a car jack."

Nice. And an obvious nod to the Gingerbread Man case. I'll never forget what Charles Kork did with fishhooks. "Trace?"

"Nothing leading. Scraped his fingernails. Found a black hair. There was some kind of white crust on the wounds, got a sample of that. Rogers at the lab is getting back to me."

"Prints?"

"Ran them locally. Nothing. Going through the National Fingerprint Database, but you know how long that takes."

"Check Jensen in the NCIC?"

"Lots of arrests. Drugs. Banging. Battery. Classic repeat offender—until a few years ago."

"What happened then?"

"Don't know. Guy seemed to just drop off the face of the earth."

That sounded a lot like Caleb Ellison.

I thanked Mason, then got on the horn to county. Max Hughes wasn't in, but the M.E., Phil Blasky, was.

"Good evening, Jack. I heard about Herb. How's he doing?"

"Stable, last I heard. You burning the midnight oil?"

"Paperwork. Just got a memo, telling me that efforts are being made by the county to reduce the amount of paperwork. The memo came with a twenty-six-page report I have to fill out, in triplicate. I'm not a fan of irony."

"Have you taken a look at Steve Jensen, transient hotel death from five days ago?"

"Mackerel man? He's scheduled for tomorrow morning."

"Mackerel man?"

"A joke one of the attendants made. Mouth full of hooks. Guy obviously took the bait. I'm not a fan of humor either."

"Then why did you call him Mackerel Man?"

"I try to fit in."

Strange bunch, coroners.

"Any chance you can tear yourself away from that interesting report and do a prelim for me?"

"When do you need it?"

I checked the dashboard. Coming up on nine o'clock.

"An hour?"

"I'll check my tackle box for my hook remover. Could use some fresh coffee, you got any."

"See you at ten."

I hung up, then plugged my phone into the cigarette lighter to charge it.

"Are we going to the morgue?"

"No. I'm going to the morgue. Note my use of the singular, rather than the plural."

"I'm free."

"And I'm not. I'm working."

"Come on, Jack. I can't go home now. It's probably wall-to-wall naked midgets."

"Doesn't that bother you?"

"Why should it? Little people need love too."

"I meant that Harry's cheating on you."

"We're not married yet. But just because it doesn't bother me doesn't mean I want to see it." She placed her hand on my arm. "Let me go in, Jack. It will be like my bachelorette party."

"Viewing a dead body?"

"I've seen bodies before."

"And it's something you're eager to do again?"

"Not really. But if you don't let me come with you, I'll keep you up all night asking a bazillion questions about what I missed."

"Holly . . . it's against the law for a civilian to enter the county morgue."

"I won't tell anyone. Cross my fingers."

She did, indeed, cross her fingers. I sighed.

"Don't talk, don't touch anything, and don't let the M.E. know you're not a cop."

She hugged me, and I almost swerved off the road.

"Holly, if we're going to be friends, we need to talk about this hugging thing."

We didn't talk about the hugging thing. Instead, the conversation shifted to tae kwon do.

"I'm working on my fourth dan. My pyonson keut chireugi are getting there. I busted a finger last year, breaking boards."

That impressed the hell out of me. Pyonson keut were thrusting strikes using the fingertips. If Holly could break boards using her fingers, she was way ahead of me.

"I'm better at kagi than chireugi." Though, if I were being honest with myself, my leg strength and flexibility weren't what they used to be.

"Where do you train?"

I couldn't remember the last time I set foot on the mat. "I haven't trained in a while. I should probably get back into it."

"It would be fun to spar with you."

Maybe, if I equated bleeding with fun. Holly had two inches, more experience, and about fifteen pounds on me. And from what I could observe, that extra fifteen pounds was all muscle. She'd kick my ass.

Instead I said, "Yeah. That would be fun."

We stopped at a chain donut shop to pick up donuts and coffee for Phil. I also got a coffee. Holly got a frozen mochaccino with extra chocolate, and three glazed donuts.

"Old habits die hard. I'll do a thousand extra sit-ups tomorrow."

The county morgue was in Chicago's medical district, on Harrison. I pulled into the circular driveway behind the two-story building and parked in a spot designated for hearses and ambulances. Before we got out of the car, I had a heart-to-heart with Holly.

"Morgues aren't very pleasant. Do you have a weak stomach?"

"I haven't thrown up in years."

I hoped she was telling the truth. I'd hate to see those donuts again.

"Try to stay professional, and if you do need to hurl, don't hurl on a corpse. Phil hates that."

"Got it."

We went in.

After I signed the check-in book for myself and Holly, the attendant took us back through the loading station and into the cooler. It smelled like a butcher shop, which essentially is what it was; racks and racks of refrigerated meat. They were operating at capacity, and over two hundred bodies lay on metal shelves, warehouse-style. Some leaked fluids. Some seemed frozen in bizarre poses. Some looked like they might open their eyes and start talking.

Holly took it all in, wide-eyed and slack-jawed.

"This is pretty freaky."

"Shhhh. Act professional."

"Check out that guy. He's hung like an elephant."

"Holly—"

"Jesus, Jack, look at it. You're single. Grab a knife and take it home."

Phil Blasky poked his head out of the autopsy room, and I elbowed Holly in the ribs to shut her up.

"Hi, Phil."

"Hello, Jack. Who's your friend?"

Holly waltzed over to him, hand outstretched. "Detective Holly Frakes. I'm a cop. Really."

I tried not to wince. Phil glanced at her hand, then glanced at his own, covered by a bloody latex glove.

Holly noticed this and patted him on the shoulder instead of shaking.

"Nice to meet you, Phil. I hear people are dying to get into this place."

Ouch. But Phil seemed just as entranced with Holly as everyone else she met, and he even offered a weak chuckle.

"A pleasure to meet you too, Detective. I've found out some interesting things, if you'll step into my office."

We followed Phil into the back room, where the body of Steve Jensen lay naked on a metal table, a block propping up his head. Beneath him was a small puddle of what I called *people juice*; not blood, but a pink, semiclear fluid that looked like the stuff at the bottom of the package when you bought a steak at the supermarket.

Phil hadn't made the *Y*-incision on Jensen yet, or sawed open the skull, but the body had been washed down.

Jensen had been a trim man, muscular, with straight brown hair and tattoos covering both arms, the motif running to guns, skulls, and naked women with devil horns.

"Average." Holly frowned. She was looking at his joint.

Phil missed it. "As you can see by the condition of the body, the body bears over thirty stab wounds of various sizes and depths. I can safely assume that the inquest jury will rule out suicide."

He chuckled again. The second chuckle I'd heard in the ten years I'd known him.

The only place to set the coffee and donuts was on a medical tray, next to some bloody implements. I hoped the cardboard box was thick and nothing leaked through.

"What's wrong with his mouth?" Holly asked.

Jensen's cheeks were sucked in, as if he were about to blow us a kiss. His lips were shredded and resembled hamburger.

Holly bent down for a closer view. "Looks like he's in serious need of some Chapstick."

Phil grabbed onto the lower lip and pulled, revealing half a dozen brass fishhooks, skewering Jensen's mouth closed. He picked up a scalpel and wedged it between the teeth, levering the mouth open, tearing the lips even further. He positioned the head so the overhead light could penetrate the mouth, and then used a water squirt pen that hung from the ceiling on a spiral hose to spray out the excess blood.

It wasn't pretty. Jensen had a puckered appearance because his tongue and inner cheeks were hooked together.

"He was alive at the time." Holly pointed. "See the bruises on his face? Someone shoved hooks in his mouth, then slapped him around to get them stuck."

Blasky put his hand on the victim's neck.

"I can feel some bumps in the throat. He probably swallowed, or inhaled, hooks as well."

I finally spoke up. "What's the cause of death, Phil?"

"This wound right here." Blasky tapped a two-inch puncture on Jensen's chest. "Thin-bladed knife, slipped between the ribs and ruptured the heart. Won't know what exactly went wrong until I crack the chest."

"He was tortured." Holly swallowed, then walked over to the corpse's legs and peered at a stab wound. "These cuts have salt rubbed into them."

Phil frowned. "Kind of silly, to interrogate a man with fishhooks in his mouth. How was he supposed to talk?"

"He wasn't supposed to talk," I said. "He was supposed to hurt."

"He hurt, all right. I ran a blood sample and did an enzyme immunoassay. His histamine levels were off the charts. This man died in agony."

"Why do some of the stab wounds look different?"

"It appears that two weapons were used, a thin, double-edged blade and a thicker one with a serrated back."

The hunting knife that Benedict's attacker left behind had a serrated back.

"Must have gotten bored with the little knife, gotten something bigger," Holly said.

"Can you tell by the angle if the perp is right-handed or left-handed?" I asked.

Phil picked up a stainless steel protractor and worked out some angles.

"The big blade was wielded by a lefty. The smaller blade, by someone right-handed."

Holly nodded. "So the killer had a knife in each hand."

"Then how could he rub the salt in?" I shook my head. "No. I have a different theory."

"We're all ears, Lieutenant."

I frowned. "I think we've got more than one killer."

CHAPTER 35

I'D BEEN NURTURING that theory since early this morning. All evidence pointed toward a meticulous guy with a blond beard, yet a sloppy redhead was the one who attacked Herb. I hadn't been able to reconcile it. But if there were two killers at work, everything fit.

The Gingerbread Man's partner had found a replacement.

Holly gave me a funny look. "Are you sure?"

"That's how it looks. One of them is probably Caleb Ellison."

"And the other one?"

I chewed on my other lip. "I don't know." I added, "Yet."

Phil Blasky picked up his coffee and took a sip, making happy smacking sounds.

"You ladies are welcome to stay for the autopsy. There's donuts."

That didn't hold a lot of appeal for me, though Holly seemed thrilled at the prospect. I stared down at Jensen's body, puzzling why he died, wondering what his link to Caleb Ellison was, and found myself focusing on his tattoos.

In the middle of his biceps, slathered with hell imagery and the machine guns, there was a small piece of skin missing, the size of a quarter. Unlike the other wounds, this appeared to be a slice, rather than a stab.

I looked lower, and a similar patch of skin had been cut from his forearm. The other arm had three similar marks, on the back of the hand, the triceps, and the shoulder.

Someone cut off a few of his tattoos. And I had an inkling why.

"Do you have an extra pair of gloves, Phil?"

"There's a box under the cart."

I pulled out a pair and tugged them on. Holly did the same, though without much enthusiasm.

"We're not doing a cavity search, right?" she asked.

I ignored her, picking up Jensen's cold right hand and spreading out the fingers, which felt like stiff rubber. I peered at the webbing, and his palm, then worked up the underside of the arm until I got to the armpit. Not finding what I sought, I did the same with the left arm. Then I scrutinized behind the ears, and the back of the neck.

"Can we turn him over?"

Phil nodded, munching on a donut. His chin had strawberry jelly on it—I hoped to God it was strawberry jelly.

"On three," I told Holly. "One, two, three."

I pulled. She pushed. Jensen tilted up onto his side and flopped toward me, momentum taking him off the edge of the metal table. The headrest went flying. I had to push my hip against his clammy, naked hip to keep him from falling onto the floor, splotching my Kathleen B top with people juice. How many damn outfits could I ruin this week?

Holly tugged on his arm, sliding Jensen back into position.

The tattoo was over his right buttock. Homemade, black ink, three letters: *DDD*.

"Son of a bitch." Holly rubbed a gloved finger over the ink. "This guy's a Disciple."

"I haven't heard of that gang."

"They're from my town. The triple *D* boys. Detroit Devil Disciples. Operate on the East side, maybe a hundred strong. They run drugs, guns, a string of crack whores. Represent for Folks."

"And you know them because . . . ?"

She offered a small, private smile. "Let's just say I've crossed paths with them a few times."

I stared at the mark. Someone had cut off the others, and missed this one because it had been in an unobtrusive spot. Removing tattoos was symbolic, like stripping a gang-banger of his colors. Either his own gang did it because he betrayed them, or a rival gang did it to disrespect him.

There was also a third possibility: to keep Jensen's identity hidden.

Mason's search for Jensen in the National Crime Information Center records revealed a criminal record, until only a few years ago. The same for Caleb Ellison. It was highly doubtful they'd suddenly gone straight. Changing identities seemed a much better prospect.

"I have a few contacts in Detroit." Holly stripped off her gloves and pulled a flip phone out of her front pocket. "Want me to see what I can figure out?"

At this point, I needed all the help I could get. "Be my guest."

Holly trotted off, phone in hand. I pulled off my gloves and bellied up to the big slop sink, where I spent five minutes trying to get the stain out of my blouse.

"Jack! I got something!"

Holly had poked her head into the autopsy room.

"What?"

"Steve Jensen is using another name. I described him to the guy I talked to, and he pinned down an alias. A quick look at his record, and we got a list of associates, one of them named Caleb."

"Caleb Ellison?"

"No. Caleb's using an alias too. The guy you're looking for is a redhead, right?"

"Yeah."

"Caleb's last known address is here in Chicago."

I hurried over to Holly, the stain forgotten.

"What's the address?"

Holly shook her head. "I want to go with you."

"Holly, dammit, this is police business."

"I got the information, I want to come with you."

"No. Absolutely not."

I felt eyes on the back of my neck. Blasky was staring at us, munching on a cruller. I took Holly into the cooler with me.

"Who did you call in the Detroit police to get this information?"

She played coy. "Who said I called the Detroit police? I'm a private investigator, remember? I have plenty of contacts."

I pushed past her, walking out of the cooler, into the loading room. I could call the gang unit in Detroit, possibly get the same info Holly did, but I had no clue who to talk to, and no idea how long it would take.

"Jack . . ." Holly caught up, tugged on my sleeve. "Don't be pissed. I just want to be a part of this."

"You're a civilian, Holly. I could lose my badge just for bringing you into the morgue."

She made a pouty face.

"Come on, Jack. All I do is spy on cheating husbands, take pictures of fat guys trying to cheat insurance companies, and chase losers who jump bail. This is something real. Something important. Do you know how many times I heard Harry tell the story about the time he helped you nail Charles Kork?"

I ignored her, signing out, leaving the morgue.

"I have his address, Jack. I can back you up."

"It doesn't work that way, Holly. I need a warrant, cops on all the exits, the Feds want a piece; you being there could ruin the bust."

"Fine. I'll get him myself."

She took off across the parking lot, walking at a brisk pace.

"Dammit, Holly! Don't make me arrest you!"

She kept walking, but offered her opinion of my authority with a single finger.

I jogged up to her, grabbed her shoulder, and she spun around in a blur, spreading her feet in a tiger stance—her hands in underhanded fists, one foot in front of the other, heel off the ground as if cocked to go off. Without even thinking, I stepped back and fell into a back stance, my rear foot planted behind me, both arms parallel to my front thigh.

I tensed for her attack, but it didn't come.

"You want to do this on pavement?" I said.

"I want to come with you."

"You can't. The last time a civilian came with me on a bust, it became a weekly TV series."

The parking lot was dark, and I couldn't read her eyes.

"Your choice, Jack. We do it together, or I do it alone."

"Or I arrest you for withholding evidence and obstruction of justice."

"You think you can? I'm bigger, younger, more experienced, and have a farther reach."

"And if you lay a finger on me, you go to jail. That would mess up your wedding plans, wouldn't it? Think, Holly. This isn't the way."

I hoped she'd back down, because she was right; I probably couldn't beat her sparring. Which meant I'd have to shoot her.

Seconds ticked by. The night air cooled the sweat that had broken out on the back of my neck. I kept my muscles rigid, tense, fighting the adrenaline surge.

"He lives in Ravenswood," Holly said.

"Where in Ravenswood?"

She came at me, bringing her rear foot up. I lifted my arms to block, but Holly didn't kick. She ran past.

Holly reached the car five steps ahead of me, throwing open the door and grabbing her Vuitton carry-all. I managed to get my fingers around one handle of the bag, and Holly gripped my wrist and dropped to a knee, twisting my arm out at an angle and forcing my elbow to lock. I released the bag.

"I'll call you when I get there." She smiled and winked.

I swung my free fist around, but she shoved me back, onto my ass, and then sprinted down the street. By the time I got to my feet she'd ducked behind a building and disappeared.

This was what I got for trying to have friends.

I considered my options. I could call in the cavalry, but Holly was too smart to get picked up by a squad car. I could go home and let fate take its course; after all, I'd tried my best to stop her. Or I could head for Ravenswood and hope she would call.

Naturally, I headed for Ravenswood.

CHAPTER 36

*J*ACK IS COMING. Alex knows.

An anticipatory smile creeps onto Alex's face.

This is working out better than expected.

The smell from the basement wafts up through the floor. Alex ignores it, deciding what to do next.

The apartment is a mess. There are things to fix, things to do before Jack's arrival.

This trap must be carefully set for it to work.

"Where shall I hide?"

Alex has seen the TV show, knows all about the time Charles hid in Jack's closet and almost killed her.

There's a closet in the living room that will be just perfect.

"In the closet. Second time's a charm."

The man enters the closet, knife in hand.

CHAPTER 37

I PARKED NEXT to a hydrant on Lincoln Avenue, just north of Montrose. Ravenswood covered about three hundred square blocks, and like many other Chicago neighborhoods was undergoing some extreme gentrification. Lured by affordable housing, rehabbers had been buying like crazy and slowly increasing the property value by rebuilding, remodeling, and repainting. The liquor stores and chop shops of years past were being replaced by Starbucks and Panera Bread franchises.

If Caleb Ellison resided in Ravenswood, he had thousands of houses, apartments, lofts, and condos to hide in.

Before I could dwell on how this case spiraled out of control, my cell rang.

"Hi, Jack. You alone?"

"Dammit, Holly. Where are you?"

"Where are you?"

"On Lincoln and Montrose."

"You're close. I'm on Bell Avenue and Argyle. I'm going into the house."

"Holly, don't . . ."

CLICK.

I jammed the car into gear and did a U-turn, racing east down Montrose, and then hanging an immediate left on Bell. Argyle was eight or nine blocks up. The area was dark, residential, all houses and apartments. Eighty-year-old oak and maple trees lined the sidewalks, parked cars lined the streets.

I got to the corner ninety seconds after receiving the call, and double-parked parallel to a Saab. I hopped out of the car and did a slow 360-degree look around.

No Holly.

I checked my cell phone to see if the caller ID had picked up her number, but she'd blocked it.

She was going to ruin this bust. Or even worse, she was going to get herself killed. And she was probably within a hundred yards. That is, if she'd been telling the truth. How could she possibly think . . .

Three cars ahead of me was a sedan, the driver's-side mirror missing.

I tugged out my .38 and approached the car. Though the street wasn't well lit, I could tell that the paint job was dark gray—Titanium Pearl. A glance at the rear confirmed it was the Eclipse.

I did another scan of the area, looking for Holly. The Eclipse was parked in front of a large Victorian apartment building, yellow brick, with a walk-in courtyard. It didn't seem like a place a serial killer would live. Too many tenants, too hard to come and go without being seen.

Next to the Victorian was a two-story red neo-gothic building, with spires on the roof. Definitely more private, but every single light in the house was on, and curtains were open on both floors.

Across the street was a three-flat. The top apartment had several lights on. The middle apartment was completely dark, and a large *For Rent* sign hung in the window. The basement window had a single light burning.

That seemed the best bet. I approached cautiously, listening for anything out of the ordinary. The house had a black iron fence around the perimeter, and the gate had been pushed inward. I walked alongside the building, into the backyard, and saw the broken basement window.

This was the house. And since a crime, breaking and entering, was in progress, I was legally entitled to enter the establishment. Holly's illegal entry had saved me the trouble of needing a warrant.

I considered calling for backup, decided to check it out first, and got on all fours, climbing backward through the ground-level window.

I'd smelled so much death in the last few days I should have been used to it, but the stench down there practically knocked me over. Worse than Packer's house in Indianapolis. Worse than Bud Kork's root cellar.

To my left, illuminated by a bare bulb hanging from the ceiling, I saw the source of the odor.

Three corpses, seated around a card table. Clothesline bound them to their chairs. Dr. Francis Mulrooney's face was still recognizable, frozen in a bloated, agonized scream. Below the neck, his rib cage had been broken open, and his own hands shoved inside the chest cavity, up to the wrist.

To his left, I recognized Diane Kork from the injuries received on the video. She'd since been dressed in a push-up half-bra, which left her blackening nipples exposed. Her head tilted back, the slash on her neck yawning open like a bucket. A big bouquet of silk flowers—daisies—were shoved into the wound.

Next to Diane was a third corpse, a man with glasses and a beard. He looked the freshest, but also had the most mutilation. His abdomen was sliced open from his groin to his breastbone, and his organs had been pulled out and placed on a silver platter on the table in front of him, like a Thanksgiving turkey. In his hands were eating utensils, a knife and fork. Atop the fork was something brown and roundish. It took me a moment to realize what it was—a kidney. Some other organ was crammed into his mouth, ballooning out his cheeks.

Besides the smell of rot was the gag-inducing odor of urine and feces, and for the first time since being a rookie I contaminated a crime scene, bending over and throwing up between my feet.

I recovered quickly enough, freeing my cell phone, calling 911 and requesting assistance. Then I looked past the decaying dinner party, sighting the staircase. I moved fast, not bothering to be silent, taking the stairs two at a time, anxious to get some fresh air.

They led to the kitchen. I came through the door in a crouch, my gun pointed forward. I checked left, then right, straining to hear some kind of movement.

The house seemed silent.

The kitchen hadn't been cleaned in weeks; fast food wrappers and pizza boxes stacked on the counters, the sink overflowing with beer bottles, the floor sticky with stains and spills.

I went through the kitchen, into a living room, which was also a disaster. Besides the empty food boxes and cans, almost every surface of the room was stacked with pornography. Magazines, videos, and DVDs, littering the table, the sofa, the easy chair, and the floor. Nasty porn too. I glimpsed a few titles: *Latex Bondage Torture. Pain Sluts. House of Agony. Seymore Blood's Human Pincushion.*

A television rested in the corner of the room, next to a closed closet door. A camcorder perched on top of the TV. Even at the distance, I could make out the large letters *RCA* on the side of it.

The room opened into a hallway, and I moved quick but cautious, leading with my gun, staying low. My finger rested on the trigger, but I was aware of the pressure, aware that Holly was someplace in the apartment.

Four doorways down the hall, all open.

"Caleb Ellison! This is the police! Come out with your hands over your head!"

"Jack!"

Holly, from one of the rooms.

"Holly, where are you?"

"Back bedroom!"

Someone came into the hall. I dropped to a knee and sighted on the head. It was Holly. I pointed my gun at the ceiling, blowing out a breath.

"Dammit, Holly, you scared the crap out of me."

Holly didn't answer. In an unbelievably quick move her hand shot up and she fired three shots in my direction.

I dropped, facedown, hugging the carpet, getting my gun out in front of me—Holly running at me, still firing—but not at me, over my head—four and five and six shots—and me turning to see the pudgy redheaded man coming up behind me, the knife falling from his hand, the closet door still swinging from when he leaped out, Holly's bullets hitting his chest again and again, blood erupting like fireworks, until he fell at my feet with his tongue hanging out and his eyes wide and empty.

Holly stood next to me, wisps of smoke rising from the barrel of her 9mm. She grinned.

"Thirty points."

I didn't understand what she meant, but then I remembered the shooting range earlier that day. Six rounds in the chest, five points each.

"Give me the gun, Holly."

I held out my left hand. My right was still curled around my .38, which was currently pointed at her belly.

"I just saved your life, Jack."

"I know. Protocol. Backup will be here any minute."

She nodded, handing me her weapon butt-first.

"You okay?" she asked.

"Yeah. You?"

"You check out the party in this freak's basement? One more and he'd have enough for bridge."

I tucked Holly's piece into the back of my pants and got to my feet. I could hear the sirens approaching.

"How much trouble am I in, Jack?"

"I don't know. You broke the law, but saved my life. And probably saved the taxpayers millions of dollars in an expensive trial."

I gazed back at Caleb Ellison, whom I could ID from his mug shot. Like Steve Jensen, he had a fair share of tattoos slathering his arms, several of them the triple *D* symbol. His chest looked like he'd spilled a plate of spaghetti on it. There was no need to check for a pulse.

"But I'll be out by tomorrow, right? The wedding is at noon, and I haven't picked up a dress yet. Which is fine with Harry, because he wants us both to get married in the nude."

Not an image I needed in my head.

"I don't know, Holly. It depends on if the state's attorney wants to press charges. Either way, it's going to be a late night."

"How about if I give you the gun and you say you killed him?"

I shook my head.

"What if I gave you five bucks?"

Which was such an absurd thing to say, I began to laugh. Holly laughed too, and we kept laughing right up until the CPD kicked in the front door.

CHAPTER 38

*F*IRST ONE'S BY those bushes."

Lorna Hunt Ellison extends both arms and points. Her wrists are cuffed together under the sleeves of her Day-Glo orange prison jumpsuit. The elastic is tight around her middle, and the legs are too long, but the color reminds her of the hunting jacket Bud used to have, the one he used for deer season, and Lorna likes that memory. She and Bud had gone hunting dozens of times, and Lorna was the one who usually brought the game down—Bud couldn't shoot for shit. He loved dressing it, though. Bleeding the carcass, stripping off the hide, butchering the meat. Sometimes he couldn't even wait for her to cook it before having a little taste for himself.

Bud.

She'll see him again. Very soon.

One of the FBI guys walks up to the tree she's pointing at.

"Right here?"

Lorna spits. "Looks about right."

She's leaning up against the squad car, looking for the spray-painted rock. This should be the right place. She wrote the directions down. *Rosser*

Park, in Liverpool, the second dirt road off of Oregon Street, heading east toward the lake. Take the road until it stops. But she doesn't see any rocks, painted or otherwise.

Lorna walks away from the car and takes a few steps onto the grass. She'd insisted they remove the leg irons, or she wasn't showing them where any damn bodies were, guaran-fucking-teed. They listened to her. What harm could an old lady do, right?

The pig with the rifle—the one who is supposed to be pointing it at her the whole time—is scratching his nuts, the rifle butt-first on the ground. Two more cops, holding shovels, are standing next to that FBI asswipe, poking them at the dirt, trying to decide where to start digging.

"Right there!" Lorna shouts. "About four or five feet down."

She looks to her right. No rock. To her left. The black sedan the Feds drove is parked there. One of the Feds is standing beside it, talking to some fatty sheriff.

Lorna looks beyond the car, to the lake. The area is mostly open: ankle-high wild grass, a few saplings, and those bushes she pointed at. The weather is cool, in the high fifties. No activity, no fishermen or joggers. Too early in the morning.

Everything is perfect, if she can just find that damn rock.

The fatty sheriff walks over, eyeing Lorna like she's something he stepped in.

"After this, you're taking me to see Bud, right? Blessed Mercy Hospital in Gary?"

He scowls at her. "That's the deal. I didn't make it, though. I don't deal with scum."

"You probably don't deal with much. An ass that fat, you probably ride a desk all day."

His eyes get dark and mean. "Watch your mouth, bitch."

Lorna spots it: a small gray boulder about a foot high, surrounded by dry grass and fewer than five yards away. There's a big red *X* on it.

"I apologize, Sheriff. You mind if I stretch my legs a little? I haven't been out in the open in twelve years."

He grunts.

"Thank you, Sheriff."

She walks slowly, without apparent direction. When she reaches the rock she stretches, then bends down to tie her shoe.

The gun is there, in an old plastic zipper bag. It's a derringer—a small, two-shot weapon that Doc Holliday always had up his sleeve in old Western shows.

She removes the gun from the bag and cocks the hammer. The overall length of the pistol is less than four inches, and she can comfortably conceal it in the palm of her large hand.

"Hey, Lorna! You copping a squat over there?"

Laughter from the men. Lorna stands up and gives them the finger, then heads back to the group. There are four cops and two Feds, and the derringer only has two rounds.

But two is all she'll need.

She walks up to the pig with the rifle, holds out her wrists to him.

"Can you take these off? They hurt."

He snickers at her, and before he can finish she shoots him twice in the left eye.

The sound is like a firecracker, two sharp bangs, and before the pig even has a chance to fall over, Lorna is dropping the derringer and picking up the rifle, a Remington 7400 auto loader with an eight-shot magazine. She kneels behind the squad car, balancing the muzzle on the hood, and aims at the closest body— the fat sheriff.

The rifle is awkward to fire with her hands cuffed, but she manages to put one between his eyes while he just stands there, looking confused. Dumb-ass desk jockey.

Several people are returning fire, the car getting peppered with bullets. Lorna ignores them. She swings over to the FBI idiot, a tall guy in a gray suit, and shoots him twice in the chest while he struggles to remove his own gun from his holster.

The near threats removed, Lorna turns her sights onto the group by the bush, thirty yards away.

In a gunfight, the longest gun usually wins. The two pigs and the remaining

Fed are too far away to hit her. Plus, they have no cover, except for the leafless, sad-looking bush they'd been digging next to.

Lorna had gone varmint hunting too many times to count. She could drop a possum from a hundred feet away.

These men were closer, and lots bigger than possums.

Lorna drops the first cop with one in the head. The second cop hits the dirt, trying to crawl into the hole they'd been digging. The Fed ducks behind the bush, which makes Lorna laugh out loud.

She shoots the cop in the neck, and then shoots the FBI idiot in the arm.

"Toss the gun!" she yells.

He throws his pistol aside and places both hands on his head.

"Stand up!"

He stands. It's like an FBI version of Simon Says.

Lorna aims, exhaling as she squeezes the trigger.

The agent's knee explodes in a spectacular fashion.

"I said, stand up! Or the next one is between your ears!"

Lorna truly enjoys watching the man struggle to get up, falling over twice, and finally managing to support himself on one leg.

She thinks about going for the other knee, but drills him through the groin instead.

Again he falls.

Lorna drops the rifle and kneels next to the first pig she killed, the one who took off her leg irons. He has handcuff keys in his pants pocket. She spends a moment freeing her wrists, and then pulls the cop's sidearm—a Sig Sauer 9mm—from his holster.

"You still alive, Mr. FBI man? Lorna will be with you in just a sec."

Lorna scans the horizon, doesn't see another living soul. The fresh air smells wonderful. Like freedom. She walks casually over to the bush, past the dead pig in the hole, over to the Fed who is on his back, grabbing his crotch with both hands and breathing like he's in labor.

"Ain't no bodies out here, Mr. FBI man. I was playing with you. Pretty sneaky, wussn't it?"

His face is soaked with sweat, but he seems more angry than afraid.

"Don't I scare you, Mr. FBI man? You Feds are tougher than I'd've guessed."

She brings up the Sig, thumbs off the safety, and shoots him in one shoulder, then the other.

There's fear on his face now. Fear and pain and some craziness too.

"You Feds are something else. You come and visit us—me, and Bud, and people like us—and you talk about trying to understand why we do what we do. Like we're some animals you're studying on some nature show on TV."

She squats down next to the Fed, a big ugly smile on her face.

"This's what happens when you play with animals, Mr. FBI man. You get bit."

He cries out, and she fires the gun and stares, curious, as the back of his head decorates the grass behind him.

Lorna doesn't know how much time she has before someone comes, so she moves fast. First, she pats down the Fed and finds his car keys. Next, she strips out of the orange jumpsuit and hurries over to the sheriff, pleased to see there's very little blood on his clothes.

She strips him, struggling with the pants, which keep getting stuck on his big feet. It takes almost five minutes, and Lorna curses at herself for taking off her own clothes before she took off his, because she's freezing by the time she's done.

Lorna dresses quickly. His shirt is too big, and the pants are too long and tight at the hips, but after she tucks this in and tucks that in and puts on the sheriff department jacket and snap-brim hat, she takes a look at herself in the rearview and is pleased by the transformation.

Next, Lorna gathers up four more guns—she can't find the one the Fed threw into the grass—and a pair of reflective sunglasses. She brings it all into the dark sedan and starts the engine.

Blessed Mercy Hospital is less than ten miles away. Lorna puts the car into gear and hits the gas. It's the first time she's driven in over a decade, and it's almost as exciting as shooting all of those pigs.

Lorna fiddles with the car radio, and finds a station that plays country. She hums along to an old Hank Williams tune.

The hospital is a mess of activity. There're media folk around, all over the roads, and Lorna drives past them and into the parking lot. She leaves the car by the ER entrance, counting seven police cars before she goes inside.

There's a handful of pigs in the lobby. Two of them eye her. She walks past, ignoring them, trying to imitate the cop swagger she's seen so many times. The nurses' station is hopping, and Lorna lets out a shrill whistle to get a little girly's attention.

"Where's Kork?"

The nurse gives Lorna a foul look. "Down the hall, to the left. Room 118."

Lorna tips her hat, slightly large for her head, and walks into the ICU. There are two cops guarding Bud's room. One is asleep in a chair. The other gives Lorna a lazy glance.

Lorna removes the hand from her pocket, the hand holding the Sig, and jams it up into the cop's armpit. She pulls the trigger three times, but only two bullets fire. The cop flops over, and Lorna glances at the gun and sees the barrel is all gunked up with blood and little bits of stuff. She drops the weapon and reaches for another, a .45 AMC tucked into her belt, which she levels on the sleeping cop's head just as he opens his eyes.

Lorna's knuckles are the last thing he sees. She fires once, then steps into the room.

Bud is sitting up in bed, a goofy grin on his face.

"Hello, my love."

"Hello, Bud."

She tosses him a gun from her other pocket, then fishes out the handcuff keys she got off that cop at Rosser Park. Handcuff keys are universal, and she unlocks Bud's thin wrist.

Bud shoots at someone in the hall, and Lorna knows that cops'll be all over the place soon. She aims at the window and puts three rounds through it, then uses her foot to kick the spiderwebbed glass onto the lawn.

"We gotta go."

Bud fires again, and Lorna drags him over to the window and shoves him through. She follows him out and looks around, trying to get her bearings. The parking lot is fifty yards to the right.

They run for it.

Neither Lorna nor Bud are in the best physical condition, but fear is a powerful motivator, and they make it to the car in under ten seconds. From first shot fired until now, less than a minute has passed.

Lorna expects the parking lot to be swarming with pigs, but the two cops she sees are running inside the ER. They probably think she's still in Bud's room.

"Keep your head down, Bud."

Lorna pulls out of the parking lot, forcing herself to drive slow and careful and not attract attention. She drives past all the reporters, turns on the road to the interstate, and merges onto the expressway.

"I knew you'd come for me, Lorna."

She reaches down, patting his bald head.

"Family takes care of its own, Bud. We help each other." She wrinkles her brow, trying to remember what to do next.

"We gotta ditch the car, get you some clothes."

"And then what?"

"Then we got a score to settle in Chicago. Against that bitch cop who took away our Charles."

She presses in the car's cigarette lighter.

"I want her alive, Lorna. She's a sinner, and needs to be taught the error of her ways before we send her to meet her Maker."

"We'll teach her, all right, Bud. She's gonna repent all of her sins. By the time we're through, she'll be repentin' other people's sins."

The cigarette lighter pops out. She hands it to Bud, the end glowing orange.

"Here you go, baby. Play with this while I think."

There's a sizzle, and a squeal, and a smell like bacon frying.

Lorna smiles.

It's good to have her Bud back.

CHAPTER 39

I WAS QUESTIONED for over six hours.

I'd forewarned Holly that the fastest way to get through it was to tell the truth. Which is what I did. It meant disclosing I'd taken a civilian to Indiana to interrogate a suspect, and then snuck her into the Cook County morgue—neither of which were recommended police procedure.

But stopping a serial killer still counted for something in the eyes of the state's attorney, and Caleb Ellison was indeed a killer.

Besides the grisly tableau in his basement, Caleb had almost twenty snuff videos, many of them duplicates of Charles Kork's collection, but some of them new. Caleb had been smarter than Kork—he'd kept his face out of the picture—but not by much; weapons he'd used in the movies were discovered in his apartment. The camcorder seemed to be a match. Caleb also had a collection of Polaroid snapshots of posed murder victims, one more revolting than the next.

Another interesting bit of evidence was discovered in his bedroom—a cache of Michigan driver's license templates, and the equipment and software to create fake IDs, including an algorithm program that generated accurate driver's license ID numbers based on name and date of birth.

Checking his database uncovered several aliases for Caleb Ellison and for the recently deceased Steve Jensen. Background checks on these aliases revealed criminal records; their paper trails had ended several years ago because they'd committed their recent crimes and done their time under false names. We still had no idea what had dissolved their partnership, or what prompted Ellison to kill Jensen so horribly. But psychos really didn't need much provocation.

The Crime Scene Unit, and the Feebies, had practically moved into Caleb's apartment, continuing to gather evidence and build a case against a corpse.

I was finally cut loose at four in the morning, without charges filed against me.

Even at that late hour, the media had camped outside the station, and in a rare moment of lucidity I gave a decent statement.

"The Chicago Police Department is a meticulous, highly tuned crime-fighting machine, unlike how it's portrayed on certain television shows. Stopping Caleb Ellison was the result of the hard work and dedication of dozens of officers, from the superintendent on down."

Maybe that would score me some brownie points.

Once home, I unplugged my phone, fended off a cat attack, took a long shower, slapped on some burn cream, tugged one of Latham's old T-shirts over my head, and crawled into bed.

I was exhausted, but unable to relax. Sleep mocked my attempts, keeping me awake with thoughts of Caleb's basement, of my mother, whom I hadn't visited in a few days, of Herb, of Harry's wedding, which I had to get ready for in just a few hours, of Holly, who was still being questioned as far as I knew, and still hadn't bought a wedding dress.

I managed about ten winks out of a possible forty, and at nine a.m. I got up to face the day. It began with a call to Herb, who was being prepped for his bypass surgery.

"I saw it on the news this morning. You're catching psychos without me. I'm obsolete."

"Sorry, Herb. Next time I'll wait until you're feeling better before I do my job."

"I appreciate it."

"How was my sound bite? Did I look okay?"

"Thin. You looked too thin. Have you been eating okay?"

Bless that man.

"Thanks, Herb. Have yourself a good operation. Don't give the doctor any trouble."

"I've got it easy, compared to you. Aren't you standing up at that idiot McGlade's wedding today?"

"Yeah. Lucky me."

"Can you swing by the hospital and pick up the gift I made for him? I haven't wrapped it yet. It's still in the bedpan."

I laughed, then realized I hadn't gotten McGlade a gift myself. The ceremony was at noon, at the Busse Woods forest preserve in the suburb of Elk Grove. Maybe I had time to pick up something on the way.

I bid good-bye to Herb, rushed through a shower, and spent all the time I saved on the shower staring dumbly at my closet, wondering what the hell to wear. A formal gown? Not to a forest preserve. Slacks and a blouse? Not dressy enough. I didn't own a clown outfit, so that was out, and finally decided on a Bob Mackie brocade suit, pink, with a white blouse. The skirt was knee length, the jacket had shoulder pads and a rounded collar, and I never wore it to work because it was, well, pink.

I matched it with a strappy pair of DKNY two-inch heels with an open toe, but had no nylons without runs in them. I used some scissors to get a good leg from two separate pairs, and held them on with a garter belt that Latham had bought me during the inevitable "naughty underwear" phase of our relationship. I didn't expect to have as much fun wearing it this time.

I kept the makeup fast and light, refreshed the cat's food and water, and rushed out the door, almost running into my weirdo neighbor, Lucy Walnut from the Sanitation Department. She was wearing the same crusty uniform I'd seen her in the last few times. Perhaps she slept in it.

Before I had a chance to ask why she was standing in front of my apartment, she bent down and picked up a flower arrangement that had been resting between her feet.

"This is for you."

Taking flowers from creepy ex-cons set off all kinds of warning bells. Walnut must have sensed it, because she shook her head.

"It's not from me. Got delivered to your place last night. You weren't home, the florist guy asked me to hold it till you got back."

I took the flowers, a vase full of roses, carnations, violets, mums, and baby's breath.

"Uh, thanks."

"Whatever."

She trudged back to her apartment, and I brought the arrangement inside.

It had a small card, and the envelope had been torn open. Walnut? I could knock on her door and yell "J'accuse!" but didn't see the point. Instead, I took it out and read the message.

I still love you too. Let's talk. Latham.

I'll admit to a very unfeminine *whoop,* and maybe a few fist pumps in the air. I won't admit to grabbing Mr. Friskers and dancing around the kitchen with him, giving him kisses on his nose. I won't ever admit to that.

I immediately called Latham, and got his answering machine. I thanked him for the flowers, and invited him to come over tonight. My cell was almost out of juice, so I turned the power off. I'd recharge it in my car.

Energized for the first time in weeks, I practically ran to my Nova and pointed it northwest, taking the Kennedy expressway to Route 53, and exiting on Higgins Road at the giant mega-mall known as Woodfield. With almost 300 stores, I was bound to find one that had a wedding gift.

Or so I thought.

If I'd been buying just for Harry, I would have gone to a toy store and bought action figures, or some kind of toy that expelled slime. If I'd been buying for only Holly, I could have gotten some sort of designer accessory. But what would be appropriate for them as a couple?

I considered bedding. First silk sheets, then rubber sheets. Since I didn't know their bed size, I passed.

Then I looked at towels, televisions, easy chairs, the complete *Planet of the Apes* series on DVD, a lamp shaped like an ostrich, his and hers golf clubs, and a large stone that you could plug into the wall and watch water trickle over the edge, which was guaranteed to relax you, though it almost put me into shock when I saw how much it cost.

I left Woodfield at a quarter to twelve and went off in search of the universal gift, booze. Luckily there was a liquor store nearby, and I blew two bills on a bottle of bubbly and managed to make it to the forest preserve with a full minute to spare.

Busse Woods occupied a good portion—over ten square miles—of Elk Grove, which did indeed have real live elk running around in it. I followed the crude map Harry had scribbled on a beverage napkin at Mon Ami Gabi a few days earlier, taking the second entrance off Higgins. It was like being transported into another world.

Chicago had many parks, and those parks had trees, but even the densest concentration of foliage still felt like it was in the middle of a city. After turning down the twisty, thin road, the woods swallowed my car up. The forest canopy was so thick in certain parts, I couldn't see the sky. I felt like I'd driven into the movie *Deliverance*.

I took the road into the thicket for nearly a mile, finally ending up at a tiny clearing with a small eight-space parking lot, two weather-beaten picnic tables, and a rusty garbage barrel. Two other cars were already there, Harry's familiar '67 Mustang and a Volkswagen Jetta. Standing beside one of the tables were three men.

I parked next to the Jetta, checked my makeup, forced on a fake smile, and went to meet the boys.

Phin wore the same charcoal suit as the other day, but had switched the blue shirt for dark gray. His black cowboy boots were polished, and this was the first time I'd ever seen Phin in a tie. He looked good. Since Phin didn't own a car, especially not a Jetta, I assumed he took a cab here.

The man next to him—the judge or reverend or justice of the peace or ship's captain or whoever McGlade had conned into overseeing this happy union—was a short man in his sixties sporting a white beard and a corduroy blazer with patches on the elbows. Hadn't seen those in a while.

And Harry . . . Harry had crammed himself into a tuxedo, one of those new styles that had a large black button instead of a bow tie. He hadn't shaved, his hair was a mess, and his eyes were so bloodshot, it looked like he'd poured ketchup in them.

"Hey, Jackie." McGlade gave me a half-assed wave.

"Holly's not here yet?"

He shook his head. "She's running late. Didn't get out of the police station until this morning, then ran out to find a dress. Heard you had some night last night."

"You too. How was your bachelor party?"

He winced. "Those little people sure can drink."

Phin raised an eyebrow. "Little people?"

"Harry spent some quality time with a midget stripper," I explained.

McGlade held up four fingers. "Four of them. Every single Willy Wonka fantasy I've ever had came true last night."

Phin raised his eyebrow even higher. "You had sex with a midget stripper?"

Harry again held up four fingers. "Four of them."

"How was it?"

"It was short."

Both Phin and Harry began to laugh.

The guy in the antique suit walked over and held out his hand.

"Reverend Antwerp Skeezix, pleased to meet you."

I shook his hand. "Antwerp Skeezix?"

"That's my Martian name."

Harry whispered in my ear. "I had a little trouble getting someone to marry us on such short notice, and I found him on the Internet."

"I'm an ordained Martianology minister," said Antwerp Skeezix. "Harry and Holly are going to be married in the Church of Martianism. Blorg willing."

"Is this legal?" I asked Harry.

He shrugged.

Phin played it straight. "I bet the honeymoon cost a fortune."

"One does not need a rocket ship to visit Mars," said Reverend Antwerp Skeezix. "Mars is a state of mental awareness, and can be reached with a carefully controlled combination of psychotropic drugs."

"I bet," I said.

"Go stand over there, Spaceboy." McGlade pointed to the garbage can. "We'll be there in a minute."

"Blorg is good." The reverend waddled off.

Phin tapped Harry on the chest. "Are you sure Holly will go for that? Being married by Timothy Leary's stupid cousin?"

"I have no idea. I don't even know if she'll show up. I just want something to make my head quit pounding."

"I've got a gun in the car," I suggested.

Our witty banter was interrupted by the approach of a taxi. Holly got out of the back, wearing a simple white sleeveless cocktail dress—silk, above the knee, and low cut. White pumps. Her hair up and her makeup perfect. She looked stunning.

The relief on Harry's face was almost comical. He practically ran to meet her, and after some hugging and kissing they joined us, McGlade's smile big enough for three people.

"Okay, let's get this party started. Hey! E.T.! Get your ass over there by those trees."

Antwerp obediently trotted to where McGlade was pointing. Holly gave me a big hug, and then Phin a big hug. After the hugfest ended, I sidled up to her and we walked to the marriage spot Harry had picked out, between two giant pine trees.

"Everything go okay?" I nudged Holly.

"No charges pressed yet. They took my gun, though. Any chance I'll get it back? That's a pricey piece of hardware."

"If you fill out all the release papers correctly, you should get it back a little after Y3K."

"Shit. If I'd known that, I would have beat him to death with my bra."

Harry played dictator, telling us where and how to stand, putting me at his side and Phin at Holly's side.

"So what do you think, babe?"

"It's beautiful, Harry. Just perfect. And you look so handsome. Isn't he handsome, Jack?"

Actually, he looked like Danny DeVito's interpretation of the Penguin in that Batman movie.

"Handsome," I said.

Reverend Antwerp Skeezix cleared his throat. "Shall we begin?"

Harry nodded, and Antwerp undid his pants. McGlade grabbed his wrists.

"Hold on there, Starman. We decided to keep our clothes on."

Antwerp frowned. "No nudity?"

"No nudity."

The reverend cast a long, sad look at Holly, then zipped up.

"Dearly beloved, we are gathered here today, under the eyes of Blorg the Almighty the Second, son of Blorg the Almighty the First, son of Merv the Invincible, to bear witness to the joining of two lives."

I watched Holly's face. It stayed serious, even at the mention of the Invincible Merv.

"Do you, Holly Frakes, take Harrison Harold McGlade, to be your lawfully wedded husband, in sickness and in health, for richer or for poorer, until death do you part?"

"I do."

And damned if she didn't look happy saying it.

"Do you, Harrison McGlade, take Holly Frakes, to be your lawfully wedded wife, for richer or for—"

"I do," McGlade interrupted.

"Do you have the rings?"

Harry shook his head. "No rings. Tonight we're both going out and getting our nipples pierced."

Reverend Antwerp stared at Holly's chest and was momentarily at a loss for words, until McGlade kicked him.

"Okay then, by the powers invested in me, by the state of Illinois, and by the planet Mars, I now pronounce you husband and wife."

McGlade and Holly kissed. Phin and I exchanged a glance like, "That was weird," and then there was more hugging, including a hug from Reverend Antwerp that a less liberated woman would call a grope.

Then we gathered around one of the rotten picnic tables, Phin and I signed some witness papers, and McGlade gave Antwerp fifty bucks and told him to take off.

"I was hoping for a glass of champagne," the reverend said.

"Go hope for it somewhere else."

Antwerp, looking confused, walked back to his car.

"Hurry!" McGlade said. "There's a wascally wabbit stowing away on your spaceship!"

"Oh, dear!" Antwerp hurried.

Holly dug into Harry's car, coming out with a large cooler. She set it on the lawn and removed two bottles of champagne, an open carton of orange juice, some plastic cups, and two packages of bologna.

"Harry, this is all you packed for lunch?"

"Ah, shit. I forgot the raspberry Zingers. Sorry, babe. Maybe we can grab a bite somewhere local. In fact, I think I've got a take-out menu."

Harry pulled something out of his pocket. He handed it to Holly, and she squealed.

"Paris! Harry, we're going to Paris!"

"Plane leaves tonight, cupcake. Which will give us plenty of time to get loaded beforehand. Mix the mimosas, Phin! I'll pass out the bologna."

Phin opened the champagne and poured.

The first toast was to Harry and Holly, may they live happily ever after.

The second toast was to Holly, may she stay out of prison.

The third toast was to Phin, whom Harry called his new best friend.

When McGlade raised his glass the fourth time, I was in his sights.

"To the best cop I've ever met, a woman who is twice the man I'll ever be. Jack Daniels."

The alcohol must have hit him pretty quick, because he was slurring. It must have hit me as well, because McGlade's words touched me, and when I reached over to pat his shoulder, everything got blurry.

"Something's wrong." Phin shook his head, like a dog drying off. He backed away from the table and dropped to his knees.

I stared at Holly. She was staring hard at her plastic glass. Then her eyes rolled up into her head and she fell to the ground.

McGlade reached for her and he also fell over.

Drugged. We'd been drugged.

My thoughts were all scrambled, like a drunken dream, but I knew I had to call for help. My cell phone was in my car. I tried to walk to it, but I couldn't feel my legs, and every step I took, my car got farther away.

"Jack . . ."

Phin held out a hand to me, then collapsed face-first onto the ground.

I kept walking, but I forgot where I was going. The car. But why? What was so important about the car?

Sleep. That's what I needed to do. I needed to sleep.

I fell to my knees. Then to my butt.

This spot looked comfortable. Nice and grassy and comfortable. I could sleep here, no problem.

I laid my head on my arm and curled up my legs.

So nice to finally sleep.

When I closed my eyes, it was to the sound of someone laughing.

CHAPTER 40

H EY, LADY, YOU okay?"

I'd been having a disturbing dream, where I was tied to a chair at a dinner table and everyone around me was a rotting corpse. When I tried to pull off my ropes, I realized I was dead too, and my blackening flesh began to slide off my bones like BBQ ribs.

Opening my eyes, I stared up at a cop with a funny hat. I read his badge. Park District Ranger.

I startled, wondering how he got into my bedroom. Then I realized my bedroom didn't have trees in it, and my bed wasn't made of grass. I sat up. The action made me dizzy, and provoked an unhappy reaction in my stomach.

The ranger grinned at me. "Celebrating a little too much, huh?"

"Where am I?" My voice sounded strange, far away.

"Busse Woods. I'm going to check your friend."

I watched him walk over to a woman lying on the ground a few yards away. Holly.

I touched my temple, which had begun to throb, and looked around. Spotted a cooler on a picnic table, a bottle of champagne next to it, a carton of OJ, two packages of bologna . . .

The wedding.

A nice surge of adrenaline helped cut through the fog, and I remembered toasting to Harry and Holly, and then realizing we'd all been drugged.

I craned my head around, searching for Harry and Phin.

They weren't there.

I saw Harry's car in the lot, along with mine. My watch told me it was a little after six o'clock. I'd been out for over five hours.

The ranger was having some difficulty rousing Holly.

"Is she alive?"

"Pulse is strong, but she won't wake up."

I felt like curling up and going back to sleep myself. It wasn't a pleasant sensation; more like a fever dream that accompanies the flu.

I managed to get to my feet and began to walk to my car, a little unsteady, but better with every step.

My cell phone was plugged into the cigarette lighter. I needed to call Harry, to find out where he was.

The message light blinked at me. I dialed my voice mail.

"Jack, it's Captain Bains. Lorna Hunt Ellison escaped from custody this morning, and then grabbed Bud Kork at Mercy Hospital. Six cops, two Feds dead. A few miles away the Indiana Highway Patrol found an abandoned FBI vehicle. No sign of either perp. It might be a long shot, but there's a chance they could be headed your way. Stay on your toes."

Yeah. Some long shot.

I wondered how they found me. Tailed me from my apartment? Possible. I was so high from Latham's call, I could have had a dozen Abrams tanks following me and wouldn't have noticed.

But if Lorna and Bud were after me, why'd they let me go?

Another adrenaline spike, which made my hands shake.

They took Phin and Harry.

I tried to reason it out. Lorna escaped, went to get Bud, and then came to Chicago. They followed me here from my apartment, and probably watched the ceremony from the forest. Then one of them snuck into Harry's car and doctored the orange juice we used for the mimosas. The drug was probably Rohypnol, or GHB, or some other easily obtainable tranq currently popular on the nightclub date-rape scene. Odorless, colorless, and a tiny amount could take effect within ten minutes and knock out a bull.

Bud must have assumed Holly was a cop, my partner. They might have also assumed Phin was my boyfriend.

They wanted to hurt us by hurting our men.

But how did they find my apartment? And how did they find tranquilizers so quickly after escaping?

And how did Lorna, who had the IQ of a tennis ball, escape from prison and rescue Bud?

Apparently I'd misjudged her.

"What's going on?" The ranger had awoken Holly, who appeared to be panicked. "Where's Harry?"

"Take it easy, miss."

"Jack? What happened, Jack?"

I gave my head a brisk shake, but the fuzzies clung to me. I managed to get over to Holly without falling on my face.

"We were drugged, Holly. Bud Kork escaped, with his girlfriend. I think they've got Phin and Harry."

Holly stared at me, her mouth hanging open.

"My husband . . ." she whispered.

I reached down and squeezed her shoulder.

"We'll find them, Holly. I promise."

"But will they still be alive when we do?"

CHAPTER 41

PHINEAS TROUTT OPENS his eyes. His vision feels lopsided, off center, and his shoulders hurt. He's in a chair, but when he tries to move his arms and legs, they don't respond.

He takes in the scene. It's a warehouse of some sort, concrete floors and thirty-foot ceilings, row after row of empty aluminum racks. The windows are boarded up, but there's a light on somewhere behind him, illuminating a decade's worth of dust in swirling motes.

Phin does a body inventory checklist, flexing his toes, legs, fingers, arms, neck, and jaw. Nothing seems damaged. But his legs are bound to the chair legs, and his hands are bound behind his back.

He jerks himself to the side, trying to get the chair to tilt or move. It's secured to the ground somehow. He pulls on his arms, hard, and feels wire bite into his wrists.

This isn't a good situation.

Phin closes his eyes, which helps him push away the panic. How did he get here?

The last thing he remembers is the forest preserve, toasting to the newly married couple.

Someone had drugged them.

Okay, but why?

Phin has enemies, probably more than his share. But no one knew he was going to that wedding. And during the cab ride to Busse Woods, Phin kept a careful eye on the rearview mirror, a subconscious paranoia that served him well in the past. He hadn't been followed . . .

That left Jack, Harry, and Holly. Jack was a cop, Harry and Holly private investigators. They undoubtedly had enemies too. Phin might have gotten caught up in someone else's revenge scheme.

A sound, a low rumble, comes from behind him. Phin can't turn far enough to see. It comes again, louder.

Snoring.

"Hey! Wake up!"

"I'm awake. I'm awake."

More snoring.

"Goddammit, McGlade, wake up!"

"Huh? What's happening?"

"We were drugged at your wedding."

"I got drunk at my wedding? There's a shocker."

"Drugged, McGlade. We were drugged."

"Is that you, Jim?"

"It's Phin. Wake up and tell me what you see."

A long pause. Phin wonders if the moron fell asleep again.

"I'm in a chair, tied up. Looks like some kind of factory or warehouse. There's a cargo docking bay off to my right, but the door is closed."

"What else?"

"We gotta get out of here, Phin. If I don't get this tuxedo returned by tonight, they're charging me for another full day."

"Concentrate, Harry. What else is around you?"

"There's some kind of office in the corner. Door closed, no lights. On my left . . . holy shit!"

"What is it?"

"This has got to be some kind of bad dream."

McGlade yelled in pain.

"Harry? You okay?"

"I bit my tongue to see if I'm dreaming. I don't think I am. Or maybe I bit my tongue in my sleep . . ."

"You're not asleep, Harry. Tell me what you see."

"I think my tongue's bleeding."

"Harry!"

"Okay. I see a long steel table. Got a bunch of equipment on it. And some stuff, new in boxes."

Phin doesn't like the sound of that.

"What kind of stuff?"

"A blowtorch. A power drill. A set of vise-grip pliers. And a chain saw."

This has gone from bad to worse.

"Maybe they're building a birdhouse," McGlade said.

"I doubt that."

"There's also a big bottle of ammonia, and some paper towels. Spring cleaning?"

"The ammonia is to wake us up when we pass out from pain."

"Oh. That makes sense. *CAN ANYONE FUCKING HELP ME! HEY! HELP! GET ME OUT OF HERE!*"

McGlade screams for several minutes.

"You're wasting your breath, Harry. No one's going to hear us."

McGlade continues to scream anyway.

Phin tunes him out. He wonders where Jack and Holly are. Were they taken as well? Are they at another location?

Are they already dead?

He has no idea how long he's been out. A few hours? A day? He rubs his chin against his shoulder, feels some facial stubble, but not much. Less than twelve hours.

Harry stops yelling. Phin listens to him grunt and struggle for a while. The sounds eventually stop.

"Man, I'm thirsty." This from McGlade. "You thirsty, Phin?"

"Don't think about it."

"I am thinking about it. How can I not think about it? If I try not to think about something, I think about it even more because I have to think about it to try not to."

Time ticks away. A plane passes overhead, low and loud. Either taking off or landing. Phin guesses they're in the northwest suburbs, someplace near O'Hare. Elk Grove has a large industrial section, not far from Busse Woods.

"I gotta pee."

Phin squeezes his eyes shut. Being tortured to death is going to be bad enough. Being tortured to death alongside this idiot is even worse.

"It's like someone's turning a vise on my kidneys."

"Let's not talk for a while, okay?"

McGlade is blessedly silent for a few minutes. Phin concentrates on relaxing his shoulders; they're beginning to cramp up. The wire is tight enough on his wrists to make his fingers tingle. It's a heavy gauge, about the width of a coat hanger but more pliable. He pumps his fists several times to get blood into his hands.

"If I die in a rented tuxedo, how long to you think they'll keep charging my credit card?"

Phin rolls his eyes. "Christ, McGlade. Does it matter? You won't have to pay it."

"Yeah, but my wife will. If they don't find my body, she'll keep getting charged every month. It could run into millions of dollars." McGlade doesn't speak for a moment, then says, "I hope she's okay. Jack too. You think they're okay?"

"I don't know."

"Maybe they got away. Maybe they're on their way to rescue us."

"Maybe."

"And maybe they're bringing cool, refreshing beverages. And a toilet."

This guy used to be Jack's partner? Phin can't understand how she let him live for this long.

"Don't take this the wrong way, McGlade, but I can't understand what the hell Holly sees in you."

"I dunno. Love is blind."

"Apparently it's also deaf. And learning disabled."

"Maybe Holly loves me because I've got so many layers. Like a big, sexy onion. I'm an enigma, wrapped in a mystery."

"You're an enigma, wrapped in an idiot. Layers? Harry, I've only met you twice, and you're about as deep as a spilled beer."

"You're just jealous. Holly and I have something special. We have trust, and loyalty, and commitment."

"Commitment? What commitment? You cheated on her four times last night."

"They were midgets. If you add them together it only counts as twice."

Phin doesn't answer. This conversation is pointless. They need to think of some way to get out of here. He didn't undergo months of chemotherapy to suffer and die in this abandoned warehouse.

But much as Phin pulls and stretches and strains, he can't free himself.

There's nothing they can do but wait.

CHAPTER 42

M Y STOMACH HURT. I didn't know if it was an effect of the tranquilizers, or the fact that I was burning up to do something but didn't have anything I could do.

The Elk Grove police were called, but they really didn't have much to do either. Our statements were taken. A few pictures were snapped. I explained to a nearly catatonic Holly what I suspected was going on with Bud and Lorna.

"So what now?" she asked. "We just wait around for them to contact us?"

"I'm going into the office, calling Indiana. Maybe they have some sort of idea where they'd go. Got someplace to go?"

"I'm going to stick around. Maybe something will turn up here."

I looked at the twelve Elk Grove cops, standing around talking sports. Nothing was going to turn up here.

"Call me if you need me, Holly."

She reached out to hug me, but it was stiff and mechanical; all of her life force had been drained from her. I explained to the uniforms I was leaving, and when nobody protested I hopped in my Nova and headed back to Chicago.

I spent most of the trip on the phone with the hospital, trying to ascertain Herb's condition. First he was still in the OR, then he was in Recovery, then there were some kind of complications and they weren't sure where he was. I asked for Bernice, but she couldn't be located. By the time I got to the district house I was on my way to a total nervous breakdown, a feeling exacerbated by the two men waiting for me in my office.

"Hello, Lieutenant. We heard from the Elk Grove Police Department that you'd be here."

"I'm really not in the mood right now, guys."

Agent Dailey made a face that almost looked sympathetic. "We understand how you must be feeling."

"I doubt it."

"We lost two good men in Rosser Park when Lorna Hunt Ellison escaped custody," Agent Coursey said. "They were friends of ours."

"I'm sorry."

Coursey looked at his shoes, which was the most emotion I'd ever seen from him.

"It should have been us. We were assigned to accompany Lorna. But when you cracked the Caleb Ellison case, we were ordered back to Chicago."

"In a way, you saved our lives, Lieutenant."

That was a karma debt I really didn't need.

"Gentlemen, I feel bad for your loss, but I'd really like to be alone right now."

"We'd like to help."

"I prefer doing this myself."

"Kidnapping is a Federal offense, Lieutenant. This is technically our jurisdiction."

I shot venom out of my eyes. "Do you really want to play fucking jurisdiction games?"

"No," Agent Dailey said. "We really want to help."

I collapsed in my chair. I had no fight left in me.

"Fine." I closed my eyes, tried to rein in some semblance of control. "What have you got?"

"We've created a new profile, with Vicky, of Lorna Hunt Ellison."

"A new profile. Great. Does it happen to mention where she's holding my friends?"

"Probably someplace close to Busse Woods, or perhaps in the woods themselves. We had a chance to interview Lorna before her escape. She's a DO offender, impulsive, erratic, very low intelligence. Bud Kork has similar characteristics, plus he's delusional and psychotic. They couldn't have planned very far ahead."

That had been my assessment. Luring victims to your house in the boonies and burying them in your basement, though horrible, wasn't the work of a criminal mastermind. But escaping from prison, rescuing Bud, then grabbing Harry and Phin took some real intelligence. A DO—disorganized personality type—couldn't muster that. It didn't make sense.

"How did Lorna escape? Give me details."

They ran it down for me.

"We recovered the derringer, and a plastic bag we believed it had been wrapped in. Lorna could have planted it there years ago."

I didn't like it.

"Then why wait until now to use it? She's been locked up for twelve years. Why didn't she pull this stunt a long time ago?"

Both Coursey and Dailey shrugged at the same time. It was eerie.

"She might have been waiting for the right moment," said Coursey.

"Or she'd forgotten about it until now," said Dailey.

"Or"—I reached for the phone—"somebody planted it for her."

I caught Ms. Pedersen, the assistant superintendent for Indiana Women's Prison, on her way out the door.

"This is a terrible time for us, Lieutenant. I feel partially responsible. I knew Lorna was capable of violence, but didn't think she could pull off something like this."

"None of us did. This isn't your fault."

"I appreciate that." And it sounded like she did. "Can I do anything to help?"

"When I visited you the other day, I asked about Lorna's visitors. You said she had none. Correct?"

"Yes."

"How about phone calls? Prisoners are allowed calls, right?"

"Of course."

"Do you keep records?"

"No. But I can talk to the guards. They'd remember if Lorna had received any calls for the last few days. Can I call you back?"

I gave her my number.

"What if Lorna had help?" I told the Feebies.

"You think she was coached?"

"Maybe someone planted the gun, and gave her instructions on how to grab Bud and kidnap Harry and Phin. The same someone who supplied her with the roofies, or whatever drug they used."

"Caleb Ellison?" Dailey asked. "He was obviously an organized personality. Sending the videotapes, leaving no evidence—"

"You saw his house, right?"

They each nodded three times. I almost looked up, trying to see the puppeteer.

"It was a mess," I continued. "Garbage and porn all over. And look at the sloppy way he broke into my partner's house. How would you profile that?"

"That's typical disorganized behavior. Clearly Caleb manifested both O and DO traits."

Maybe, but something bothered me. Some nagging little doubt that made me think I was missing the bigger picture. I gave the Crime Lab a call, surprised that Officer Hajek was still in this late.

"Hi, Lieut, I was hoping you'd call. Get my messages?"

Only now I noticed the voice-mail light on my phone, blinking on and off. Some detective I was.

"What's up, Scott?"

"Got some results back. That burned bag you brought me? Analyzed the contents. Mostly clothing, and some glass and plastic fragments. I think they were toiletries: toothpaste, deodorant, hair spray, face cream, cosmetics."

"Cosmetics? You mean makeup?"

"Yeah. Which goes along with the burned hair sample you gave me. There were traces of spirit gum on it. I think it was a fake beard."

I pictured the Identikit photocopy; a man with a blond beard.

"So it was part of a disguise kit?"

"It could have been. And that bullet casing you found . . ."

My phone beeped. Call waiting. I told Scott to hold on.

"Lieutenant Daniels? It's Ms. Pedersen. Lorna received three calls over the last week."

"Do you know who they came from?"

"No. But the guard I talked to said it was a woman, Midwestern accent."

"Thanks." I switched back to Hajek. "Tell me about the bullet."

"Nine millimeter."

"Anything off it?"

"Nothing. But I did get something off that message machine I took from the University of Chicago. I digitized the tape and ran it through a filter, did a few comparisons."

"And you found out it's a woman's voice."

"How did you know that? That was my big surprise."

A woman had called Lorna, so it made sense a woman left the messages on Mulrooney's machine. The fake beard could have made a woman look like a man. With the sunglasses, and the hood, it would have been easy to fool the desk sergeant downstairs. And Al the car rental guy—when he greeted me, he didn't have his glasses on. He couldn't see a damn thing. Al had also mentioned the man who'd rented the Titanium Pearl Eclipse had a cold.

But it wasn't a cold. It was a way to hide a feminine voice, by coughing and speaking low.

I asked Hajek to hold on, digging into the pile of papers next to my fax machine, the ones I'd gotten the other day from the Gary Police Department. Dozens of pages on the Kork family. Criminal records and tax records and utility bills and school records and there it was—a death certificate for Bud's daughter, Alexandra.

"Scott? I need you to do two things for me. Is the Caleb Ellison evidence there yet?"

"Came in this morning."

"Caleb's computer?"

"Rogers is working on that right now, one room over."

"Connect me with him. In the meantime, get your hands on the gun used to kill Ellison."

"You got it." He transferred the call, and I crossed my fingers, hoping I was wrong.

"This is Rogers."

"Dan, it's Jack Daniels. Are you in Ellison's database?"

"As we speak. It's filled with both the real names and the made-up names. Not a smart way to make fake IDs. We'll probably get a few dozen arrests out of this."

"Check a name for me. Alexandra Kork."

I heard fingers *tap-tap-tap* on a keyboard, Rogers humming softly to himself.

"Got it. Made a Detroit driver's license, a bunch of years back."

"What's the new name?"

I held my breath.

"Frakes," he said. "Holly Frakes."

Son of a bitch. Harry's new bride was the killer. It all made sense, in hindsight. I couldn't believe I'd been so easily duped.

"Put me back on with Hajek."

"He's standing right next to me. Here."

"Lieut? I've got an empty nine-millimeter shell from Caleb Ellison's house. It's a match."

I thanked him and hung up the phone.

"Bud Kork's daughter is going by the name Holly Frakes," I told the Feebies.

"Where is she?"

"Still in Elk Grove, I think. She called my cell but blocked the number. Can you guys access my call records?"

Dailey looked at Coursey. "Not only that, we can use satellites to triangulate the signal."

"It'll take a little while to set up."

"How long?"

"An hour, if we move."

"We might not have an hour. If Harry and Phin are somewhere near Busse Woods, she could be with them right now."

Doing God knows what to them.

CHAPTER 43

ALEX KORK, WHO now uses the name Holly Frakes, pulls Harry's Mustang into the warehouse parking lot. She discovered the place a few days ago, and it's one of the reasons she insisted on getting married at that stupid forest preserve. Though Alex is a strong girl, hauling a two-hundred-pound man around is hard work, and takes a long time. Privacy is essential.

Here she has plenty of privacy.

This entire area, for several square miles, is industrial. Factories, warehouses, and shipping yards. This building is currently between tenants. And since it's Sunday night, there isn't a single person anywhere near here.

It's the perfect place to kill someone slowly.

Alex gets out and opens the garage door. She pulls the car inside the loading dock, parks, and closes the door behind her.

This next part is going to be fun.

"Holly? Holly! Holy shit, it's you! Thank God you're here, baby! I have to piss so bad the change in my pockets is floating."

Alex approaches Harry and Phin, both still securely wired to the heavy frame metal chairs. They're back to back, a few feet apart, and the chairs have been bolted to docking anchors in the concrete floor.

No way of escape, no matter how hard they struggle.

"Hi, Harry."

Alex sits on his lap and grinds on him, playfully. She curls a finger in his hair and twists a lock.

"Quit screwing around, Holly. Grab those pliers off the table and untwist these wires."

"Pliers? Sure." Alex giggles. "Just a second."

She leaves Harry's lap and circles the table, smiling at all the wonderful toys.

"How did you find us, Holly?" Phin tries to turn his head around to see, but can't.

"Easy. I just followed my heart. Nothing could keep me from the man I love. My precious husband." Alex picks up a tool. "How about this one, dear?"

"What are those? Tin snips? Yeah, that oughta work. Bring them around to my hands, baby."

"Or how about this one?" Alex picks up something older, something she knows very well.

"What the hell is that? A hairbrush? Can't you do that later?"

"It's not a hairbrush, Harry. Not anymore. Instead of bristles, it has rusty nails sticking through the end. Father used it on me, when I was bad."

McGlade makes a face. "You're not making sense, Holly."

Moment of truth time. Alex gets close. She wants to gaze into his eyes when she tells him.

"My father's name is Bud Kork."

"I thought your last name was Frakes."

"Kork, Harry. Doesn't the name sound familiar?"

"Kork? Yeah, Charles Kork was that psycho that I . . ."

McGlade stops talking. His mouth opens, but nothing comes out. His eyes become comically wide.

"That psycho was my older brother, Harry. The only man I ever loved."

Harry's face twists from confusion to mirth.

"This is a joke, right? You're getting me back for that time I accidentally used the rear entrance. I told you, baby. It was dark. I was working by feel."

"Why do you think I always turned out the lights when we had sex, Harry?"

McGlade doesn't answer.

"Scars, Harry. Along my back. I had a lot of plastic surgery, but it still doesn't look right. Want to see?"

"Not really. Scars freak me out."

Alex plants her feet, rears back, and slams the hairbrush onto McGlade's thigh. The nails penetrate a good inch, anchoring themselves into bone.

McGlade screams like a train whistle.

Alex basks in his pain, his fear. It's like sunlight on her face. That single scream is worth all of the time she invested, all of the gropes she endured. To finally have this man all to herself, for her to enjoy, is simply delicious.

As McGlade sobs, Alex walks over to Phin. His eyes are cold, emotionless. He's going to be fun to break.

"What's the matter, Phin?" Alex pouts. She caresses his chin and runs her hand over the back of his head. "Don't you like me anymore?"

"I was wondering why you married McGlade. Now it makes perfect sense."

Alex brings her face to within inches of his.

"I married him for revenge."

"You married him because you're out of your fucking mind."

The smile leaves her face. Alex steps back, centers herself, and finger-strikes Phin in the abdomen. The blow forces air out of Phin's lungs, and he grunts in pain.

"You had a hand in it too. You helped Jack and Harry find my brother. I'm going to make you pay for that, Phin."

"I want a divorce!" screams Harry McGlade.

Alex gives Phin a kiss on his forehead, then turns her attention back to Harry.

"You have to remind me, my dear husband. What are you again? Left-handed, or right-handed?"

Harry spits on her.

"I'm glad I made you sign that prenup, you crazy psycho bitch!"

"I think you're a righty. Let's start with that one, then."

She lowers the tin snips to the fingers on McGlade's right hand. Puts the pincers around his middle finger.

"Don't worry, Harry. You won't bleed to death. That's why I bought the blowtorch."

Snip.

Harry's screams are like candy.

CHAPTER 44

THE DOOR GAVE on my third kick, and I twisted my ankle badly enough to bring tears to my eyes.

Special Agent Dailey and Special Agent Coursey waited in the hallway, citing statutes about breaking and entering, illegal search and seizure, speaking without raising my hand, etc.

I didn't think Harry would mind, considering I was trying to save his life.

McGlade used to live in Hyde Park, in a little rat hole apartment. Since hitting it big with *Fatal Autonomy*, he'd moved to a penthouse on the GC—the Gold Coast. Heated garage. Twenty-four-hour doorman. And a damn good front door, which I hurt myself getting through.

The condo dripped opulence, which isn't to say it was attractive or tasteful. Harry decorated like a child-king rules a country—with enthusiasm, but no intelligence.

The carpet was deep, expensive. While the furniture all screamed wealth, the styles were confused. An art deco table breakfront. A colonial dining room set. Art nouveau chairs and a rococo sofa. And beanbags. Lots of multicolored beanbags.

The walls displayed pricey-looking paintings and drawings: oils, watercolors, acrylics, pencils. Some postmodern, some minimalist, some classical. The only common theme was their subject: naked women.

A plasma TV was the centerpiece of the most hi-tech entertainment center I'd ever seen, boasting stacks upon stacks of blinking stereo and video equipment. It was like Harry had gone into a Sharper Image store and said, "I'll take everything."

The place was clean, to the point of fastidiousness. Unusual for Harry. I'd had the unfortunate displeasure of visiting his last apartment, which was like a landfill, only roomier.

I wasn't sure what I was looking for. Holly/Alex had spent some time here. I doubted she'd left any clues; Holly was too smart for that. But I had no other leads, and I had to do something. Waiting around my office for another videotape to arrive wasn't in my game plan.

The kitchen was larger than my whole apartment. Copper pots hanging from a rack on the ceiling. A center island with a six-burner stove and a grill. A microwave large enough to defrost a whole pig.

"You find anything?"

One of the Feebies, calling from the hallway.

"Some pictures," I yelled. "Hoover in a cocktail dress."

The kitchen let out into a hallway. I limped into the bedroom first. A king-sized bed dominated the room, dead-center. On the right side of the bed was a control panel. I had no desire to find out what it controlled.

The next room was all shelves containing videos and DVDs, many of them still unopened in their plastic wrappers. The room after that was a spare bedroom, which looked unused. Lastly, at the end of the hall was a closed door that had a plaque on it that said *Spy Room*.

The spy room contained electrical gadgetry, and a lot of it. Infrared cameras. Listening devices. Night-vision goggles. A biohazard suit. Plus a large collection of remote control cars, helicopters, and airplanes.

I had no idea McGlade was such a techno-geek.

"Lieutenant Daniels! The police are here."

I followed the voice back out into the hall, and indeed four of Chicago's finest were surrounding the Feebies.

Which made sense. If Harry loved electronics this much, he probably had a silent burglar alarm. I hadn't seen the arming panel when I came in, but I hadn't been looking for it.

We coddled the cops, who were willing to overlook the criminal breaking and entering but still had to file a report in case Mr. McGlade wanted to press charges. I also arranged for the door to be fixed, so no one could walk in and steal all of Harry's goodies. And he had lots of goodies.

"Are either of you car buffs?" I asked the Feebies in the elevator going down.

"I know a few things," said Dailey. Or maybe it was Coursey.

"How much is a 1967 Mustang worth?"

"Depends on the mileage, the condition, and the model."

"Assume everything is mint or rebuilt."

"Maybe forty or fifty thousand. If a lot of custom work had been done on it, maybe more."

Harry loved his car. He's had it for as long as I've known him. If he pimped out his condo like that, he would have also pimped out his ride. And if he pimped out his ride, he'd want to protect it.

Back in my humble Nova, I radioed in a stolen vehicle—Harry's Mustang. Then I gave my location and requested for any nearby squad cars equipped with LoJack tracking equipment to give me a holler if they got a ping.

Chicago adopted LoJack a few years ago. The LoJack company sold transmitters that were hidden in cars. If a car was stolen, a police report automatically activated the transmitter, which emitted a silent radio signal, revealing its location using global positioning satellites.

LoJack helped us locate stolen cars. I was betting Harry had one in his Mustang, and I was also betting that Holly had taken his car rather than a cab, which meant we might be able to track her right to Harry and Phin's location.

Lots of betting involved with this plan.

"Roger, Lieutenant. This is car 88, just received confirm on LoJack, have the vehicle moving north on La Salle, just passing Adams. Over."

Sometimes betting pays off.

"What's your twenty, car 88?"

"South on Columbus, east of Randolph."

I was on La Salle and North Avenue, about two miles away.

"Car 88, maintain pursuit but do not engage. Repeat, do not engage. We don't want to spook her."

I kicked my car into gear and headed south on La Salle, hoping the Feebies had the good sense to turn on their scanner and follow at an inconspicuous pace. Which, knowing them, was hoping a lot.

"Suspect is at Washington, continuing north on La Salle."

I stopped at a red light on Division, squelching the urge to blow through it and set a new land speed record. Holly would recognize my car. I needed to remain calm and focused, keeping a safe distance.

Arresting her was the wrong move. Holly wouldn't give up Phin and Harry's location, even with physical persuasion. Though I was having a hard time reconciling the calculating murderer with the woman I'd spent most of yesterday with, I knew Holly would die before telling me where they were. She was too competitive, her desire to win too strong. She wouldn't take losing well.

The smarter move was to follow her and hope she led us to my friends. Which should work . . . unless they were already dead and in her trunk.

"This is car 88. We're west on Van Buren, turning north onto La Salle."

"Keep your distance, car 88. I don't want her spooked."

"Roger that."

The light changed. I stayed the course, weaving in and out of the sparse traffic. In the rearview, I noticed the Feebies' sedan, stuck to my bumper as if I were towing them.

"Dailey, Coursey, if you're on this frequency, loosen up the tail. You're crawling up my muffler."

They must have heard me, because they pulled back to almost half a car length.

"Suspect just passed Wacker Drive, continuing on present course."

I was coming up on West Chicago Avenue. Less than ten blocks away from

Holly. I turned left on Chicago. I'd try to flank her by running parallel on Dearborn, two blocks over.

"Suspect has stopped at the corner of La Salle and Kinzie."

I passed Clark, and pulled up to a fire hydrant on Chicago and Dearborn to wait.

"This is car 88. We're still on La Salle, coming up on Washington. Suspect is still on Kinzie."

A honk, behind me. Then several more. I looked in the mirror, and saw the Feebies were parked in the middle of the street, blocking traffic. This didn't go over well with the long line of commuters forming behind them.

"We're approaching Wacker Drive. Suspect is still stopped on Kinzie, one block ahead. Please advise."

"Hold position. Wait for her to move."

More honking, along with several colorful suggestions that perhaps the Feds might move their car. I watched in the rearview as a motorist actually stepped out of his vehicle and walked up to the Feebies, in a manner that made the vintage newsreels of a ranting Hitler seem genteel.

"Suspect is still holding at Kinzie, please advise."

Shit.

"Approach with caution, 88. If suspect is still in the car, pass her without stopping."

"Roger that."

Now Dailey was out of the car, showing the angry motorist his ID. The motorist responded by showing Dailey one of his fingers.

"We're approaching Kinzie, and see a black Ford Mustang parked alongside the street. No driver. Over."

Double shit.

I pulled out into traffic, made a U-turn, and headed back to La Salle. This time I floored it, wincing from the pain in my right ankle, which had swollen enough to break my shoe strap. I blew the light on La Salle, jerked the wheel hard to the left to avoid a collision, and raced toward Holly, nine blocks to go.

"You're looking for a white woman, mid-thirties, long black hair, a hundred and thirty pounds, very attractive. She might be wearing a white dress, but she's probably in street clothes. She has ID in the name of Holly Frakes."

Eight blocks. A green light, and I sailed through, easing the car up to forty-five.

"No one within sight matches that description. My partner will search on foot. Over."

Seven blocks. I chanced a quick look in my mirror and saw I'd lost the Feebies. Maybe they'd been torn apart by angry motorists.

"Awaiting okay to approach the Mustang, over."

"Hold, 88. I'll be right there."

I flew past Ohio street, then had to slam on the brakes to avoid rear-ending a bus that pulled in front of me. My ankle screamed at my decision, but the rest of my body was grateful not to have died. I swung into oncoming traffic, passed the CTA, and slowed down when I got to Hubbard, keeping my eyes open for Holly.

I didn't see her, but I saw Harry's Mustang parked along Kinzie. I pulled in behind it and limped over. When I looked inside, I understood why Holly had fled.

"Dammit, McGlade!"

Harry, in all of his disposable income wisdom, liked gadgets so much he not only purchased a LoJack, he also had a police scanner, mounted under his dash.

Holly had heard our entire radio conversation.

Triple shit with pink sugar on top.

I turned a full circle, my gaze drifting upward to the sky, cursing my failure. If I'd only maintained radio silence. Hell, if I'd only looked a little closer at Holly during the time I'd spent with her. Of course she was a killer. I should have known it from the start. Who else would have married McGlade?

Stupid, annoying, obnoxious, repulsive Harry McGlade.

God, I hoped he was okay.

CHAPTER 45

PHINEAS TROUTT WIPES his nose on his shoulder. The blood has slowed to a trickle.

He's not sure how long ago Holly left. An hour, maybe ninety minutes. She worked on McGlade for what seemed like an eternity, until the poor son of a bitch passed out.

Phin lives in a seedy part of Chicago. He's met pushers and bangers and hookers and pimps and johns and murderers, but he's never seen anything as cold-blooded as Holly. She isn't human.

For his part, McGlade had been pretty stoic through the ordeal. He screamed, for sure, but there was no begging or pleading.

There will be, though. Nobody can take that kind of agony for an extended period.

Phin wonders if McGlade has gone into shock. Might not be a bad thing. At least he'd be beyond the pain.

"How you doing, Harry?"

McGlade moans. "Got any aspirin?"

"Other pair of pants."

"Nuts."

Phin has to ask. His imagination has been running wild. "How's the hand, Harry?"

"Doesn't hurt much, because there's not much left to hurt. Hope my screaming didn't disturb you."

"Actually, you interrupted my nap. Try to keep it down next time."

"I'll try. Sorry about that."

He admires Harry's guts. His respect for the private eye goes up a few notches.

"The hand the worst of it?"

"This damn rusty nail thing in my leg hurts worse. Dirty as hell. I can feel the tetanus, surging through my veins. Though I guess dying of tetanus might not be a bad thing right about now."

Phin understands pain. He understands it more than most people. When there's nothing else to focus on, pain can become all-consuming. Crippling. The psychological aspects of it are just as bad as the neurological effects.

If he keeps Harry talking, maybe the pain won't be so bad.

"So your full name is Harrison Harold McGlade?"

"Yeah."

"Your parents named you Harry Harry?"

"Yeah."

"That's pretty funny, don't you think?"

"This from a guy named Phineas Troutt."

McGlade's voice is getting weaker. Phin can hear the strain.

"At least I don't have to piss anymore," McGlade says. "When she cut off my thumb, I wet my pants."

Phin has to grin at that.

"Nothing to be ashamed of, Harry Harry."

"All you dry pants guys say that."

"Maybe it's a good thing. There's ammonia in urine. Maybe you disinfected that rusty nail puncture."

"Didn't reach. I was pointing in the other direction."

A minute passes.

"I can see my fingers," Harry says.

"How's that?"

"They're on the floor in front of me. Think a doctor can reattach them?"

To burned flesh? Phin doubts it. But he says, "Sure."

"Assuming we get out of here."

"I'm working on it."

Listening to a man having his fingers removed and the stumps cauterized with a blowtorch can galvanize a person into action. Damage to himself be damned, Phin begins to twist his wrists in their binding. The wire is thin, and bites into his flesh.

"What are you doing?" Harry asks. "Using your psychic powers to call the other members of the Justice League?"

"I'm going to break this wire."

"It's too strong. You'll cut your hands off first."

"Either way I'll be free."

"Good plan. If it doesn't work, I've got a plan too."

Phin winces. He can feel the blood start to leak down his palms.

"What's your plan?"

"When she comes back, I'm going to swallow my own tongue and choke to death."

"Good plan."

"Yeah. That'll show the bitch."

Phin continues to twist. Back and forth. Back and forth. The wire cuts like a blade, but it's loosening just a little.

That, or it's in so deep, it just seems like it's looser.

"GODDAMMIT!" McGlade's scream scares the hell out of Phin. "GET AWAY FROM THAT, YOU SON OF A BITCH!"

"Harry? You okay?"

"YOU BASTARD! I'LL HUNT YOU DOWN AND ROAST YOU!"

It sounds like McGlade is losing it.

"Harry, what's up? Who are you screaming at?"

"Goddamn rat. Ran off with one of my fingers."

Phin isn't sure how to reply to that.

"My middle finger, I think."

"I'm sorry, Harry."

"That was my favorite finger."

"Maybe we can get it back."

"Ah shit. I can see it, in the corner, holding it up."

Phin starts to laugh.

"The rat is giving you the finger?"

"Kiss my ass, Phin. It's not funny."

Phin uses the laughter to twist even harder, his thick wrists bending the wire millimeter by millimeter.

"What's it doing now, Harry? Using your finger to pick its nose?"

"It's eating it. Corn on the cob style."

Back and forth. Back and forth. *Flesh is stronger than steel,* Phin thinks. *Determination is stronger than steel. Pain is temporary. Don't stop. Don't stop . . .*

"Uh-oh."

Phin hears the dripping sound, feels the hot liquid pour down his fingertips.

The wire has gone in too deep and severed something important. A vein. Or maybe an artery.

There are about ten pints of blood in a human body. When more than four pints are lost, the situation becomes critical. Shock ensues, and then death.

Phin knows this, and wonders how to proceed.

Either I'll make it, or I won't, he thinks.

Not seeing any choice, Phin resumes twisting.

CHAPTER 46

MORE COPS WERE called, and a four-block search of the area conducted. There was no sign of Holly.

I went through the motions, but I knew she wouldn't be found. Especially since she now knew we were after her.

What a disaster.

The Feebies were sympathetic. They promised to keep trying her cell phone to get a fix on her position. I didn't hold out much hope for that either. Anyone who watched TV knew that cell phones could be traced, and Holly had more knowledge than most. She wouldn't use her phone again.

I got back to my apartment a little after ten, and was surprised to see Latham sitting on my sofa.

My happiness was short-lived. Next to Latham, holding a semiautomatic to his head, was Bud Kork.

I reached for my holster and stopped cold when I felt the gun press against the side of my head.

"Hands up, pig."

Lorna. She'd been hiding behind my door.

I lifted my hands above my head, watching as her pudgy fingers tugged out my Colt. Using one hand, she released the catch and opened the cylinder. After shaking the bullets onto the floor, she tossed the gun aside.

"We've been waiting all night for you. Your boyfriend was kind enough to let us in."

I glanced at Latham, precious Latham, dressed in a suit and tie, a bouquet of roses on the floor at his feet. His red hair was shorter than I'd ever seen it, almost a buzz cut. His green eyes, so sparkly and full of life, looked tired and dull. One of them bulged, black and swollen, and a nasty gash on his forehead left a trail of dried blood along the side of his face.

"I let myself in with my key," he said. "I wanted to surprise you." Latham offered me a weak smile. "Surprise."

Lorna reached behind her and slammed the door, her eyes never leaving mine.

"Sit on the sofa, pig. We're gonna have us some fun."

I stole a glance at my burglar alarm. I hadn't punched in the disengage code. If the alarm went off, the police would be here within three minutes.

But the panel was dark, no blinking light. Latham. He knew the code too. They must have made him deactivate it.

If I lived through this, I really had to get the hell out of this apartment.

I limped to the sofa, sitting down next to Latham. The warmth of his body next to mine should have felt good, but instead I only felt emptiness.

Lorna waddled up to me, keeping the gun on my head. She wore red sweatpants, so small her legs looked like cellulite sausages. Her top was equally tight, a T-shirt that had a faded *INDIANA DUNES* graphic on the front, distorted by her small breasts and belly rolls.

"So Bud and me, we spent a long time thinking 'bout what we wanted to do to you, while we drove up here. Bud, tell her how upset I was when I heard 'bout little Caleb on the radio."

"We heard it on the radio," Bud said. "Lorna was upset."

Lorna's face became the dictionary definition of hate. "You *murdering pig*."

I watched her finger tremble on the trigger. She was holding an automatic, looked like a .45. A big gun. I winced.

"It wasn't me. Alexandra killed him."

"Horse pucky!" Spit flecked off Lorna's liver-colored lips. "You did it, you liar! Tell her, Bud!"

"Alexandra is an angel. The helper and defender of mankind. It's what her name means. She's the one that helped Lorna."

Bud's gun hand was shaking, from the Parkinson's. He sat on the other side of Latham, too far away from me to make a grab for it. He held a 9mm, looked like a Glock. The hammer was cocked back. One little muscle twitch and Latham was dead, and Bud was a twitcher.

Lorna came closer. I could see the blood caked under her fingernails.

"Any more lies, pig, and we'll cut out your lying tongue."

I snuck a quick glance at Latham. His hand brushed against mine. I wanted to grab on to it, hold it tight. But keeping both hands free was the smarter move.

Poor Latham. If I hadn't ever called him, he wouldn't be here facing this.

"Where was I?" Lorna stuck out her tongue and chewed on it, her face scrunched up in thought. "Bud, where was I?"

"We heard about little Caleb on the radio."

"Right. Poor baby. He loved his mama so much, and you killed him. So I'm driving and thinking how to make you pay. And Bud's in the kitchen, with the stove."

"The kitchen?" Latham asked. I gave him a subtle elbow and a look that said, *Don't antagonize the dumb animals.*

"We was driving one of those recreational camper vehicles," Lorna said. "Got it on the highway."

Bud added, "That's where we got the clothes."

I looked at Bud again. He had on a loose pair of jeans and a bulky red sweater with a big green Christmas tree stitched onto the front. I could guess what happened to the poor owners of the camper.

"So Bud's doing what he does with the burner, yellin' and cryin' and punishing himself to cleanse his sin, and I realized that's what we're gonna do to you."

Bud touched his chest. "Burns hurt. Hurt real bad."

I pictured Bud's gnarled flesh under the sweater, and figured he knows of what he speaks.

"So let's the four of us go on into the kitchen. We got something on the stove we think you're gonna like, pig."

That was my cue to get up. I did, followed by Latham and Bud, who kept the shaky gun pressed to Latham's temple.

What a crummy end to my career. To be killed by the Ma and Pa Kettle of crime.

Our merry troupe walked into the kitchen, and I could smell something cooking. I followed my nose to a pot of vegetable oil, bubbling away on the stove top.

Lorna grinned at me, showing her discolored baby-sized teeth. "Hot oil's a bad burn, cuz it sticks to you."

"I done it before." Bud nodded his head, his chicken neck wiggling. "Bad burn."

Lorna cackled. "And we gonna pour it on your little piggy head. Make us some bacon."

Bud also laughed, which quickly became a deep, chesty cough.

I decided that having boiling oil poured on my head wasn't in my best interest. I'd take a few bullets before I let that happen.

"Fine." I tried to sound matter-of-fact. "I'll do it myself."

I limped over to the pot, reaching for the handle, but before I took two steps Lorna got in front of me.

"No need to rush this, pig. You go sit yourself down. Relax a bit."

I took a step back, kitty litter crunching underfoot. Mr. Friskers had made yet another mess of my kitchen. Where was he, anyway?

I saw the slightest movement, in my peripheral vision. The cat. Perched atop the refrigerator, in pouncing position.

He was eyeing Lorna.

"I'll be doing the pouring honors."

Lorna stole a quick glance behind her, looking for the oil. Before she could grab it, ten pounds of screeching, clawing feline leaped from the fridge and launched itself at her face.

I dove to the side, skidding across the kitty-littered linoleum, Lorna screaming, Mr. Friskers screaming, Bud yelling, Lorna dropping the gun and trying to pull the cat off her face, Latham reaching down for me, his hand touching mine.

"Run!" I yelled at him. "Get help!"

Bud turned to us, aimed at Latham.

His shot was high, burying itself into the ceiling.

Latham held my eyes for just a second, a second that told me he'd be right back, promised me he'd be right back, and then he dashed out of the kitchen.

"GET THE CAT! GET IT OFF ME!"

Lorna's screaming was so shrill, she sounded like a police siren.

I tried to get to my feet, gasping at the pain in my ankle. Bud fired again at Latham, who kept low as he ran out the front door.

Safe. He was safe.

But I wasn't.

Bud peered down at me and wrapped his fingers in my hair, pressing the gun against my left eye.

"BUD! HELP ME! GET THE CAT!"

Bud looked at Lorna, then at me, then at Lorna, then at me. He eventually removed the gun from my face and aimed at Lorna. His hand jittered and shook, and Lorna spun like a dervish, Mr. Friskers sticking to her face like Velcro.

"HELP ME, BUD!"

Bud fired the gun at Mr. Friskers.

The bullet caught Lorna in the exact center of the N in DUNES on her stolen T-shirt.

Her wailing stopped mid-yelp, and she pitched forward onto the floor.

Mr. Friskers, the ride over, hopped off her head and trotted out of the kitchen.

Something between a sob and a scream escaped Bud's mouth. He swung the gun at me, his fist shaking so badly, I was sure it would go off.

"Save her! Save her!"

I crawled to Lorna. The exit wound in her back left an indentation the size of a cereal bowl under her shirt, which quickly filled with blood. Blood also spread out under her in a rapidly widening pool.

I grabbed a towel hanging from the refrigerator handle and pressed it against her wound. With my free hand, I searched the flab of her neck for a pulse.

I found it for three erratic beats, and then it stopped.

"Save her!"

I stared up at Bud.

"She's dead."

Bud opened and closed his mouth, like a fish trying to breathe air. The gun remained pointed, more or less, at me.

He whispered, "She's not dead."

"You killed her, Bud."

"No, no, no, no . . ."

"She loved you, and you shot her . . ."

"An accident. I tried to help her."

I held out my hand.

"Give me the gun, Bud."

For the briefest instant I thought he would, but then his eyebrows creased in anger.

"NO! You're a harlot! A liar! A devil! You controlled that cat, made her attack my Lorna!"

"Did I make you pull the trigger, Bud? You're the one that pulled the trigger." I stared at him, hard. "You've sinned, Bud."

Bud's face lost color, and though he was looking at me, his eyes seemed to be focused on something else, something beyond me.

"I've . . . sinned."

"You're a sinner, Bud. And you must atone for your sins. Give me the gun."

"I . . . need punishment."

"Yes you do, Bud. I'm a police officer. I can punish you."

"Punish me?"

"Thou shalt not kill, Bud. You've committed a terrible sin. But we can make it right. Let me have the gun."

"I can make it right."

Bud turned, facing the stove. I glanced around for Lorna's gun, but couldn't find where it had skidded off to.

"O my God," Bud began his contrition. "I am heartily sorry for having offended You, and I detest all my sins . . ."

"Bud, don't—"

I crawled backward like a crab, inching my way out of the kitchen, not wanting to watch but unable to turn away as Bud Kork plunged his hand into a boiling pot of hot oil.

His scream was inhuman.

I flipped onto my front and was using the doorway to get to my feet, just in time to see Latham walk through my front door, Holly at his side.

CHAPTER 47

ALL THINGS CONSIDERED, I was getting real sick of the Kork family.

Holly pressed her gun, the Wolverine, tight under Latham's jaw, hard enough to force his chin up. She wore jeans, a sweatshirt, and heavy construction boots—the same boots she'd worn while shooting at me in Diane Kork's burning house.

"Hello, Jack." Her smile was dazzling, without a hint of the sickness that it hid. "Look who I found running down the hallway, pounding on people's doors. He even asked me for help. Isn't that ironic?"

Holly closed the front door using her foot. Behind me, Bud whimpered like a kicked dog.

"This is Latham, right? You described him to me in the car. You were right. He's adorable."

Latham's eyes, so full of hope and promise a minute ago, had gone back to being blank and dead.

"Handcuffs," Holly said.

"In the bedroom."

"Let's go get them."

Holly kept her free hand on Latham's arm, and the three of us walked into the kitchen.

When Holly saw the mess, she began to laugh.

"Looks like I missed the party."

She gave Lorna a contemptuous kick, then turned her attention to Bud, who was curled up on the floor in a fetal position, shivering and cradling his burned hand. It was lobster red, pocked with blisters, puffed out to about twice the normal size.

"Hello, Father."

"Alex . . . my baby . . ."

Again I scanned the floor. Both Bud's gun and Lorna's gun were around here someplace.

I spotted his Glock, on the floor next to the stove. Holly spotted it too. She pulled Latham over, moved the Wolverine from his chin to his belly, and did a quick bunny-dip, scooping up Bud's gun with her free hand. She pointed that gun at me.

"Want to see how good I am left-handed?"

"Not really."

"Then head for the bedroom."

My handcuffs were on the nightstand, next to the bed. Holly spent a moment standing in the doorway, taking everything in.

"That's the closet my brother hid in?"

"Yeah."

She stared at it, almost reverentially, then ordered me to cuff Latham's hands behind his back and step away.

"I'm sorry," I told him.

His lips were a tight, thin line. "I'm getting used to it."

"That's right." Holly nudged Latham. "You were alone with my brother for a while."

Latham raised an eyebrow. "Your brother?"

"This is the Gingerbread Man's sister," I said. "The guy in the kitchen is her father."

Latham stared at Holly. "You folks are in some serious need of family counseling."

Holly's lips formed a pout.

"Are you saying you didn't like my brother?"

"He kept drooling on himself and trying to grab my ass."

Holly apparently didn't think that was funny, and cracked Latham on the back of the head with the butt of her Wolverine. He fell to his knees.

I sprung forward to help him, and got the Glock shoved in my face.

"Stay cool, Jack. We're just getting started."

Though I put on a brave front, staring down the barrel of a gun scared the crap out of me. It hadn't happened that many times in my career, but each time it did, the feeling was the same.

I felt a hot spot, like a laser beam, where the gun was aimed. I knew what guns could do. The damage they caused. The death they brought. Staring at something so deadly made my heart race and my throat constrict and my palms sweat and my knees turn to mush.

All she needed to do was exert a few pounds of pressure on that trigger, and I no longer existed.

It was kind of like the feeling you get after narrowly avoiding a car accident. That sick, hollow feeling of dread, knowing what might have happened.

Except with a gun, what might have happened might still happen.

"Where's Harry and Phin?" I managed to say.

"Funny you should ask. That's where we're going. I have a whole week of festivities planned."

"They're still alive?"

Holly smiled her seductive smile.

"Jack, look how cute you are, all full of hope. Yes, they're still alive. I plan on keeping all of you alive for as long as possible. As you can imagine, I put a lot of work into this whole production. I want to enjoy the fruits of my labors."

I eyed the Jewel bag, containing the Kork videotapes and files, sitting next to my TV.

It also contained Kork's hunting knife, which I'd checked out of evidence.

Holly caught my furtive glance.

"Something interesting in the bag, Jack? Let's see."

She turned both guns on me and walked over to the bag.

"Videos. Are these the ones Charles and I made?"

I nodded.

"Did you watch them?"

"Yeah."

"Did they make you hot?"

"They made me sick."

"That's because you're limited, Jack. You don't allow yourself to see the big picture. Power is a turn-on. Having control over someone's suffering, over someone's life and death, is like the best gift in the world. After making one of these videos, Charles and I would have the most mind-blowing sex."

Yuck. Yuck yuck yuck. Having sex after murdering people was bad enough, but sex with your brother?

"That's even more disgusting than having sex with McGlade."

"There you go, Jack. Getting all judgmental. You've met Father. Can you imagine what growing up in that house was like? The abuse that Charles and I had to endure? All we had was each other. It was the purest kind of love in the world."

Holly got dreamy-eyed.

"What about Caleb?" I said. "You grew up with him too."

Her face became hard.

"Caleb was trash. He had it coming. For the longest time it was just me and Charles. Then Caleb came into the picture. Charles treated Caleb like a brother. Where did that leave me?"

"And Steve Jensen?"

"Caleb was easy to manipulate. Jensen wasn't. He had to go. You were right, when we were in the morgue. Two people killed Jensen. Me and Caleb. Then I killed Caleb, and I'm going to do the same thing to you, and to everyone who ever hurt Charles. I'm his avenger."

I didn't want to play psychoanalyze the psycho, so I changed the subject.

"Those videos should be burned."

"Grab the bag. Then go back into the kitchen."

She kicked Latham, who was kneeling with his face on the bed. The back of his head was matted with blood.

"Move your ass, loverboy, or I'll kill you here."

Latham managed to get to his feet, and he was the first to stagger out of the room. I went second, the Wolverine pressed to my back.

Bud was still curled up on the linoleum, shaking so badly I could feel the vibrations through the floor.

"How do you feel, Father?"

"Hurts . . . hurts bad."

"But pain is good, right, Father? Pain is cleansing. Isn't that what you taught us?"

"Washes . . . washes away sin."

She moved one gun off me, onto him.

"And you've got a lot of sin to wash away, don't you, Father?"

"Lots of sin . . . lots . . ."

Holly pulled the trigger, shooting her father in the side. Both Latham and I jumped at the sound. Bud's eyes snapped open and he let out a low, agonizing moan.

"Gut shot. Supposed to hurt really bad. Does it hurt, Father?"

"Yes . . ."

Holly looked at me and stuck the Glock in the front of her jeans.

"It's not really his fault. You should hear the stories about what my grandparents did to him. But that's not an excuse. Some people just shouldn't be allowed to have children."

She turned back to her father. I knew what was coming and couldn't watch. I squeezed my eyes closed.

"The Lord may forgive you, Father. But I don't."

I heard the sizzle, and then the piercing scream as Holly dumped the pot of oil onto her father's head.

The scream was blessedly short. I opened my eyes. The ruin on the floor that was once Bud had passed out.

"Grab your boyfriend, Jack. It's time for us to go."

I held Latham by the elbow. His gait was wobbly, and I was limping, but I managed to get him out the kitchen.

"Where's your car?"

"On the street in front."

"Okay, let's . . ."

Holly paused, staring down at Mr. Friskers's catnip mouse toy. She smiled.

"I didn't know you had a cat, Jack. I just adore cats."

I bet she adored cats. In the same way she adored human beings.

"What's its name?"

"Mr. Friskers."

Holly frowned. "What a shitty name. Why'd you name him that?"

"That was his name when I got him."

"Call him."

I considered what Holly would do if I said no.

"Mr. Friskers! Come here!"

As expected, Mr. Friskers didn't come here.

"What makes him come?"

"Nothing. The cat doesn't like me."

"So why do you have it?"

"It's my mother's."

"Your mom is a vegetable, right? Get rid of the damn thing. I'll even help you. Here kitty, kitty, kitty . . ."

Holly made kissy sounds.

I willed the cat to stay put. The gunfire had probably scared him to death, and he was probably hiding under the couch, or the bed.

"Here he comes. That's a good kitty."

Mr. Friskers trotted right up to Holly's feet. I felt something die in my heart. Nasty as that cat was, I'd gotten used to the damn thing.

"Wow." Holly reached a hand down to him. "You're an ugly one, aren't you?"

Mr. Friskers gave her a vicious swat across the back of her hand and bounded away.

I didn't try to hide my grin. "I think you hurt his feelings."

Holly lifted her hand, noticing the blood. She licked it away, then raised the gun to my head.

"Find the cat, Jack. He's coming with us."

Rather than argue, I dropped the bag, hobbled over to the sofa, got down on all fours, and peered underneath it.

"Is he there?"

"Nothing but a family of dust bunnies and a peanut M&M."

"Move it, or I'll turn your boyfriend into a girlfriend."

She pointed the gun at Latham's crotch, a move that made him noticeably uncomfortable.

I crawled over to the dining room table, and I spotted it.

The .45 Lorna dropped when Bud shot her.

I didn't bother to question how it got eight feet out of the kitchen. Instead, I scrambled for it as fast as I could.

"There he is!" I pointed, stretching out, reaching for the gun, wrapping my hand around the butt and bringing it around to Holly, thumbing off the safety, aiming at her head and squeezing the trigger.

Click.

Empty. Stupid Lorna had run out of bullets.

Which was why I freaking hated automatics.

This delighted Holly.

"Jack, I wish you could have seen your face when you fired and nothing happened. It was priceless. You would have killed me too. Damn, that was fast. I didn't even have time to bring my gun up."

I blew out a deep breath and came very close to crying.

"Maybe you can load it with that M&M you found."

I clenched my teeth, determined not to let her see me break down. And then my cat, my mean, stupid, annoying as hell cat, came out from behind the easy chair and touched his head to my hand, demanding to be petted.

I held him close.

"Do you have a cat carrier?"

"Closet. On your left."

Holly went to the closet, took out the small cage, and tossed it to the floor.

"Pack him up. It's time to go."

The next few minutes were a blur. I crated Mr. Friskers and the four of us left my apartment, went down the stairs, and climbed into my car. Holly and Latham in the back, me and the cat in the front. I drove.

"Get on the expressway, head for Elk Grove. Anything funny and I kill Latham, then you. You remember how good a shot I am."

"I remember you missed me at Diane Kork's house."

"Missed you? I nicked your ear. That's what I was aiming at. I didn't want to kill you, Jack."

"Why not? You could have killed me a dozen times already. Why haven't you? Why go through all of this?"

"I'll tell you when we get there."

I didn't think I wanted to know the answer.

CHAPTER 48

PHIN IS LIGHT-HEADED. He figures he's lost at least two pints of blood, probably more. Even a slight movement in his wrists sends ripples of agony up his arms.

But the wire is bending. He can feel it.

"How you doing, Harry Harry?"

"I'm ecstatic. After all, it's my wedding day."

"Don't feel bad. All marriages start out a little rocky."

Harry snorts. "When I asked for her hand in marriage, I didn't expect her to cut mine off."

Phin grimaces, the wire grinding against exposed tendons. But he's got almost a full inch of play now. Just a little bit more and he'll be able to get his hand free.

"What was I thinking, Phin? That a woman like Holly would marry me. She's beautiful, smart, sexy . . ."

"A lunatic."

"We all have our little faults. You know what the sad part is? I didn't even see it coming. I was all caught up in myself, and I never stopped and questioned what was going on."

"It happens, McGlade. Don't beat yourself up over it."

"I had no clue. Not one. We talked. We laughed. Even the sex was good. I mean, I'm no porn star, but what I lack in size I make up for in speed."

Phin offers a weak chuckle. He pulls hard, trying to slide his right hand out of the wire. His wrist is slick with blood, and he's got his binding almost up to his thumb.

"But it seemed genuine. For that thirty seconds, she really seemed to be enjoying herself."

"You lasted thirty seconds? What are you, Superman?"

Harry laughs, but it comes out forced. "Okay, maybe I was inflating the numbers a little bit to impress you. But that's not the point. The point is, I was so wrapped up in myself, I had no idea I was marrying a crazy woman who wanted to kill me."

Phin grunts in pain. He's almost there. "Self-delusion is a powerful thing, Harry."

"Except my self-delusion killed us both."

"Try to stay positive."

"I am positive. I'm positive we're both going to die."

"We're not dead yet. And I think I've got something to make you feel a little better."

"Nothing can make me feel better. Except maybe killing that damn rat who ate all of my damn fingers."

"This will."

Phin yells, tugging as hard as he can, and his battered wrist pops out of the wire.

He's free.

Phin brings his hands around and looks at his wrists.

Ugly. Most suicides looked better.

"Phin? Are you okay?"

Phin tugs off his tie, wraps it around his right wrist, and ties a knot using his teeth.

"I got my hands free. I'm working on my legs."

He takes off his shirt next, winding it around his left wrist, trying to stop the blood. Then he digs into his cowboy boot, and pulls out the Kabar folding knife he keeps strapped to his calf. It's a seriously tough piece of hardware, with a three-inch serrated steel blade that can cut through a car door.

Phin slips the blade between the wire and his ankle and twists. The heavy gauge wire breaks with a *ping* sound.

"Phin? How you doing, man? Let me tell you, if you get us out of here, you'll be my best friend in the whole world."

Phin switches legs, prying at the wire. "That's okay, Harry. I'll help you anyway."

The second wire snaps free, and Phin gets to his feet. He's dizzy, but exhilarated. He turns around, looks at Harry.

The poor guy's hand looks like a well-done filet mignon.

"You free?"

"I'm free."

"Phin, you magnificent bastard! I love you. I'm going to make you a character on *Fatal Autonomy*. I think Ricky Schroder is looking for work."

"What the hell does *Fatal Autonomy* mean, anyway?"

"I dunno. The network thought it sounded cool. How's my hand look?"

"Like it should have a baked potato right next to it."

"Hurry up and cut me free. And get this filthy rusty brush out of my leg. I can feel the lockjaw setting in."

Phin takes a step toward McGlade, then hears a car pull into the docking bay. Holly's back.

He goes to the table, looking for a gun. There's plenty of reloading equipment: scales, empty shells, lead ingots, a bullet mold, even some baton rounds. But no guns.

The garage door opens.

Phin considers facing her head-on. But he's weak, and woozy, and only armed with a knife. Holly is a martial arts champ and probably armed to the teeth.

Still, he has to try.

"I'm going to try and stop her, Harry."

"Can you cut me loose first?"

"No time."

"At least pull out these nails. Phin!"

Phin grips the Kabar in his weakening hand and quickly locates a good place of attack.

"Stay quiet, Harry Harry. This will all work out."

But the words feel like a lie leaving his mouth.

CHAPTER 49

ALEX MAKES JACK open the garage door. She's never been this excited before. She's killed many people, and has always taken pleasure from the act, but she's practically giddy with joy at what lies ahead.

Four victims. Plus a cat. Good for a week of entertainment. Possibly two, if she restrains herself a little bit.

"Get the cat," she orders Jack. Her gun points at Jack's face. She flinches. The cop doesn't like guns being pointed at her. That will make what's coming up very interesting.

"How about the videos?" Jack asked.

Why would Jack be so interested in the videos? Alex keeps the pistol on Jack's head and digs her hands into the plastic Jewel bag.

There's a very big surprise at the bottom. Underneath the VHS tapes is a plastic bag containing a hunting knife. Alex holds it up, her pupils dilating.

"Was this my brother's knife?"

Jack doesn't answer. But she doesn't have to. Alex quickly tears away the plastic and grips the weapon in her left hand. There's still some dried blood clinging to the blade. From the last time Charles used it.

Alex decides the knife will see some further use. Tonight.

She tucks it into her back pocket and yanks Latham out of the car, ordering him and Jack into the warehouse. Everything has succeeded beyond expectation. She tells Jack to close the door behind them, and then parades her and Latham over to Harry and . . .

Phin is gone.

There's a puddle of blood under his chair, and some loops of wire.

Rage swallows Alex, and she rushes at McGlade and cracks him across the face with the Wolverine. His head rocks back.

"Where is he?!?"

"He went to catch a movie. Said he'd be back later." Harry grins, his teeth streaked with blood. "Hiya, Jackie. Come to lend me a hand?"

Alex lifts the pistol to hit McGlade again, and notices Jack rushing at her from the side.

Training takes over. Alex pivots on her hips, snaps her leg out, and kicks Jack straight in the chest.

Jack makes an *oomph* sound and collapses onto the concrete.

Alex turns back to Harry, then looks around the warehouse. She's only known Phin a short time, but he isn't the fleeing type. He would have taken Harry with him.

Unless he didn't have time to.

Which meant he'd only freed himself a few minutes before they arrived.

Alex puts herself in his shoes. He's injured himself escaping. Probably weak. He may have a knife, or some other hand weapon. There are lots of places to hide, but he's not thinking about hiding. He wants to get himself into a position to pounce.

Alex spent several years in the Marines. She knew about ambushes. People usually don't think three-dimensionally. They'll look around at eye level, but rarely look up high or down low.

Alex glances up, and sees Phin crouching on the top rack of the aluminum shelving unit, alongside the table with all of her equipment.

Had she gone to the table, he could have dropped the fifteen feet down and hurt her. Possibly killed her.

A smart place to attack from. But now that she sees him, he's simply target practice.

"Hello, handsome." Alex aims the Wolverine. "Let's do this the easy way."

Both Jack and Harry scream the word *NO!*

Alex fires twice, and the bullets hit home. Phin tumbles through space, spinning and bleeding. He smacks the table, hard, then bounces off and sprawls onto the floor like a dropped rag doll.

Jack begins to cry.

"You see, Jack. This is why I didn't kill you, or Harry, earlier. Even though I had plenty of chances."

Alex walks up to the fallen lieutenant, drinking in her misery.

"You never knew my brother. Sure, you exchanged a few words with him. But you didn't *know* him. He was something you chased. Hunted. Your prey."

She turns to Harry, tenderly touches his bruised cheek.

"I could have hunted you the same way, but what's the satisfaction in that? You were as unknown to me as Charles was to you. So I chose to get to know you. To spend time with you. To fully understand what I intended to destroy. And you got to know me, as well. Don't you feel betrayed, Harry? Isn't it so much worse, being killed by someone you love?"

"Love?" Harry shakes his head. "You're just another notch on my belt, baby. Those midgets last night were twice the woman you are. And no icky scars."

Alex pats McGlade on his leg, the one with the rusty nail brush sticking in. He howls.

"I owed it to Charles to do it this way. To eat this dish nice and cold. I could have taken you at any time. You too, Jack."

Alex goes to Latham, pushes him over to the shelving unit.

"Unfortunately for you, cutie, you just got in the way."

She uses Jack's keys to uncuff his left hand, pulling his arm through the metal scaffolding before cuffing it again.

Jack is still on the floor, huffing and crying. Pathetic.

Alex goes to the table, sets the Glock and the Wolverine next to her bullet-making equipment.

"So here's what's going to happen next. I'm going to give you a chance to save the day, Jack. Isn't that generous of me? But you'll have to prove yourself."

As Alex talks, she loads the guns.

"You're going to have to prove you're better than me, Lieutenant Daniels. You think you're woman enough?"

Alex sticks the Wolverine into the waist of her jeans, then approaches Harry. With one hand, she unbuckles his belt.

"Can't get enough of the love stick, eh, Mrs. McGlade?"

"I couldn't even find it half the time."

"Maybe you would have enjoyed it more if you pretended I was a blood relative."

Alex tugs off the belt and tosses it in front of Jack.

"Stand up and put that on."

Jack, her face streaked with tears, slowly stands up and winds the belt around her waist.

Alex presses the gun into Jack's neck and drags her, by the belt, over to an open area of the warehouse. Using her left hand, she removes the Glock from her jeans and shoves it into Jack's belt.

Alex puts her lips next to Jack's ear and whispers, "I'm going to prove, once and for all, I'm better than you are."

Then she walks backward, slowly, keeping a bead on Jack's chest.

When she's forty feet away, she stops, tucking the Wolverine into her waistband.

"You think you're faster than me, Jack?" Alex smiles. She's never felt this alive before.

"Draw, whenever you're ready."

CHAPTER 50

A CALM CAME over me. The same calm I felt when I was in Diane Kork's bathroom, with the house burning down around me. I stared at Holly, perhaps fifteen yards away from me, a dazzling smile creasing her perfect face, and I knew I was going to die.

Holly was better than me. She played me, and Harry, for fools. What she said about getting to know us to hurt us worse was true.

If I'd just been grabbed by her and killed, it would have been bad enough. But coming from someone who I knew, someone I trusted, and not seeing it coming; that was like a gut punch.

And to add injury to insult, she just killed my best friend, and was going to kill the man I loved, and me, and my cat. And even stupid Harry, whom I found myself developing a soft spot for. A very small soft spot, but a soft spot nonetheless.

I looked at Latham, and mouthed "I'm sorry." He was crying, which made me feel even worse.

In my head, I said good-bye to Herb, and to my mother.

"Come on, Jack!" Latham yelled. "You can do it!"

But staring at Holly, I knew I couldn't do it. She would put ten rounds into my chest before I even got a shot off. The woman was better than me at everything. She wouldn't have set this little scenario up if she didn't think she'd win.

"Anytime, Jack. Or would you prefer I try this with Latham instead?"

My knees were rubber. My mouth went dry. My hands were shaking worse than Bud's.

I couldn't win.

Latham said, "You can do it, Jack! I love you!"

I couldn't win.

Harry said, "Jackie, just drop the bitch so we can go home."

I couldn't win.

Holly said, "Or maybe I could play this game with Mr. Friskers. I don't think he'd be as scared as you look right now."

I couldn't win I couldn't win I couldn't win.

But goddammit, I could sure as hell try.

I reached for the Glock, tugging it from the belt, bringing it up and at the same time stepping forward—Holly went for the body shot, and a profile is harder to hit—and my arm fully extended and I watched as Holly's eyes went wide and she grabbed for her gun and fired first, but I wasn't going to be duped this time by trying to outdraw her, I was going to make sure my shot counted and I took careful aim and felt the wind as her slugs tore the air in front of me and I squeezed the trigger and fired.

Her head snapped back as if on hinges, and she sprawled out onto the concrete floor, her gun skittering off into the darkness.

Cheering, from Latham and Harry. I walked toward Holly, saw the blood streaming down her face, and then limped over to Phin, digging at his neck, feeling for a pulse.

He surprised me by opening his eyes.

". . . buttons . . ."

The relief I felt was tangible.

"I'm getting an ambulance, Phin. You're going to be okay."

"Bullets . . ." he moaned. Then he said *buttons* again.

But it wasn't *buttons*. It was *batons*.

Batons were specialty bullets, used by police for crowd control. Made of rubber. Non-lethal.

I looked up at the table, saw Holly's bullet-making equipment.

She wouldn't have risked killing me so quickly. She had other plans.

I heard Harry and Latham yell just as Holly kicked me from behind.

CHAPTER 51

THE BLOW KNOCKED me sideways. I rolled with it, tucking in my head and coming up in a kneeling position, my arms up to block.

I saw little flashes of light, and my vision was lopsided, but I was able to see Holly—her face a Halloween mask of blood and rage—move in and attempt another front kick.

Instinct took over. I swiped away the kick with my left forearm, and my right hand formed a fist and I gave her a sharp jab in the inner thigh.

Holly yelled, retreating two steps. That gave me time to get to my feet. I kicked off my heels and adopted a ready stance, left foot behind me, keeping the weight off my injured right ankle.

Holly wiped a sleeve across her eyes. Her forehead was bleeding like mad. Though baton rounds weren't lethal, they were still like getting pegged with a slingshot. The blood in her eyes was to my advantage, and I used it.

Biting back the pain, I swiveled my hips and brought my left leg forward, aiming the kick at her chest. Holly leaned away, as I expected, and I brought the left foot down and moved forward, going into a round kick with my right foot.

I extended my knee and felt my heel connect with her chin.

The shock of contact made me gasp and see red, but Holly took the worst of it. Both of her feet left the ground and she hit the floor ass-first—not the preferred landing on concrete.

Pressing my advantage, I lunged forward, wanting to get on top of her and strike at her face or throat.

I was too hasty. Holly scissored her legs out and swept my feet out from under me. I also hit the ground hard.

When a fight goes to the floor, the stronger opponent usually wins. Holly wasn't only stronger, but her Marine training probably made my police academy training look like ballet. I rolled backward, two or three body lengths away, before getting up on my knees.

Holly moved like lightning, and hit like a baseball bat, throwing a roundhouse punch at my face that I barely deflected in time, taking the hit on the left shoulder.

My whole arm went numb.

She followed up with an equally vicious kick to my chest. I bunched up what little pectoral muscles I had, but her big construction boot knocked the wind right out of me and I went skidding backward across the dusty floor on my butt.

I let momentum take my legs up over my head, and rolled to my feet. My lungs tried to take in air, but they weren't working. It's a terrifying feeling, not being able to breathe. I'd been hit in the diaphragm before, and knew that in just a few seconds the muscle would stop spasming and allow me some air, but rationality doesn't mean much in the throes of panic.

Holly sensed my struggle, and came at me with snarling, bleeding fury, taking two running steps and launching herself into a jumping double kick.

I slipped the first kick, but the second caught me under the chin, cracking my lower jaw into my upper jaw, spinning me around like a top.

I would have hit the floor, but instead slammed into the metal shelves, and was able to grab on and keep from falling.

My breath came back, and I gulped it in, began to choke when something got caught in my throat, and spit out a chip from one of my teeth.

My right ankle was pudding. I kept my weight on my left foot and clutched the metal railing.

"I thought you were third dan," I said through the new gap in my front teeth. "You fight like a yellow belt."

Holly wiped the blood from her eyes and fell into her cat stance, her palms flat and fingers extended for pyonson keut.

"And that wedding dress made your ass look huge."

She yelled, "KIYAA!" and struck with her fingertips at my neck. I pivoted my head around and her fingers met the steel bar supporting the giant shelf.

The shelf won.

I executed an elbow strike, cracking her across the cheek. An illegal move, but hey, no refs.

Holly hit her head against the shelving unit, and I grabbed her hair and helped her hit her head two more times. There was no tae kwon do name for that maneuver, but it felt great.

I was going for thirds when her hand grasped my wrist and she dropped all of her weight down to one knee, flipping me onto my back.

Before I could get my hands up, she used the knife edge of her good hand to break my nose.

I'd never had my nose broken before, but I know she did indeed break it because I heard the snap and the pain brought fresh tears to my eyes.

Again, using blind instinct, I rolled away. The rolling intensified the pain and dizziness I felt, and when I came to a stop I titled my head to the side and threw up.

"Jack!" I heard Latham yell, but he seemed very far away. My vision was a kaleidoscopic mess, but I could make out Holly stumbling toward me, looking like Sissy Spacek at the end of *Carrie*, bloody and murderous and out of her freaking mind.

A foot away from me, still in his cat carrier, was Mr. Friskers.

"Hang on," I told him.

Holly lunged.

I picked up the carrier and thrust the corner into Holly's face. She staggered back, and the door popped open. Mr. Friskers hopped out, gave each of us a disappointed look, and ran off into the shadows.

I switched my grip to the carrier handle, got to my knees, and hurled it at her.

She ducked it, and came at me again.

Standing up wasn't going to happen for me. It looked like I had a small pumpkin growing out of my foot. My nose made even the tiniest movement of my head pure torture.

Holly looked to be faring better. Her right hand was mangled, and she had some visible bumps on her head, but that didn't seem to slow her down.

"Enough of this bullshit."

She reached into her back pocket and pulled out the hunting knife. Charles Kork's knife. The one I'd so cleverly tricked her into bringing along.

How quickly things could go from bad to worse.

I got onto all fours and crawled away as fast as I could. Harry was the closest thing to me, so I headed for him, reaching out my hand for his chair, and then I felt Holly's iron grip on my bad ankle.

That pain was bad enough. But when she slashed the blade across my thigh, I thought I'd died and gone to Pain Hell.

I twisted around, the pain giving me superhuman strength, kicking out at Holly with my good foot and knocking her off me.

I stretched out my hand, fumbling for Harry's lap, my fingers locking around the handle of a what looked like a hairbrush, but when I pulled it out McGlade yelped and I saw that instead of bristles it had a dozen nails sticking out of the end.

Holly jumped at me, bringing down the knife.

I let out a war cry, my reptile brain screeching with rage and fear and pain, and my left arm blocked the downward arc of the knife while my right swung the hairbrush with everything I had, digging into Holly's face, and tearing much of it off.

Holly spun in a semicircle and hit the floor.

I sat there, clutching the brush, breaths coming out in ragged gasps, waiting for her to get up so I could give her a second helping.

She didn't get up.

"I wet my pants again," Harry said.

I crawled over to her, not looking at the ruin that was once a gorgeous face, not listening to the gurgling coming out of the hole that was once a beautiful mouth, taking the knife out of her hand, digging around in her pockets until I found my handcuff keys.

Dragging myself across the floor, I uncuffed Latham, who hugged me gently and kissed my fingertips.

"Nice job, Jack. I forgot how exciting life with you was. We've been apart for months, and not one person has tried to kill me in all that time."

"So you're taking me back?"

"You couldn't keep me away if you tried."

"Hey lovebirds!" Harry yelled. "Can you save the kissy face for later and get me the fuck out of here?"

Latham ran off to get help. I stared at Phin, and he gave me a weak thumbs-up.

Returning to Holly, I cuffed her hands behind her back and pulled off her shirt to try to stop some of the massive bleeding coming out of her face. It didn't help much.

"Use a tourniquet," McGlade suggested. "Put it around her neck."

I crawled over to Phin, not wanting to move him in case of a spinal injury. He had two bullet wounds in his left shoulder. Holly hadn't wanted him to die, probably because she wanted him around for a while to torture.

I slipped off Harry's belt and tied it around Phin's arm to slow the bleeding. Then I picked up some tin snips off the table and crawled to Harry, setting him free just as the sirens howled in the distance.

Harry hugged me.

"Thanks, Jackie. I owe you one."

"Just take me off that damn TV show."

"Take you off? Do you know what kind of amazing episode this would make? Shit, Jack, we'd hit number one in our time slot."

"Harry . . ."

"Fine. You're off."

The sirens got closer, and Latham came back in, toting my cell phone. He sat beside me, holding me tight. And I began to sob. But it wasn't from pain, and it wasn't from shock. It was from pure relief.

A purring sound made me turn around. Mr. Friskers was sitting in McGlade's lap, a dead rat in his jaws.

"Good kitty," Harry said. "Good fucking kitty."

And he continued to pet him until the ambulances arrived.

CHAPTER 52

WE WERE ALL taken to Alexian Brothers Hospital in Elk Grove. Latham got stitches. I got stitches too. I also had my nose set and packed, which hurt worse than when Holly broke it, and had a cast put on my ankle for a bad sprain. Phin needed five units of blood, but came out of surgery in good shape.

And Harry—I actually felt sorry for Harry. He had to have his ruined right hand amputated.

"Don't let them do it, Jackie," he pleaded as they wheeled him into the OR. "That's half my sex life."

I patted his shoulder. "You'll get one of those cool robotic hands, like on James Bond."

That made his eyes light up.

"I'll be able to crush cans and shit like that?"

"Yeah."

"Do women like those things?"

"They're sexy," I told him. "You'll have to fight the women off."

Alex Kork, whom I knew as Holly Frakes, also needed surgery. She had skin removed from her buttocks, her hips, and her stomach, to try to reconstruct her face. From what I heard, it wouldn't help much. She'd spend the rest of her life looking like a patchwork quilt.

I also finally got through to Herb, and spoke with an exhausted Bernice.

"Everything went fine. He's doing great. I'm watching what's happening on TV. Are you okay?"

I squeezed Latham's hand.

"Never better."

"Herb wants to talk to you."

"He's awake?"

"He's still a little dopey. But then, he's always a little dopey. Here he is."

"Jack! I'm watching you on TV. It was Harry's wife all along?"

"Yeah. How's that for a shocker?"

"Well, at least now it makes sense why someone would marry that moron. For a while there, I thought there was something seriously wrong with the universe."

"How are you doing?"

"Good. Just like an oil change. You gonna come visit?"

"Hell yeah."

"Bring donuts."

Latham and I were discharged at around three in the morning. As expected, my apartment was a full-blown crime scene, infested with cops.

Bud Kork, gut-shot and burned, had died on my kitchen floor next to his common-law wife.

I picked up some essentials and spent the night at Latham's new condo. With the cat, of course.

"I bought this king-sized bed with you in mind," he told me.

"Might be a while before I'm ready to break it in."

"We can take as long as you need."

Between the two of us we had three black eyes, twenty-three stitches, a nose full of cotton, and a twisted ankle, but we managed to break it in that night.

I fell asleep wrapped up in Latham's arms, a goofy, chipped-tooth smile on my face.

The next few days were spent playing catch-up. I visited the office and finished my reports, and Captain Bains told me the superintendent was considering a promotion for me. I visited Herb and brought him Cinnabons. I visited Mom and told her everything that happened. I visited Harry, and he showed me his stump and moaned about the tetanus shots he had to get. I visited Phin, who thanked me for a wild weekend. And I visited Alex.

She had two armed guards at her door, and another one that sat inside her room. She lay on top of her sheets, bandages covering most of her body from the many patches of skin they'd harvested trying to reconstruct her face. Her head was swaddled in gauze, mummy-style. Her hand was cuffed to the bed frame. A single blue eye peered out through the cotton, fixing on me when I entered.

"Hello, Jack. Thanks for coming."

Her voice sounded weak, muffled by her dressings. I sat down in the chair next to her.

"I hear you've been cooperating with police. Telling them everything they want to know."

"Just listening to my lawyers. They want to use an insanity defense, obviously. Poor abused child grows up confused and alone. Some bullshit like that."

"Do you think you're insane?"

She shrugged. "What do you think?"

"I think there's something seriously wrong with you. Maybe you'll be able to get some help. Professional help."

"I doubt it. I killed my last four shrinks."

I leaned forward.

"Why did you want to see me, Alex?"

"You can call me Holly if you want."

"Why did you want to see me?"

"The doctors, they didn't want me to see my face yet. But last night I got up and went to the bathroom and took off my bandages in the mirror. I look like someone stapled some raw pork chops to my face."

If she wanted sympathy, she was preaching to the wrong choir.

"I'll be scarred for life, Jack."

"You already were," I said.

Holly didn't seem to have anything else to say, so I got up to leave.

"Jack."

I stopped. Waited.

"You beat me this time. But it isn't over."

I gave her a final glance.

"It's over," I said, and left the hospital.

That night, in Latham's bed, I had a strange dream. I was at the shooting range, and no matter how carefully I aimed, I couldn't hit the silhouette.

But rather than frustrate me, I found it funny as hell. Every time I missed, I laughed like crazy. It was one of the most wonderful dreams I'd ever had.

My cell phone woke me up.

"Ms. Daniels? This is Julie, over at Henderson House."

Henderson House. The long-term care facility where my mother lived. I checked the clock, saw it was three in the morning.

The fear washed over me like a wave. I'd been expecting the worst for so long, but found myself unable to handle it.

"Is it Mom?" My voice quavered, my eyes filling with tears.

"Yes, it's your mother. It happened just a few minutes ago. She's come out of her coma."

Had I heard correctly?

"Mom's out of her coma?"

My talking woke Latham up. He hugged me in the darkness.

"Not only is she awake, but she's completely lucid. Can you come over here, Ms. Daniels? She's asking for you."

Several Months Later

THE ALLEY WAS dark, and I shouldn't have gone in there. It was just plain stupid.

But into the alley I went, following McGlade, gun drawn and moving in a crouch.

"I see something." Harry had his gun out as well, a much larger gun than mine. "Cover me."

"No." I tugged his arm back. "It's my turn to go first. You cover me."

"Jack, this is dangerous. Don't fight me on this."

Without listening I pushed past McGlade and broke into a run. I stopped in a Weaver stance, legs two feet apart, both arms stretched out in front of me, steadying the gun—

—silhouetted by the street light behind me.

A perfect, easy target.

"Freeze! Police!"

The first shot caught me in the stomach, blood gushing out before me like a fountain.

I fell in slow motion, three more shots ripping into my chest and shoulders, spinning me around, painting the brick walls with blood before I hit the pavement.

I heard Harry yell, and watched him run out to me, firing into the alley as he ran, grabbing me by the collar and dragging me out onto the sidewalk, leaving a smeared trail of red.

"Harry . . ."

"Shh. Jack, don't talk."

I looked down at the ruin that was my chest, blood pumping out in a ridiculous amount. McGlade tried to press down on some of the wounds. I cried out in pain.

"I've got to get help, Jack."

He tried to stand up, but I stopped him, grabbing his hand.

"It's . . . it's too late, Harry . . . too late."

"Hold on, Jack."

A single tear rolled down my face. I put on a brave smile.

"You'll get the guys. Right?"

"Of course I will, baby. Count on it."

I blinked a few times.

"Everything's getting dark, Harry."

McGlade knelt down, propped my upper body onto his lap, and put his arms around me.

"I'm here, Jack."

"Harry . . . I . . . I need to tell you something." I was whispering. "Come close."

"I'm all ears, Jackie."

"All . . . all of these years . . ."

McGlade now had tears in his eyes too.

"I'm listening."

"I . . . love . . . you . . . Harry . . . McGlade . . ."

Harry bent down, and his lips touched mine. When he pulled his head back, my eyes were wide and staring into space.

I was dead.

Harry cried out, lifted his head back, and screamed and screamed and screamed.

TO BE CONTINUED . . . appeared at the bottom of the screen. Then the image froze and faded to black.

My mother clicked off the TV with the remote control, frowning at me.

"That was crap. Pure crap. You never would have gone into the alley like that."

I shrugged. "At least I won't be back next season. You want a beer?"

"A beer sounds wonderful. Let's get good and plowed and order a pizza with extra everything." She made a kissy sound, and Mr. Friskers bounded into her lap.

"You sure you want everything, Mom?"

Mom smiled, and it was beatific. "Absolutely. I've got a lot of eating to catch up on, Jacqueline. I've got a lot of life to catch up on."

She reached for my hand and held it tight. I held it just as tight, never ever wanting to let go.

"You know what, Mom? That makes two of us."

ACKNOWLEDGMENTS

Every book, the list of people I need to thank gets longer . . .

To fellow scribes: Barbara D'Amato, James O. Born, Lee Child, Blake Crouch, Bill Fitzhugh, Jack Kerley, William Kent Krueger, David Morrell, PJ Parrish, and M.J. Rose, for their words, encouragement, and inspiration.

To those in the book biz: Robin Agnew, Augie Alesky, Lorri Amsden, Elizabeth Baldwin, Jim Berlage, Terri Bischoff, Jane Biro, Chris Bowman, Linda Brown, Bonnie Claeson, Diana Cohen, J.B. Dickey, Moni Draper, Tammy Domike, Judy Duhl, Luane Evans, Dorothy Evans, Bill Farley, Beth Fedyn, Dick File, Marilyn Fisher, Holly Frakes, Steven French, Fran Fuller, Sandy Goodrick, Diane Gressman, Maggie Griffin, Joe Guglielmelli, Maryelizabeth Hart, Patrick Heffernan, Jim Huang, Rick Jensen, Steve Jensen, Jen Johnson, Jon Jordan, Ruth Jordan, Steve Jurczyk, Bob Kadlec, Richard Katz, Edmund and Jeannie Kaufman, Carolyn Lane, Steve Lukac, Sheldon MacArthur, Bobby McCue, Dana Mee, Laurie Mountjoy, Jim Munchel, Karen Novak, Cynthia Nye, Otto Penzler, Henry "Hank" Perez, Barbara Peters, Sue Petersen, Sarah Pingry, Taryn Schau, Terri Schlichenmeyer, Matt Schwartz, Cindy Smith, Terri Smith, Kathy Sparks, Laura Stanz, Dave Strang, Jim & Gloria Tillez, Barbara Tom, Maria Tovar, Susan Tunis, Chris Van Such, Lauri Ver Schure, Linda Vetter, Janine Wilson, Chris Wolak, and the many others who have helped spread the word—if your name isn't here, blame the typesetter!

To the publishing folks: Lauren Abramo, Ellen Archer, Alan Ayres, Michael Bourrett, Susie Breck, Anna Campbell, Regina Castillo, Jane Comins, Natalie Fedewa, Nicola Ferguson, Brad Foltz, Miriam Goderich, Jessica Goldman, Laura Grafton, Dick Hill, Amy Hosford, Eileen Hutton, Navorn Johnson, David Lott, Bob Miller, Phil Rose, Will Schwalbe, Michael Snodgrass, Abby Vinyard, Katie Wainwright, Miriam Wenger, Kimberly West, Westchester Book Composition, and Raynel White.

The amazing Leslie Wells.

Jane Dystel, who kicks major booty.

Barry Eisler and Jim Coursey, for their first draft insights.

Family and friends: Laura Konrath, Mike Konrath, Chris Konrath, John Konrath, Talon Konrath, Latham Conger III, George Dailey, Mariel Evans, and Jeff Evans.

And of course, Maria Konrath. I couldn't write a word without her.